Bolan wouldn't stop until he was dead

Every enemy dead provided Bolan and his forces with more ammunition, transportation, fuel, even clothing. Laud would be expecting the Executioner to stagger in, weakened, worn-out, running on empty.

That was enough for Bolan.

Ahmur Ibn Laud was a monster, but he was a genius at war-making.

The only thing Laud didn't count on was Bolan being an equal to him.

Monster for monster.

Genius for genius.

Laud was going to meet his executioner, and when that time came, they would both learn whether the Divine Sword was keen enough a weapon to stave off the Executioner's wrath.

MACK BOLAN ®
The Executioner

The Executioner

Don Pendleton's ®

HARD
PURSUIT

A GOLD EAGLE BOOK FROM

W®RLDWIDE.

TORONTO • NEW YORK • LONDON
AMSTERDAM • PARIS • SYDNEY • HAMBURG
STOCKHOLM • ATHENS • TOKYO • MILAN
MADRID • WARSAW • BUDAPEST • AUCKLAND

First edition June 2004
ISBN 0-373-64307-1

Special thanks and acknowledgment to
Doug Wojtowicz for his contribution to this work.

HARD PURSUIT

A man who has to be convinced to act before he acts
is *not* a man of action... You must act as you breathe.
—Georges Clemenceau
1841–1929

I will pursue justice as long as I have a breath left
in me. I am a man of action.

—Mack Bolan

THE
MACK BOLAN®

LEGEND

Nothing less than a war could have fashioned the destiny of the man called Mack Bolan. Bolan earned the Executioner title in the jungle hell of Vietnam.

But this soldier also wore another name—Sergeant Mercy. He was so tagged because of the compassion he showed to wounded comrades-in-arms and Vietnamese civilians.

Mack Bolan's second tour of duty ended prematurely when he was given emergency leave to return home and bury his family, victims of the Mob. Then he declared a one-man war against the Mafia.

He confronted the Families head-on from coast to coast, and soon a hope of victory began to appear. But Bolan had broken society's every rule. That same society started gunning for this elusive warrior—to no avail.

So Bolan was offered amnesty to work within the system against terrorism. This time, as an employee of Uncle Sam, Bolan became Colonel John Phoenix. With a command center at Stony Man Farm in Virginia, he and his new allies—Able Team and Phoenix Force—waged relentless war on a new adversary: the KGB.

But when his one true love, April Rose, died at the hands of the Soviet terror machine, Bolan severed all ties with Establishment authority.

Now, after a lengthy lone-wolf struggle and much soul-searching, the Executioner has agreed to enter an "arm's-length" alliance with his government once more, reserving the right to pursue personal missions in his Everlasting War.

Mack Bolan was no superman, though with the help of a compact Aimpoint scope atop his M-16 A-2 rifle, he had a superhero's ability to see as far as an eagle. He kept the safety in place on the sleek weapon, not wanting to accidentally trip the match-grade trigger of the modified-for-silence M-16. Complete with a foot-long GEM-Tech suppressor, the rifle was a swift, quiet instrument of death, and in the hands of the Executioner, it was also his tool of judgment. He lay flat across the roof of the old villa, atop sunbaked curved shells of clay that layered across the top of the old Moorish-inspired architecture. Bolan propped on his elbows, waiting for the rest of his prey to show up in the courtyard below.

This hit, on the outskirts of Cairo, was a two-for-one.

The Executioner ran over the events that led to this night, and the plan that brought him here. While Hal Brognola had his arrangements with Bolan to take out targets in service to Stony Man Farm, ultimately for the good of the United States, Bolan also had the freedom to take personal missions in his War Everlasting. Brognola contacted the Executioner about two men responsible for blood, tears and suffering across three continents. This time Mack Bolan surprised Brognola. The targets were long marked for justice, and the Executioner was fully prepared to deliver their judgment.

Target number one was Yong Kit Ho. Ethnic Vietnamese, but a member of the People's Republic of China's SAD—equivalent to the American CIA. He was a mover and a shaker in back alleys from Pakistan to Japan. Yong wasn't known to pull the trigger on anyone, but he always provided the triggers—and the rest of the guns—to anyone who was disrupting an enemy of the PRC. Yong's visit to Egypt was something that had interested an American CIA man, J. R. Rust. Rust and Bolan had kept quiet channels open over the years.

Bolan knew the value of keeping communication and intel outside of his ties with Stony Man Farm and Hal Brognola. Bolan's relationship with the government was arm's length, and he was at his most comfortable as a lone hunter—a shadow hunting shadows.

Target number two was Qurif Kissad, a member of Hamas. Bolan had warred before with the radical terrorist breakaway organization of the Palestine Liberation Organization. Kissad's very existence and presence in Cairo meant that he was fair game for the Executioner. This man was a killer, and he had gunned down soldiers and innocents alike. There was also talk that this particular parasite convinced the young and disenfranchised of the West Bank to become human bombs. The Executioner had encountered the type around the world, monsters willing to sacrifice the lives of a nation's future for a goal of pure hatred. It was a given that Kissad was meeting with Yong to bring hell to Israel and the Palestinian territories.

Anything that the Executioner could do to break apart this meeting of the minds would seem to be a matter of reflex for him. But Mack Bolan didn't do anything on pure reflex. He was a thinking soldier who constantly planned, even if it was only a few seconds ahead based on the environment. The only things Bolan was missing from this plan were his .44 Magnum Desert Eagle, left in the States to make room for the multipurpose M-16, and a ride home. Brognola's urgent cell phone communiqué gave the Executioner some options for a ride home, and

Bolan had supplemented his Beretta 93-R with a weapon he'd been thoroughly wringing out for possible field use. A tiny Beretta 9000S, complete with polymer frame, was tucked away. What made the small pistol so attractive as a backup gun was the fact that it could take the 15- and 20-round magazines of its big brothers, the Beretta 92-F and the Beretta 93-R. It could also handle the same high-powered 9 mm hollowpoint bullets that Bolan made for himself, or had made for him by Stony Man Farm.

Bolan didn't expect it to get down to the stubby Beretta. Too many unexpected things, however, had come at Bolan in his life for him to ever be complacent, even on a simple hit and git like this one. A complacent soldier quickly became a dead soldier.

Above the courtyard, with lamps lighting the ground level casting shadows and the clay shells concealing him, the Executioner was nearly impossible to see. His face and hands were darkened by combat cosmetics, and he wore a combat blacksuit. The snug garment was laden with hidden pockets and hugged his powerful frame so nothing would snag. Even though he was nearly invisible, Bolan kept the scope's lens cap folded to provide a shade for the front lens.

Yong sat in the courtyard of the hotel, smoking a cigarette, lounging lazily in a Technicolor nightmare of a shirt and a cream summer-weight suit. Yong was unarmed, but around the courtyard, three men who wore dark suits and black sunglasses were obviously packing iron.

Hair slicked back, the SAD man looked as if he were living the life of a Hong Kong action movie gangster, complete with long, dramatic drags on his cigarette. He smirked, looking at one of his bodyguards, then reached over and took a sip from a tumbler of brown fluid.

Eat, drink and be merry, the Executioner thought, the scope magnifying Yong's features.

Tonight, you die.

The bodyguards were reacting to something that the Executioner couldn't quite see. He regretted his position didn't give him a better view of what was right under the balcony where a main hallway emptied onto it. Bolan had scouted the killing box, though. This would at least give him a bit of an edge. Earlier in the day, dressed in khaki shorts and a T-shirt, and armed with the Beretta 9000 in his pocket, he'd gone on a soft probe of the courtyard.

There were only three hallways that led to escape. The Executioner perched on a rooftop of a wing that didn't have a first-floor hallway running through it. Bolan was confident with the M-16, he could deny Yong and Kissad the hallway entrance he couldn't see, as the balcony gave cover only to someone standing directly in the archway. One step beyond and the Executioner could blow off feet and legs. The other two hallways were well within the Executioner's arc of vision, which meant they were well within his line of fire.

Bolan didn't intend to stay on the rooftop all night, though.

He gave one last check to make sure that the curved roof tiles, an inch thick and two feet by two feet, would hold his weight. He anchored bungee cords to two of the heavy shell tiles and clipped a harness around his waist. With a simple roll, he'd be down to courtyard level within seconds if necessary, and the fast-release belt clasp would allow him freedom of movement to take on all comers.

Well, this time, the comers were Kissad and his people.

Show time.

On the barrel of the M-16 he'd attached a boom mike, designed by his longtime friend and fellow soldier Hermann "Gadgets" Schwarz. Weighing less than twelve ounces, the boom mike had the range to pick up conversations from the courtyard, and was connected to Bolan's combat harness, where a 14.5 ounce receiver ran its line up to his ear. Another little outside the channels bit of hardware.

Even though Gadgets was one-third of Stony Man Farm's Able Team, the electronics genius had supplied the Executioner with high-tech surveillance gear since practically weeks after Bolan began his crusade against Animal Man. Gadgets kept Bolan in a supply of electronic surveillance goodies, often lending the big guy raw prototypes for testing. Though Bolan himself was no electronics specialist, the suggestions he made to Gadgets allowed Able Team and Stony Man Farm to profit from Bolan's field testing.

The M-16 mounted super-ear was a prototype, something that would be as useful sweeping for errant enemy footsteps in a jungle as giving a crusading sniper a chance to listen in on his enemies. It was a system that was inspired by the U.S. Army's Land Warrior system, where rifles had lasers and remote optics mounted on the barrels. Gadgets took the concept a step further. If seeing around a corner was a good thing, then seeing and hearing around a corner, or at a distance, was even better. By putting everything in place on the silenced sniper rifle, it cut down on the extra gear that had to be carried. In the old days, Bolan would have needed a separate, rifle-sized shotgun microphone to get the kind of up close and personal eavesdropping ability the M-16 now provided.

Kissad walked in, flanked by a pair of his own hardmen, dressed in a simple white shirt and khaki pants. His right pocket was bulging with the presence of a pistol. The hardmen who flanked him wore loose leather jackets, and had to have been sweltering even in the slowly cooling Egyptian evening, but the jackets were a must to conceal their hardware. From the size, Bolan figured them to be armed with nothing larger than a MAC-10 or mini-Uzi. Heavy-duty armament, definitely more than the Chinese contingent was packing. Bolan made a mental note to give the Hamas hardmen his attention first.

The Executioner depressed the activation stud on the super-ear.

"You're running late," Yong said.

Bolan was grateful for Yong's English. The Executioner's knowledge of Arabic was passable, and his Chinese good enough to order an authentic meal at a restaurant, but otherwise, the Executioner would have been out of luck if they'd gotten to speaking in technical terms. Still, he was prepared, just in case. The receiver for the super-ear also had a wire hooked to a flat, seven ounce MP3 recorder that could hold up to an hour's worth of music. Gadgets had discovered an understated bonus for the device. It could record an hour of conversation if needed. With a good computer and a satellite link, Bolan could transmit the compressed data in a mere five minutes. If the pair started talking in Arabic or Chinese dialects, he'd have them recorded for later translation.

Kissad nodded. "I'm running late."

Yong frowned. "You're awfully cool about it."

Kissad smirked. "Because you simply don't matter to us anymore."

Bolan perked up at that. The vultures were falling out?

The Executioner slipped the selector on the suppressed sniper rifle to full-auto. Just in case business started early.

"I don't understand," Yong said. "I have promised you everything you need."

"You've promised us everything, but someone leaked your presence to the U.S. Embassy," Kissad growled. He glowered as he paced back and forth.

Bolan's steely blue eyes narrowed at that. He'd have to let Rust know about the leak in his office.

"But what about your boat?" Yong asked.

Boat? Bolan made a mental note of that. Why would Hamas need a boat?

"I've got it covered," Kissad answered. "And I do not need some Chow Yun Fat wannabe parading across the city and attracting every hairy eyeball from our enemies."

Yong sneered and stood. "Just who do you think you're talking to?"

Bolan watched Kissad's fast draw from his pocket. He almost felt admiration for the blazing reflex motion. The revolver flashed and blasted, five explosive fireballs bursting from its muzzle as Kissad's hardmen began unleathering their heavy-duty pieces. Sure enough, they were Uzis, as Bolan had figured, and he tapped off a 3-round burst into the gunner on the left before his weapon was halfway out of his jacket. The hardguy shuddered, bullets ripping into the front of his chest.

Others were making up for the stealth rifle. The courtyard was now filled with the crash and thunder of close to a dozen weapons as men dived for cover, sweeping at one another in panic fire. These men were thugs and terrorists. Marksmanship under fire was not one of their skills. Kissad's men were burning off their clips fast, without even acquiring a target, while the Chinese bodyguards were ponderously slow in trying to aim from the shoulder and fire. Entire magazines were being emptied in panicked sweeps of fire that mostly chewed up walls and furniture.

Only one of the Chinese bodyguards took a hit, a glancing wound that drove him to the ground, but he crawled behind a stone column and reloaded his empty CZ-75 knockoff, leaning around and continuing to return fire. He actually managed to tag one of Kissad's gunners with three shots, but only after blasting through a whole 15-round magazine. The gun locked open, and the bodyguard swerved back, the column he hid behind sparking and casting off gouts of crushed stone dust as bullets hammered it.

Kissad took cover behind an overturned table, revolver emptied after pumping shots into Yong. Bolan tracked a burst across the tabletop, giving the M-16 its head. All he got was a cloud of flying splinters and a suddenly alert terrorist for his trouble.

Kissad was too fast, physically and mentally. He began shouting something over the din of the firefight. The terrorist grabbed a limb on Bolan's first target and dragged the body closer to the table. The body wasn't as much an issue as the Uzi on its chest. Bolan fired down at the corpse, trying to knock away the Uzi, but the torso was jerked behind the shade of the overturned table before the burst tracked into it. Kissad was armed, and Bolan didn't waste time with a curse.

The soldier didn't need a translation for the words "up there!" in rushed Arabic, as suddenly the shadows around him were filled with shattering clay. The Executioner kicked off the rooftop, rolling over the edge in a blur of motion. For the space of a few heartbeats, he was weightless, his body hovering in midair, then he was cutting loose with the weapon, tumbling forward. Mack Bolan may not have been Superman, but for a moment, he was in full free flight, the bungee cords on his waist still flapping loose behind him, no slack taken. Instead, the slack was off on the suppressed M-16, bullets ripping out the can on the barrel in a harsh, prolonged fit of coughing. Kissad still bellowed for his men to sweep the roof with gunfire. The gunners were cutting loose, aiming too high, with no fire discipline as they let the recoil of their weapons yank their fire even higher. Gravity, however, pulled the Executioner down. The M-16's bolt locked back on an empty chamber. The magazine had run dry while he still descended. Bolan let the rifle swing on the sling around his neck. His hand flashed to his hip, used to the massive grip of the Desert Eagle, but instead, finding the stubby little Beretta 9000, which cleared leather in an instant. He stiff-armed the Beretta and hammered off three quick rounds, somehow coring a Hamas gunman as he was still slowing on the bungee cords a heartbeat later.

The whole course of events took less than two seconds.

Bolan's boots hit the clay bricks of the courtyard at the same time as his first kill with the Beretta 9000 crashed face first to the ground. Flexing his knees to absorb the shock, the soldier tracked for targets even as the gunmen tried to take into account the sudden flash of blackness that was in their midst. Sending a dose of 9 mm pills into another of the Hamas hit men Bolan found himself in the shadow of the same table that had protected Kissad's life moments ago. Gunmen started scrambling to get to him.

The Executioner took a splinter of a second to grab the

taped magazines on his M-16 and flip them, bringing a fresh 30-round load to bear. He swept the charging handle and stripped a fresh round off the top of the new magazine.

The first Hamas man into view ran across at pelvis level, the muzzle of Bolan's assault rifle humming as bullets ripped through the suppressor. The guy tumbled into eternity with his pelvis broken and his belly filled with hot lead and bone chunks. The terrorist hot on his heels tried to slow down, but Bolan swept the scope's dot sight on him at chin level. Another stroke of the match-grade, full-auto trigger, and a geyser of skull and brain matter erupted from the fledgling volcano that used to be a terrorist's head.

The Chinese men were still shooting, and Bolan spotted Yong laying near to him, snarling and firing off rounds from a Chinese Makarov copy. The SAD man had torn open his Hawaiian-style shirt, revealing a dark blue vest beneath. Somewhere under all that there also had to have been a holster that clipped to his body armor.

Bolan rolled to his right, hard, before Yong could put together the fact that the newcomer to this battle was no friend of his. As he rolled behind a massive stone pot, Bolan spotted Kissad, heading down one of the hallways. The borrowed Uzi in his fist spit lead, brass casings tumbling in the air as he laid down covering fire for his own retreat. His fellow Hamas hardmen be damned while Kissad saved his own skin.

The easy shot on Yong would have to wait, because the Executioner refused to let the gunfight spill onto the street. No terrorist was worth an innocent life cut down in a cross fire.

Bolan rolled into view, exposing himself to Kissad's remaining killers. Fate intervened as Yong and his remaining bodyguard were cutting loose with their pistols. The hail of gunfire flickered both ways, and Kissad spun away from the battle, racing down the hall. Again, Bolan stroked the trigger, and 5.56 mm tumblers spit out of the blunt suppressor on the sleek M-16.

Kissad suddenly windmilled his arms, his legs shot forward from under him. His body bounced to the ground and his Uzi clattered along floor tile. The Hamas man clawed and groped, hunting for his weapon as sweat glistened on his forehead, drool pouring from a corner of his mouth. Qurif Kissad was suffering, but the Executioner spared a mercy burst for the terrorist.

Mack Bolan was not a man who believed in cruel or unusual punishment, even for the worst of Animal Man's minions.

Kissad's headless body twitched, and Bolan turned his attention back to the gunfight.

Yong was perched over his bodyguard, trying to control the bleeding of the dying man.

Honor, even among thieves, Bolan thought. He stood and pocketed the magazine from the partially depleted M-16.

Yong was whispering to the dying man in Chinese as Bolan drew a fresh magazine and slapped it home, this time pulling the charging handle in order to get the SAD agent's attention. Yong looked up, his eyes full of fury.

"I assume you speak English," Yong said. "Make it quick."

Bolan shouldered the rifle and put a single round into the dying bodyguard's forehead.

Yong turned from the mercy shot, his cream-colored suit now spattered pink from blood. He stood and faced off with the Executioner, eyes unwavering.

"Mossad?" Yong asked.

Bolan shook his head, lips a tight line across his craggy face.

"It doesn't matter. I don't suppose you could be bought off?" Yong suggested. The guy knew when his time was up.

Bolan shook his head again. "There's not enough money on this planet. Not for you."

Yong smirked and nodded. "I kind of figured that. Kissad accused me of thinking I was in a John Woo movie. You *are* a walking John Woo movie."

Yong looked down the hall at the dead terrorist, then sighed. "It was fun while it lasted."

"The party always has to end sometime," Bolan told him.

Yong shrugged and held the pose, closing his eyes and spreading his arms. A signal that it was done and over with.

Bolan put a single bullet just above the bridge of the SAD man's nose, blowing his brains out through the back of his long, flowing hair.

Once again, the courtyard was quiet, except for the sound of dripping blood.

The Executioner reached for the super-ear's controller, turning it off.

If there was one thing the Executioner didn't need to have recorded for posterity, it was the sound of dripping blood.

"GOOD JOB, STRIKER," Hal Brognola said in congratulation over Bolan's line. The cell phone was hooked into Bolan's laptop, which had a satcom link back to Stony Man Farm. Between the phone's encryption, the satcom's encryption and the tight, direct line transmission setup of the system, it was unlikely that anyone would ever have a chance of hearing what Bolan and Brognola were saying to each other. Still, the Executioner wasn't going to bandy about words, nor be careless with information.

"Any problems?" Brognola asked.

"No. Tell Cowboy the new Tupperware worked great," Bolan returned.

Brognola cleared his throat. "Huh?"

"He'll know what I mean," Bolan replied.

Brognola grunted an affirmative. "I assume everything went well with Gadgets's little experiment, too."

"It was an earful. I uploaded the conversation. Maybe you can make sense of it," Bolan said.

"Yeah, Bear gave me a transcript as soon as you sent it," Brognola confirmed. "Voice recognition typing. Will wonders never cease?"

Bolan smiled at his friend's comment. "Sometimes the gee-whiz James Bond gear makes up for the stress."

"Does that do it for you?" Brognola asked.

Bolan gave a chuckle. "I actually don't have time to stress out. I'm too busy living in the moment."

Brognola groaned. "All these years of me and my antacids, and now you clue me in on that samurai zen crap."

Bolan grinned. It wasn't often he got to provide someone else with a chuckle. Usually, he was straight man to the gallows humor of his friends and partners Jack Grimaldi and Gadgets Schwarz. "I wouldn't worry about it. You'll still need the antacid for Bear's coffee."

"I heard that," Aaron "The Bear" Kurtzman clicked in. "We were doing some checks, and we found out about that possible boat link."

Bolan was ready to take on another leg of this particular mission. "Give me a location. I'll stop in and look—"

"A little late, Striker," Kurtzman cut him off.

Brognola spoke up. "You're not the only one who has his own projects going."

"I'm sending you the info dump," Bear explained. "Good news is, they're your ride home if you want it."

"I'll take it," Bolan answered. He listened as his phone crackled for about ten seconds, Bear's data transmission sizzling down the tight beam channel.

Bolan read the screen of his laptop, skimming quickly.

The boat that the Farm assumed was being talked about was a yacht owned by a terrorist known as Ahmur Ibn Laud. Laud was the commander of an al-Qaeda breakoff organization known as The Soldiers of the Divine Sword of Allah. The U.S. Justice Department arranged to get a joint strike force over to Egypt for the purposes of catching Laud, and finding out more about the Divine Sword, whether it was a true splinter—made of members who had grown dissatisfied with al-Qaeda's lot, or if the Divine Sword was something much more complex. According to Kurtzman's information, Laud's boat was docked in a marina at Alexandria, just up the Nile from Cairo.

Around the time that the Executioner was passing judgment on Yong and Kissad, a joint U.S. Marshals Service and FBI Hostage Rescue Team moved in on the yacht, took Laud prisoner and whisked him away to a C-130 parked just outside of

Cairo. It was a quick operation, and moving Laud away from Alexandria was done to prevent his terrorist buddies from interfering with the transport team. Whatever al-Qaeda cell was operating in Alexandria was unlikely to think about contacting a cell in Cairo once their boss was snatched.

It was a good plan on paper, especially with the presence of a U.S. aircraft carrier creating a good red herring. Bolan figured that the C-130 would more or less hug the coast and move out over international waters only to avoid flying over Libya.

A minimum of risk, Bolan figured. The big lifter would be vulnerable to faster moving aircraft, to which al-Qaeda supposedly had no access anymore. Not since U.S. bombing raids had obliterated the Taliban's air forces. Or so it seemed.

A lot of aircraft could have been sent elsewhere, and all it took was a single good airplane with some serious firepower to take down a Hercules. Even most of the Third World aircraft, which could barely break 400 miles per hour in flight and only be fodder for an F-16 fighter, could tear apart a Hercules. That would require planning and training though.

The thought nagged the Executioner for a few moments. It would take planning, especially if someone was setting a trap. Was Ahmur Ibn Laud willing to sacrifice his own life to kill American lawmen?

"Striker, you okay with the flight? If not, we could just get you on a helicopter out to the carrier group, and I can send Jack to bring you home," Brognola interrupted his reveries over the sat phone.

"No. I'm fine with the flight with Laud," Bolan answered. He didn't give voice to the idea that he might be stepping into the jaws of death, but for Mack Bolan, that was a given with every footstep he took.

Gleaming coils of stainless steel writhed around Ahmur Ibn Laud's wrists, binding them together so that he had only three inches of play between them. Another ten-inch length of the stainless chain clung fast to the loop of unyielding links around his waist. The same loop dropped a length to his ankles where yet another chain finished the job of binding him so that he shuffled in strides no longer than the space of one of his own feet. Barely able to move, Laud saw the task of creeping up the rear ramp of the C-130 Hercules as emasculating and tedious, making him seem like some feeble old man.

But Laud was not a man to allow a moment of discomfort to get in the way of himself. He moved with dignity, head up, crystal blue eyes clear and penetrating into the shadows under the tail of the massive plane. Let these Americans chuckle and chortle, watching him with relaxed bemusement, for they were clasping a scorpion of the desert to their bosom, thinking to contain the killer's true sting when all they had done was band his pincers.

He worked his way slowly, certainly, up the ramp, the hot wind across the Egyptian airfield blowing in from the desert. His shoulders began to cramp, but he ignored the pain. The three-hour drive and the blistering heat informed him that he was no longer anywhere near Alexandria, where the American lawmen had come to his humble little yacht, stormed aboard and taken him under arrest.

They sent eight armed men to arrest one, in the middle of the night, at a small marina where no one was armed. The Americans so readily accepted the fact that he was theirs for the taking.

Just as Laud had arranged it.

Two men showed alertness, one of whom was a dark-skinned man. He'd done all the speaking to Laud, reading him his Miranda arrest rights for covering all bases—and ordering him to cooperate, all in fluent Arabic. Laud put up a halfhearted struggle. The man, almost a black man by complexion, still had the aquiline nose and the wavy black hair of a man whose bloodline ran deep through the Mediterranean.

The American Arab watched him like a hawk, quiet and serious, his hand never far from the pistol in its hip holster.

The only other man who could not relax and grin as if it were time for a beer was a baby-faced, stocky man with blue eyes and blond hair. He stayed at the bottom of the ramp. While the false Arab watched him, the other looked out on the horizon with what Laud believed the Americans called "the thousand-yard stare."

"Jonny, Hadji, would you two relax?" one of the Americans said. He was wearing a lightweight windbreaker with the letters FBI emblazoned in bright yellow across the stylish black nylon. "This isn't Hannibal Lecter."

Laud was confused for a moment at the FBI man calling the Americanized Arab "Hadji." It was more appropriately a Pakistani or Indian name. He didn't have the blunter nose and straighter hair of someone from the subcontinent. Then he remembered from his brief time in America, a cartoon show about two young boys and their guardians. The boys were named Jonny and Hadji. The resemblance was there for the men, and probably even more so when they were much younger.

Laud filed this away for future reference. Obviously these

two men had known each other for a long time, perhaps since childhood. A threat to one would give the other pause.

Ammunition for the future.

Laud repressed a smile, remaining impassive and shuffling toward one of the benches on the C-130's interior. He paused, seeing a man wearing an army uniform and carrying a gear bag. This man was tall, more than six feet, but tightly muscled. The sleeves of his BDU blouse were rolled up, revealing impressive corded muscles. His closely trimmed black hair was plastered to his sweat-slick forehead. The man sat down comfortably, as if he had spent most of his life on the big transport aircraft. He had to have been a longtime soldier, Laud guessed. Or maybe something more, considering he was alone, and hitchhiking on a plane that should have been reserved for the American team and himself.

Cold blue eyes regarded him as the man sitting at the end of the bench tried to act the role of a tired soldier. It didn't work for Laud, and the hard gaze probably pierced his own thoughts. There was a meeting for a moment, two iron wills holding to see who would blink first. Then Laud reacted to being prodded in the side by "Hadji."

"Sit down," Hadji told him. Laud felt his knee buckled out with a simple nudge, reflex dumping the al-Qaeda commander back onto the bench. He landed with the thump of clumsy flesh and jingling chains.

"All right," Laud answered in perfect English. He brought up his smile now, the smile of certainty that he had everyone's number on this plane, even the hard man at the end of the bench.

"Face front, and no smiling," Hadji ordered.

Laud looked forward. "I don't take orders from sidekicks too well."

There was no response for a heartbeat. American racism was such a wonderful ally in making even the most devoted lawman blink for a moment. "I don't care, Ahmur. You murder people for a living, and used to crawl on your knees for handouts from a pack of cannibals who starved, raped and murdered almost an entire nation."

The muzzle of the side arm pushed Laud's thickly bearded chin up so the two men were looking face-to-face now.

"If you want to get into a pissing contest about who holds the moral high ground, just remember your bladder's empty, and you're headed for a five-by-eight cell forty feet underground until your trial."

Laud feigned a frown.

Hadji holstered his pistol, halfway between anger and satisfaction. He stepped back, returning to a level of professional alertness, emotion drained from his face.

Laud wondered whether that professionalism would be when he was on his knees, handcuffed, with a pistol at the base of his neck.

The good times were coming.

"Don't let him get to you, man," David Kowalski suggested, sitting down next to Orlando Wazdi after the brief confrontation.

"I'm not," Wazdi lied. He wished he were telling the truth, but he thought he'd at least done a good job of covering up on the surface. Apparently not, though. Laud was watching him with bemusement, and Ski was immediately at his side trying to provide moral support.

"The gun on his chin might come back to haunt us when this punk gets to trial," Ski said.

Wazdi's gut churned for a moment, but he willed it back under control. "All right. No more macho shows of who's the boss."

"Yeah. It's too long a flight. Once we get in the air, we can relax," Ski told him. Wazdi glanced down at Ski's lap and saw he still had his Remington 870 shotgun resting there, finger against the trigger guard, only a heartbeat away from cutting loose with a blast of buckshot. The muzzle was pointed right at Laud's legs and crotch as he sat.

Wazdi managed a smirk. "You're gonna blow his kielbasa off?"

Ski nodded. "If they try to take him back, I'm aiming low. They say over here an emasculated man is not even worth a woman."

"You're a sweetheart. The misogyny of my roots is always one of my favorite subjects," Wazdi answered.

"Wazz," Ski groaned, "your roots are the north side of Chicago. Maybe Miami."

Wazdi kept watching Laud. They were speaking low enough, and were far enough away from him that he couldn't hear the details of their conversation.

"Just because Poland never had much to contribute to the world doesn't mean you can't get a little groove back to the Motherland."

"Yeah? Where would Maxwell Street be without the Polish?"

"Probably dumping too many onions on some other meat by-product."

The ambient sunlight was dying out as the rear ramp was being hydraulically lifted into place. The plane itself was starting to shake and rumble with the drone of the engines of the big bird powering up. The interior lighting wasn't much compared to the harsh blaze of the Egyptian sky, but Wazdi had adjusted to it.

As soon as the loading ramp latched firmly shut, Ski flipped over the 870, jerked the bolt on the shotgun and ejected the round from the chamber. If he needed a fresh round, he could strip it off the magazine with a simple tromboning of the slide. Plus, he had his pistols if need be.

"My favorite part," Ski muttered.

"We're not on board one of those little Buddy Holly-killing puddle jumpers, Ski. We're aboard a Hercules," Wazdi reassured his childhood friend. "We're not going to crash."

Ski was afraid of heights, despite the fact that the two friends went skydiving and bungee jumping together on the rare weekends that they weren't neck deep in cases. The last real jumping they did was when they were training at a secret facility in Virginia's Blue Ridge mountains, when they were part of what they knew only as the Blacksuit Program. They'd had months of farmhand work, combat training and nighttime patrol at a facility a short distance from Washington, D.C. He'd like the camaraderie there, and the "instructors" taught him things that were very street relevant. That stuff then got passed on to his coworkers, information that could mean the difference for survival.

Wazdi's mood became grim with the appearance of Special Agent Quentin Best. The guy in charge of the Laud snatch wasn't someone who would have been picked for the Farm's work. First off, he wouldn't stoop to doing hay bailing or fence post repair for a good part of the day, and he suffered from NIH-ilism. Not nihilism the political theory that the destruction of modern society was the only way humankind could survive, but the near-fatal disease when someone in charge had his head up his ass and ignored any concepts "not invented here."

"All right, Wazdi, you can stop watching Laud," Best said, smacking him heartily on the shoulder.

Ski tensed like a rottweiler responding to an attack on his owner, but Wazdi gave an out-of-sight wave.

"You don't have to be his personal bodyguard. You're just the translator," Best continued, smirking.

Wazdi nodded, letting the condescension wash over him like a summer drizzle. "Yeah."

Best chuckled. "Don't take it personally. We got him, and your buddy and his team kept their peepers peeled on the drive over. You didn't see them going over their boundaries."

"All right," Wazdi answered with the same interest he'd show an ant nibbling at grains of sand on his boot.

Best tensed. "Listen. There's a chain of command here, and I expect you to show me some damn respect. Don't you like working for the team?"

"I love it," Wazdi returned defiantly.

Best went nose to nose. "Then listen up. I don't care if you cry discrimination. I'm not going to put up with your insubordinate bullshit."

"I didn't see any insubordination," Ski spoke up. Wazdi flinched.

Best glowered. "I didn't ask your opinion. Move it. I want this space reserved for real FBI only."

Ski stood, which wasn't very far. He was five foot eight, but built like a fireplug. Best towered over him by four inches and had a lean, gangly frame.

"Wazz works for the FBI. And he respects your rules. I don't, so I can pretty much speak the truth when I say you're not acting too damn professional," Ski challenged.

"I'll report you to your supervisor if you don't back off," Best growled.

Ski grinned. "Go ahead. Unlike you, my supervisor actually respects the brains of the people working under him."

As Best reddened, Wazdi grabbed Ski's elbow. "Come on. You need a time out. Sorry, sir."

Wazdi felt a little resistance at first, but the bulldoglike Ski eventually followed along as they moved up the bench. Best's crew of sycophants surrounded him and began to compliment him for a snatch and grab gone well.

"You gotta work for someone better," Ski muttered as they sat across from a quiet man.

"I work for the Federal Bureau of Investigation, Hostage Rescue Team. Best just happens to be a small part of that," Wazdi answered.

"Well—" Ski broke off.

Wazdi, still watching Best and his people laughing in front of Laud, looked up at his old friend to see why his train of thought was still boarding at the station.

"Wazz!" Ski hissed.

Wazdi got slapped on his arm when he didn't look to where Ski was pointing.

The big guy, having settled into what looked like a combat

nap, was very familiar to the two. The only name they knew him by was Striker, and he wasn't a constant visitor to the Farm, but when he showed up, people got excited. A pair of icy blue eyes flicked open and looked at the pair sitting across from him.

He just nodded, put a finger to his lips, then closed his eyes again.

Wazdi blinked for a moment, got the message, then relaxed, nudging for Ski to do the same. But he couldn't resist commenting, "You're right, Ski."

One icy eye opened slowly, looking at him as he spoke.

"He does, he does look like him," Ski said.

The eye widened some, and he started to sit up.

"Yeah, Striker does look like Race Bannon," Wazdi said.

The big man shrugged, then slumped back down to rest, relieved.

THE EXECUTIONER WAS surprised to see two former blacksuits on the flight. He was relieved by their presence, though. These were competent, highly trained men he would probably be able to call on if something happened. He wasn't sure what could happen, but he'd gone over the facts of how easily Laud was smoked out by the combined team in Alexandria. Most overseas arrests by similar task forces had been of terrorists who weren't actively involved in operations, but also had gone off with similar ease. Laud, a ranking member of al-Qaeda, was still active in keeping the international terrorist organization in business.

Eight men had walked onto the marina where Laud parked his yacht, stormed the decks and nary a peep filled the air.

The phrase "suck play" kept rolling over and over in the soldier's head.

Not one sentry was present.

Not one bodyguard.

Not one roommate.

It could be that Laud was cocky, and let his crew go on shore leave. After all, the yacht was docked.

No, the two men sitting before him had felt the tension, too. As if another boot were about to be dropped, and this one had cleats. He stirred from his physical dormancy, rested from the drive to the plane, and looked at the pair. A wave of his hand and they stepped across, kneeling beside him.

"This was a trap," he said to them.

"This is from the news file marked 'duh,' Striker," David Kowalski quipped.

Orlando Wazdi gave his friend a jab with his elbow. "Serious time. Use big boy language."

Bolan ignored the icebreaking comedy act. "The name's Stone. Colonel Brandon Stone."

"Yes, sir," Ski returned. He hummed a familiar movie theme, inspired by Bolan's self-identification. This too he let pass, but his lips tightened in a slight smile.

"He doesn't have an off switch, does he?" Bolan asked Wazdi.

Wazdi shook his head. "Only a volume switch. Feel lucky. He's in happy mode now. Cranky, he's a whole lot worse."

Bolan nodded. "Duly noted."

"Colonel Stone," Ski spoke up, a little bit of reverence in his tone, "what do you think is going to happen?"

Bolan looked over. "Laud isn't suicidal, but I don't think this plane's getting as far as the coast."

Ski looked at the floor. "Great."

KANSID YASSIF KEPT the Lockheed T33 tame as he swung the aircraft low and over the Nile, watching the C-130 Hercules taking off in the distance. At five hundred miles per hour, the jet, formerly part of the Pakistani air force, wouldn't stand a chance against most things in the sky these days. It was considered a close support aircraft by third world nations. Using its cannon and rocket pods for peppering ground forces who couldn't scramble out of the path of a five-hundred-mile-an-hour bullet, it could rain precision fire across a football field in the space of a heartbeat.

Yassif regretted the fact that he never had a chance to be a real fighter pilot. Instead he took potshots at easy targets on the ground, never getting the joy of seeing an enemy airplane spout a thick tendril of choking smoke as it began its wounded descent to the waiting earth below. This day, however, he'd finally get his dream. The Lockheed was sold under the counter by a Pakistan air force colonel to his friends in the great crusade for Islamic theocracy that was the Taliban.

The Hercules in the distance was a sitting duck for the smaller, more agile craft. Fitted with 23 mm cannon and rocket pods, he could literally blast the plane into confetti.

However, this was only to be a force-down. It would still count as a kill. Yassif's cannons blowing engines and one wing apart, perhaps stitching a pilot. Ahead, in the desert between Egypt and Libya, helicopters waited to pick up Laud, and a few extra, juicy prizes.

Yassif kept the Lockheed low and ready.

It was almost time to start the show.

Captain Michael Yates continued his regular sweep of the instruments on the C-130, making sure everything was running smoothly. His copilot, Lieutenant Josephine Grant, and their navigator, Alan Stewart, were keeping their eyes on the skies from their respective points of view. Flying over a desert was a risky enough business, as had been proved in mishaps from Iran, to Afghanistan over the years.

The Herky bird had a history of being able to go anywhere and survive almost anything, but the whims of fate were as deadly as antiaircraft guns. Complacency, Yates thought, could turn a routine flight into a moment of life and death. You missed one detail, and the next thing you knew, you got a big picture—usually through the windshield as the sky and the ground twisted in a struggle to be on top before everything became ground. Relaxation was not a part of Yates's language until all wheels were on the ground, he was in the pilot's lounge and Scotch whisky was nestled in a tumbler in his hands.

"What the...?" Stewart spoke up, checking the radar.

"Whatcha got?"

"We had a blip at four o'clock," Stewart said.

"Any radio traffic?" Yates asked.

"Nothing, and there wasn't enough time for it to register any IFF," Stewart answered. He tapped the screen, as if to goad the mystery contact out of hiding.

"Think we should radio Cairo to see if they have anything in the air over here?" Grant asked. She was keeping her eyes peeled now.

"I would, but we have some very dangerous cargo on board. Let's not call attention to ourselves by ringing up Cairo," Yates decided. He directed Stewart to contact the aircraft carrier.

"Maybe they have something in the sky with some better eyes than we've got," he explained.

"Gotcha, Cap," Stewart answered.

Yates gave the engines on the Herky Bird an extra goose, pushing them as close as possible to their 360 mile-per-hour maximum speed. He didn't want to get caught flat-footed.

Maybe complacency had crept into his routine. He had been flying these missions since just after the FBI grabbed the psycho who shot up the CIA front gate. The FBI and U.S. Marshals were making more and more of these grabs after a successful arrest and extradition from Pakistan. The Hercules had been made an integral part of it. It was one of the few aircraft with the range and endurance to go anywhere. It was also a common sight on airfields around the globe, so the mere presence of the big transport wouldn't set off alarms.

Except, maybe this time it did, Yates thought as his gaze went from the gauges to the windows, wishing he had a better view. Ahead, the desert was not as flat as they often showed it to be in the movies. Dunes rolled and undulated like waves at the speed they were moving, and he didn't think that the radar on the Hercules could spot anything flying low to them. It was a principle of stealth technology that uneven surfaces deflected radar beams, so they would not bounce back as contacts.

His stomach tightened as he listened to Stewart's hushed murmurings. Yates pulled up the intercom. Maybe it was time to get someone looking out for their backs, too.

ORLANDO WAZDI watched the flight technicians head toward the portholes along the sides of the cabin. He tried to relax, but his muscles drew even tighter at that sight. "They're worried," he whispered.

"Someone must have spotted a tail," Bolan stated. He sat up from his brief catnap.

"So what do we do?" Kowalski asked.

"Take a look out one of those little windows and see if there's some bad guys on our tail," Wazdi returned.

Kowalski chuckled nervously. "Great. Then we fire up the Batplane and chase after them."

"Batplane?" Bolan asked.

Wazdi spoke up to alleviate his friend's tension.

"You mean you don't have an inflatable jet aircraft inside your gear bag?"

Bolan grimaced.

Kowalski swallowed, paled for a second, then steeled himself. "Looking out for trouble could help."

Wazdi felt a surge of pride as his childhood friend went back. The flight crew regarded the blond marshal for a moment, but didn't want to say anything. Wazdi and Striker went to the opposite side of the cargo bay.

Best's voice cut through Wazdi's concentration as he peered through the porthole. "Wazdi, what the hell are you doing?"

"Playing spot the mummy," Wazdi sniped. "Any moment now, the computer-generated face of Arnold Vosloo will come tearing up from the desert in the form of a sandstorm and try to eat us. But it is written by the ancients that the big mouth of the FBI might be able to scare him off."

Best sneered. "Listen, smart ass…"

Bolan put his hand on Wazdi's shoulder. "There!"

Wazdi turned and caught the shape of a distant speck. "It's so far away."

"At the right speed, it'll be right on top of us in no time," Bolan mentioned.

"Got a rocket launcher, maybe?" Wazdi asked.

"Don't get nervous on me now," Bolan said.

The big man lifted a pair of binoculars to his eyes. "It's a Lockheed. The thing's got two hundred miles an hour on this bird."

"Lockheed? What?" Best asked.

"We have an enemy aircraft shadowing us," Bolan explained, turning and speaking solemnly. "Get your men ready for a possible crash."

"Who the hell are you?" Best challenged.

Bolan didn't bat an eyelash. "Colonel Brandon Stone. This aircraft is under threat of a shootdown. Get your people prepared now!"

Best flinched, for once silenced. Wazdi wished he had an easy chair and a tub of popcorn to watch the big-mouthed FBI commander's squirming, when the plane shook. A hole the size of his fist was torn in the hull of the transport and everyone dived to the floor, ducking.

"Get in crash position! Get in crash position!" Best ordered, his voice soaring into a squeal.

Wazdi, his face resting on the waffle pattern of the C-130's deck, didn't blame the guy. Only the man they knew as Striker was staying up and moving now. Wazdi pushed himself up and followed the big soldier from the Farm.

Whatever was going to happen, he wanted to be right there, and this guy seemed to be a lightning rod for action.

THE EXECUTIONER TURNED because he knew what was going to happen next. The moment the enemy plane started shooting at the Hercules, the transport craft's minutes were numbered, and those doomsday numbers were tumbling like brass from the breech of an M-16 on full-auto. If the pilots could get the plane to the ground without crashing or without getting knocked out of the sky by a salvo of cannon fire, then there was a chance Bolan and the lawmen could fight off an assault.

If they landed without being jarred to senselessness, or worse, killed.

The odds weren't in their favor, and only seconds remained

before the Lockheed would begin its return run with the heavy 23 mm cannon that had torn ruthlessly through the fuselage of the big transport. Bolan raced toward Laud. Everything in this suck play revolved around him, and the Executioner's instincts were to make sure that the prisoner wasn't returned to his people still breathing. He charged up the deck and slipped, slamming against the wall and nearly toppling completely to the ground. A strong hand reached out and grabbed his shoulder, hooking him up before Bolan was completely floored, and he saw Wazdi looking after him.

"Slippery deck," the FBI man commented.

"Laud's going to make an attempt at a breakout," Bolan said as he reached for his Beretta 93-R.

"I'm going to make sure he makes it to trial. No one's above the law," Wazdi challenged. He drew his own weapon, a SIG-Sauer P-226.

"So why are you filling your hand?" Bolan asked, trying to ignore the irony of Wazdi's declaration to him.

"If Laud fights back, I will shoot. And then I'll do everything to make sure he survives after I've stopped him," Wazdi said.

The FBI man moved forward, and Bolan allowed the young idealist to have his chance.

The Executioner's faith in the system swelled at the sight of a passion for justice that rivaled his own.

MIKE YATES HELD on to the controls for dear life, knowing he didn't have the sheer muscle power to swing a multiton aircraft, but putting every ounce of his strength into the desperate effort to keep the plane straight.

"Hydraulics are going dead!" Grant screamed. Her voice grew shrill with controlled panic, her hands and eyes moving with methodical, mechanical precision as the C-130 rocked again, hitting another rumble of turbulence that was punctuated by the sudden impact of rounds from the Lockheed's jackhammering cannons.

Wind rushed in the cabin, and Grant suddenly wrapped her arms around the stick. Yates looked back and saw a gaping cavity in the side of the cockpit, the navigator Al Stewart dangling by one hand on the crooked edge of the hole.

"Take the controls!" Yates ordered.

"Mike, no! He's gone!" Grant shouted back.

"Take the—"

Suddenly, with a rush of clarity, he saw the whole picture. Through the hole, he saw Stewart hanging on, but his eyes were empty and lifeless, his jaw slack, tongue rolling from parted lips. Farther down his body, the worst of the nightmare scenery emerged. Below Stewart's rib cage, tatters of his flight suit flapped and ripped in the wind. There was nothing more than shreds of skin, and a long, flapping rope hanging loose from the bottom of the rib cage, twisting and swirling like an enormous earthworm.

Yates's jaw dropped in horror. He was looking at a dead man, hanging on out of pure reflex, a literal death grip on the metal. Already the hand was gray and bloodless, the rest having been dumped out in a smearing spray over the Egyptian desert.

"Mike! Mike, goddammit!" Grant shouted.

Yates spun back to the controls and powered the Hercules hard into a bank, using the engine controls as an improvised rudder, using pure thrust and drag to steer. The black shape of the Lockheed darted up from under them, retreating in the distance, dancing in and out, faster than the Hercules by a half. "Jo! Landing gear!"

Grant looked at him, then reached for the controls. She jerked the hydraulics. "It's frozen!"

"We need the drag to slow us for an emergency landing!" Yates shouted.

The wind was a seething, thundering beast holding its very own death metal rock concert inches behind them. Communication was only possible through the loudest of bellows, and Yates was already getting heady from the rushing oxygen and the urgent shouting.

Grant put all her strength into it. She was a slip of a girl, bony elbows and waist, with chin length, flat and flaxen hair. He morbidly wondered if he ever could have had a chance with her, and wasn't in a hurry to throw away such a thought. She looked up at him with big, terrified eyes, full lips pressed flat in an effort to crank the landing gear on manual.

"It's coming!" she shouted.

Yates kept on the throttle, steering and understeering. They had a chance.

Maybe he would have a chance with her when this was all over.

GUNFIRE SUDDENLY STARTED blasting on one side, and Wazdi turned, seeing Laud holding a pistol.

The terrorist was chained up, but one hand was free, the back of his still-chained hand bitten through and bloody. Wazdi had noticed the freshly stitched cut on the back of the man's hand when they had grabbed him in Alexandria, but he didn't think anything of it. He cursed himself.

Any man who would have himself shot out of the sky would also be insane enough to surgically implant a handcuff key that he could only get to by chewing through his own flesh.

An FBI man, Rafferty, was down, and Laud was diving behind the injured lawman. Wazdi brought up his pistol, but the plane was bouncing like an insane bull, and anything resembling a precision shot would have meant death for his partner. He glanced back to check on Striker, who was putting away his own pistol.

At least they wouldn't have to fight over Laud living or dying. It was now a game of hand-to-hand, except Laud had no such qualms about using his own gun.

"Gun!" Wazdi announced over the din of rushing wind and distant cannon fire.

He dived to the deck, gunfire blasting over where he'd been a moment ago, and he watched as Striker moved with catlike skill and speed toward the terrorist. Turbulence hurled both men around so much that Laud emptied five more shots. All missed the big man as he finally closed to strangling distance to the terrorist. Wazdi got to a three-point stance and kicked himself forward, bursting with all the speed he could muster. While he had played basketball in college, he wasn't too bad in pickup games of touch football, and he lunged like a spear toward the trio of Rafferty, Striker and Laud. He didn't know who he was going to hit, but he intended on trying to bring all three of them down and separating them.

Wazdi's feet left the floor, and he sailed, almost weightless, seeing Striker with one hand on Laud's wrist, his other hand on the terrorist's throat.

Time stopped.

MIKE YATES GOT the Hercules down almost on the deck. He was keeping the plane going, and Jo Grant was still cranking on the landing gear to get it into position.

"Brace for impact!" Yates screamed.

Grant looked up, and the look on her face said that Yates had to be kidding.

The captain reversed throttle anyway. The landing was going to hurt like hell, but they still had a chance.

The Lockheed swung in the distance again, and this time swooped into a head-on charge at them. Yates looked up at the little black dot.

"No, no, no," he muttered. "Give us another half mile, you fucker!"

Grant fixed the gear in place with a loud cranking clack.

It had been only a heartbeat from when Yates saw the Lockheed bearing on a suicide course for them.

Except it wasn't suicide for the Lockheed.

Flickering cannons winked at the cockpit, and thunder filled Yates's ears. He glanced back over his shoulder and saw Jo Grant try to raise her hands to ward off the hell coming at them, but as she brought up each arm, it was shorn away by a slow-motion thunderbolt of flaming lead. The next impact struck her dead center, and she didn't suffer the loss of her arms too long, the explosive shell mercifully putting her out of her misery and into eternity in a fountainous explosion of gore.

Yates closed his eyes as the thunder continued, smashing across the console of the Hercules, making the gauges vomit forth their gears and dials in eruptions of volcanic shrapnel that peppered the entire cabin, punching tiny needles into his own skin that were only a hint of the horrible end that was yet to come.

When the cannon shells impacted, tearing through his legs, Yates felt nothing, no pain, no separation, and he wondered vaguely if this was what Stewart had felt when he had been blown in two. Just a senseless moment with no pain, no pleasure, total numbness and overwhelming peace.

The Hercules slammed to the ground, wheels hitting the sand, digging in and snapping off as the big transport belly flopped down. The impact lifted the legless Captain Yates out of his seat. He tumbled in midair, looking back and seeing that the Hercules was still holding together, a big bird as mighty as the Greek hero she was named for.

There was a chance that people survived back there.

Yates's peace was complete, and he had left his shell of a body before it was slammed into the back of the cabin by sheer inertia.

MACK BOLAN HELD on to Laud with all his strength, but the terrorist was slick with his own blood, and even with one hand chained down, the man had strength and guile. A knee slammed hard into the Executioner, and Bolan felt himself tumbling as the airplane was dropping hard, as if they had hit a wall.

Gravity went to nothing, and for the second time in twenty-four hours, the Executioner was completely freed from gravity by the laws of physics. Space tumbled beneath him, and Laud twisted hard. Bolan tried to hang on, but in the temporary zero gravity of the hard plunge, he had no leverage while the tightly bound Laud was able to tuck everything tight to his body. Arms and legs dangling loose, Bolan was in for a bad crash unless he tightened up.

Out of the corner of his eye, he saw Wazdi, floating toward them, almost as if he were on slow-motion film. Body outstretched, the FBI man was making for the clot of men, hands clawing outward as if he were some black panther, pouncing on his prey. Bolan twisted and saw Laud tuck and somersault beneath Wazdi, who swiped at him.

There was no time for any other reactions, the moment was gone, and physics once more grabbed hold of the men in the cargo hold. It didn't just grab hold, it latched on like alligator jaws with crushing force, grabbing human beings and yanking them back and forth like so many rag dolls. Bolan himself was only half tucked for his collision with the bulkhead. His shoulder and biceps were slammed hard into unforgiving aircraft aluminum. Bolan's head bounced, mostly off his compressed shoulder, but he got enough of an impact on the fuselage to see stars for a moment, an explosion of fireworks that left him dazzled.

Wazdi and the lawman Laud was holding hostage came flying into him, the force slamming them into a dog pile atop him. Knocked breathless, the Executioner could barely move, his entire body flattened by enormous forces.

Moments later, Bolan could breathe as both men rolled off, and he himself came tumbling to the floor, shocked, dazed and half conscious.

The plane wasn't moving anymore, and the only thing Bolan could hear was his blood rushing like a freight train.

On his hands and knees, stunned and blinking blood from his eyes, Bolan tried to recover his senses, Suddenly he heard chain saws ripping through the far end of the hull.

Bolan lifted his head, which felt like it weighed a ton, and saw Laud hurrying toward the fresh rents in the side, shouting. The Executioner's shaken brain translated barked Arabic into urgent English.

"Get them! Get them all! I want them all executed!"

At the sound of Ahmur Ibn Laud's barked command, the Executioner fought his way out of grogginess and into a kneeling crouch, hands stabbing at the grips of his Berettas stuffed in their holsters. Both sleek Italian pistols filled his hands, and he cut loose a savage burst of gunfire at the nearest violation of the fuselage. He saw the mangled chain saws and the hull peeling away to allow AK-47-armed gunmen to dive in. Bolan caught the first pair of Laud's terrorist followers with six 9 mm hollowpoint rounds that sent them crashing to the ground like the Hercules had only moments before.

Other archways had been opened in the fuselage, tongues of shorn metal flapping away as chain saws died in the desperate and savage effort to slice through the aircraft's hide. Motors burned, blades bent, chains shattered. They had done their job, giving the terrorists access. Daylight and 7.62 mm ComBloc rounds poured through the fresh holes in the airplane, sizzling through the cargo hold at chest height, sweeping to take out anyone standing and fighting. Bolan reckoned the gunners were certain almost anyone would be kept cowering on his belly at such a blistering onslaught.

Mack Bolan wasn't almost anyone.

The Executioner did go to his belly, but he raised his Berettas, aiming at one gunman who advanced into the belly of the grounded beast. In his desert Tri-Color BDUs, he had been "camouflaged" as just another soldier heading home on a pickup flight. In the darkness of the broken hold, he was a fuzzy tan wraith, his uniform picking up and reflecting the seeking streams of sunlight, and helping bring more steel-cored hornets sizzling at him. Bolan would have preferred to have been in his blacksuit for this fight, using the shadow-blending stealth aspects of the skintight war suit to give him an edge over the invading gunners. But it, along with the M-16 he'd have liked to be pitting against the dozen barking and blasting AK-47's was halfway down the length of the big transport in his war bag, in the middle of a heavily armed clot of terrorists. That didn't matter. Bolan wasn't a soldier who wasted time wishing for better equipment—he made do with what he had, and let fly with another salvo of Parabellum rounds. He watched as another gunman twisted, stitched across the chest and throat with lethal 9 mm rounds.

To one side, a thundering fireball lit the shadows and another of Laud's terrorists jerked as if swatted by an invisible jackhammer. The hostile invaders turned their attention of savage return fire toward the fading muzzle-blast, and Bolan caught the faint flicker of Dave Kowalski's blond hair flash. The former blacksuit was in motion, diving out of the way the moment his finger tripped the trigger. Bolan recalled another blond shotgun expert, Carl Lyons, teaching that the blazing fireball of a 12-gauge combat shotgun might have issued forth instant stopping power, but it also made you a much more attractive target for enemy guns. Kowalski tripped another roaring blast of fire, then ditched the shotgun, diving behind a support strut as bullets chased after the fireball. The marshal doubled back and tucked into a ball, narrowly escaping a seething swarm of hunting autofire.

Bolan cut loose again, the Beretta 93-R in triburst mode, chopping down two more gunners with two bursts into one man, three in another, the salvo of slugs sending the pair tumbling. The gunners returned their attention to him, and Bolan pressed himself tight behind an equipment locker, steel-cored bullets stopped by whatever was inside the aluminum shell of the locker. The soldier didn't have much room to move, but he reloaded both Berettas as the terrorists continued their savage salvos.

Orlando Wazdi rejoined the ranks of the conscious. Even though he was groggy, he still managed to burn off half a magazine from his SIG-Sauer P-226, drawing fire and tagging one more terrorist. It was Wazdi's turn to duck a withering barrage that stitched the fuselage behind him. This gave the Executioner a heartbeat's respite.

Bolan took it, breaking into a run and firing off single shots as he rushed to Wazdi's side. Hooking the FBI man's arm, Bolan dragged him back toward the cover of the flight deck, pulling him through the entrance hatch as he ran empty on the little backup Beretta. Bullets tore the air around him while he returned fire, unaimed, but focused again, chest height, hoping to keep the injured and dazed lawmen out of the lines of his fire. He didn't want to hit one by accident. Wazdi tumbled, all arms and legs, behind the bulkhead and Bolan brought up the machine pistol. Time to look for Kowalski, and anyone else in a fighting mood.

The smart-mouthed marshal had stopped midrun, firing a gun in each hand. Bolan gave a shout and tapped off two tribursts to give the man cover fire. Kowalski took the heads-up and hauled toward the entrance of the portal, more tribursts sizzling from the Executioner's Beretta. Under a flaming blanket of copper-jacketed cover, Kowalski dived through the hatch and scuttled out of the way.

"You okay?" Bolan asked, ducking back to reload.

"We're on the ground. We're not crashing. A few bullets don't really freak me out," Ski replied. He dumped the empty magazines of both his pistols and reloaded them. One was an odd, hammerless Colt-style .45 automatic, and the other was a hammerless Beretta with a short barrel.

"Beretta and a Colt?" Bolan asked.

"Para-Ordnance LDA and a DAO Beretta. My teaching guns. I'm an ex-Marine and I couldn't stand all the 9mm or .45 debates, so I use both to show they're both all right."

"Don't get him started, Striker," Wazdi said, reloading. "He'd give a lecture during a firefight on a sinking and burning ship in the middle of a monsoon."

"My mistake," the Executioner apologized. He looked to see what Wazdi was watching.

"They're only tossing harassing fire this way right now. Not coming any closer than the last injured one of our guys," Wazdi said. "We must be too much of a headache for them."

Bolan's icy blue eyes narrowed. "Not good. Not good at all."

AHMUR IBN LAUD crouched restlessly, listening to the crackle and pop of war being waged behind him, and the wash and roar of helicopter rotors before him. In the crash, he'd lost the handcuff key he'd had placed under the flesh of his hand. But that one moment of possession had freed an arm, allowing him to snatch an unwary lawman's pistol when Yassif made his presence known. Two shots, and the lawman was dead, or near enough.

He'd heard the name Rafferty shouted out, and he now weighed Rafferty's handgun in his hand, a high capacity .40-caliber Smith & Wesson. He wouldn't have any more ammunition for it, and he'd burned most of the shots getting to freedom, firing at the tall, powerful man and Jonny and Hadji. They kept low, and probably didn't notice much of his activity since his loyal elite had made their entrance.

Laud looked at Turiq, a fumble-handed young man, kneeling before him, trying to get the bolt cutters onto the chain.

"Hurry, damn you! There is battle taking place, and I sit here like a eunuch!"

The bolt cutter clipped the chain connecting his left arm to his waist, and Laud shrugged free.

"Finally!" He cuffed the youth. "What is your mental malfunction?"

"Apologies, sir," Turiq said. He put the bolt cutter to the chain linking Laud's ankles and fought the grips, pressing with all his might, growing red-faced.

Laud shoved the boy off, grabbing the bolt cutters for himself.

"Find me magazines like this one from the captured Americans! And the same ammunition." Laud shoved the Smith & Wesson magazine into the red-faced teen's hands. Turiq spun and was gone in an instant.

Laud turned and pulled the one full magazine he'd been able to grab off the American, Rafferty, and slipped it into the pistol's empty butt. He did a press check, and there was the flat nose of a .40-caliber hollowpoint round inside the breech. He could at least be some part of the fight for thirteen shots.

Chain dangling from his waist, Laud charged back to the Hercules and crouched behind his men, who were guarding the entrances of the big aircraft.

"How many?" Laud asked.

"Three left inside," said Kadal, one of his men. "But they are behind a bulkhead. The steel is too much for our rifles to penetrate, and we left the grenades in the helicopters because you said you wanted living prisoners."

Laud nodded. "Understandable. Have we got the rest?"

"Everyone yet living, except those three," Haffriz said. "Our men found four dead."

Laud did some quick arithmetic. "Thirteen prisoners executed will be enough of a shock to the Americans. How many did we lose?"

"Six," Haffriz said before his hair fluttered on one side of his head. He stood for a moment, his eyes having lost their focus. Blood poured down both of his temples, and he stumbled into the sand, leaking blood and brains.

"Seven," Kadal amended. "And three injured."

Laud grabbed Haffriz and tossed his corpse to one side,

blasting away with the captured American pistol. He liked the recoil on the weapon. It felt powerful and the brass kicked out, big fireballs of angry flame spitting into the darkened depths of the hollowed-out aircraft. He'd put out five shots and ducked behind cover, a salvo of bullets chasing him. The terrorist grinned. "I like this gun."

He shoved the pistol into his waistband and then scooped up Haffriz's Kalashnikov. Kadal watched him.

"What shall we do, sir?"

"Lay down fire. We'll leave one helicopter behind. Load the prisoners onto the other ships," Laud ordered, "and get Yassif on the radio. I want him to blast this wreckage."

"To root them out?" Kadal asked.

"Right. The Lockheed either will kill them, or it will demoralize or injure them. Once that's done, we can send in the team from the last helicopter and pick them up. Already dead bodies are good to make any carnage look worse," Laud said.

Kadal nodded. "I'll stay behind for that."

"Return with these men," Laud said. His voice was stern and hard.

Turiq returned, his arms full of magazines. "Sir..."

Laud grinned, plucked one and found it was what he wanted. He pocketed several, discarding the ones that weren't needed. He ended up with seven magazines for his new pistol. "Thank you, lad."

The boy nodded, beaming at the praise.

Laud turned, fired off half a magazine into the shadows, then shoved the Kalashnikov into Turiq's hands. "You will stay with Kadal and recover the dead men."

Turiq watched, blinking as the helicopters kicked sand into his eyes, and Laud turned and walked toward the quintet of helicopters idling on the dunes.

KANSID YASSIF acknowledged Laud on the radio.

"Yassif, I want you to blast the wreckage. We have people

who might cause us trouble. Then you can return to the airstrip," Laud said. "We'll be leaving one helicopter and Kadal's team behind to do the clean up."

"I copy, Ahmur," Yassif answered. He banked the Lockheed, throttling up into the turn. "Make sure your men are clear of the C-130."

"I will," Laud replied.

Kicking out sixteen thousand pounds of thrust, the T33 almost literally stood on one wingtip, g force nudging Yassif deeper into his acceleration couch. He loved the power of the agile little striker, and leveled out as he saw the smudge of the crippled craft as a dot on the horizon. Helicopters took to laboriously slow flight, pulling away from the transport and swinging to the north. Yassif throttled back, wanting to savor this, bringing the T33 down to a mere 325 miles per hour.

The pilot activated the fire control for the 77 mm High Velocity Artillery Rockets that rested in two 19-shot bundles under each wing. The fat barrels of explosives were capable of leveling a city block. Unaimed, they wouldn't be precision firepower, but they would be enough to dig any force out of the Hercules, or turn them to paste with a direct hit.

He aligned the crosshairs and tripped the trigger.

The rockets cut loose in a hissing flash, multiple warheads spitting outward in a cascade of steel and flame that tore two smoky wounds in the sky before him. The 77 mm rockets started hitting the ground, striking close to the C-130, spewing sand into the sky with eruptions of the heavy warheads. The explosions began walking across the desert, and Yassif was satisfied to see the fuselage crumple, buckle and fold under multiple impacts. One huge, flat wing and engine caught another series of the rocket-propelled shells and disintegrated in a fury of splinters, flame and smoke.

It was an orgy of explosive savagery, the desert heaving and spitting sand into the sky along with the smoke and cordite from the detonating artillery rockets. The Hercules twisted, its cockpit rolling away like a guillotined head under the shattering forces dumped onto it.

"All right, Kadal," Yassif said into his radio. "The bodies should have hit the floor by now."

"If not, they still will," Kadal announced. "Thanks, and may the wind be at your back!"

Yassif did a wing wiggle, then tore off across the sky, once more enjoying the thrill of life at six hundred miles an hour.

ORLANDO WAZDI ALMOST felt like he did the morning after he went to a Fishbone concert with his friend Dave Kowalski, ears ringing and head pounding from the avalanche of concussive force and tumbling against the bulkhead.

At least at the Fishbone concert, he had cool music, got tanked on beer and got laid by a groupie.

Here he only got percussion, groggy from smacking his head on a bulkhead, and screwed by a terrorist who was out to make a big statement about how powerful his organization was.

He got to his knees and saw Striker was up already, a cut bleeding on his forehead, and another trickle of blood coming from one nostril.

"They'll be sending in a mop-up crew," Bolan said. It sounded as if he were trying to talk through a pillow, and Wazdi knew that his ears were still recovering from the cannonade.

Wazdi gave his head a shake, and swallowed hard.

"Where to?" Kowalski asked. His face was a red mask of painted blood, but Wazdi couldn't make out where the cut was that caused the blood flow. Even his white-blond hair was dyed pink over his forehead.

"Up to the cockpit," Bolan said. This time, it came through more clearly. "We'll wait to see which way they come in, and we can make a retreat from there."

Wazdi nodded, half numb, following in the big soldier's footsteps. Bolan paused at the entrance to the cockpit, and looked back.

"It's not pretty up here," he said, profound fury soaking and drowning his words, pulling them into a morass.

Wazdi and Kowalski followed, and the FBI man felt his stomach clench hard. He hadn't eaten, thankfully, because the carnage of shattered flesh, bone and organs was a nightmare splattered across the confines of the compartment. He slipped momentarily on a squishy piece of gore, and grabbed a handhold on a wrecked section of instrumentation.

He glanced at a man-sized hole, a yawning exit torn by shells that had sliced the cockpit from one end to the other.

"Shouldn't there be three people here?" Kowalski asked, pensive. He looked back over his shoulder, a bit of paranoia creeping into his voice.

Bolan pointed to the hole that Wazdi was looking at. "One must have been sucked out."

Wazdi knelt, looking at the most complete of the bodies, a man sawed off at the top of his legs, staring sightlessly from blue eyes. Yates, his name tag read. Dirty blond hair poked out from under his flight helmet, which was askew on his head.

"He saved our lives," Wazdi said. Deafness was rumbling up and around his head, darkness churning at the corners of his vision, cold blood sluicing through his veins.

"They both did," Bolan said, leaning over Yates and closing his eyelids. "She was right on top of the landing gear manual control."

Wazdi looked over at the mess that was the other body. "She?"

"Look at the legs and hips," he said sadly.

Wazdi clenched his eyes shut and turned away. Only then did he open his eyes. He saw his friend Kowalski go green. "I'd rather not," he whispered.

Bolan's voice cut through the turmoil. "We'll attend to them later. Right now, we have to stay alive."

The sadness had retreated from the big soldier's voice. Not completely, but the warrior was focused now.

"We're taking that helicopter," Bolan added.

The ice in Wazdi's chest grew a degree colder for a moment, then broke apart, melting into hot lead, flushed with adrenaline.

"After Laud?"

Bolan locked eyes with the FBI lawman. "You said you wanted to bring him to justice."

Wazdi whispered a silent prayer for the flight crew, then looked to the big man from Stony Man Farm. "Lead the way, big guy."

From years of experience, the Executioner knew that a Huey could pack up to twelve men on board, armed to the teeth and ready to fight. Without a good look at the ship, Bolan couldn't tell how many were in the mop-up crew that he was expecting, but there was one major concern on the big man's mind.

Were there door gunners?

Two M-60s raining lead on any armed resistance would be catastrophic, to say the least. Right now, the Executioner and his blacksuit partners were armed only with handguns and knives. Pitting those against AK-47s was a troublesome enough prospect without a rain of 7.62 mm damnation from above.

Besides, Bolan needed the helicopter in flying condition. If Laud was going to be tracked down, Yates and his crew avenged, and most importantly, if Best and his people were to be rescued, they had to take flight on enemy wings.

Hard pursuit was the order of the moment.

Bolan had come on board to stop the deaths of fellow soldiers, and while he had no full count, the four he knew were dead were four too damn many. They were unacceptable losses in the war against terrorism, because even blood for blood, the soulless savages responsible for this attack were not worth the sacrifice of the good people fallen in resistance to Animal Man.

Blood vengeance wasn't the Executioner's goal anyway. He

wanted only the knowledge that future victims would not suffer the same loss and pain that had the Executioner on his War Everlasting.

These thoughts appeared and vanished in the moments it took Mack Bolan to thread the suppressor on his Beretta 93-R. He looked to the other two men with him. While the warriors of Able Team and Phoenix Force would have been ideal backup in this fight, especially if they were fully loaded with their usual state-of-the-art weaponry, they were busy elsewhere. The team of "Jonny and Hadji," however, former blacksuits from Stony Man Farm, were well-trained men, and proved their ability during the crash and subsequent firefight. Even with their help, though, Bolan was going to need stealth to even the odds in close-quarter battle with Laud's Soldiers of the Divine Sword. The Beretta 93-R was the only silenced firearm between the three, but not the only quiet weapon.

Like Bolan himself, Wazdi and Kowalski had the wherewithal to have knives on their bodies, both having at least two knives, a fixed-blade and a folding backup knife. What surprised Bolan most was Orlando Wazdi's possession of a trio of shaken—the so-called ninja throwing stars, or more often misnamed shuriken.

"The stocky little Hispanic guy from the Farm got me interested in these again," Wazdi confessed.

Bolan remembered now. Rafael Encizo, one of the founding members of Phoenix Force, was a man who held an almost encyclopedic knowledge of blades from cultures around the world. Encizo was also a student of shuri-jutsu, the Japanese art of throwing weapons. He was introduced to the deadly throwing stars by fellow Phoenix Force founding member, and the first fallen soldier of that team, Keio Ohara. Once a student, now the master, Encizo honored his lost friend's legacy by sharing with the Farm's blacksuits another potential life-saving weapon in their personal arsenals.

In addition to the throwing stars, Wazdi also had a Cold Steel

Tantō and a folding CRKT knife. David Kowalski, in addition to a Gerber LST folding knife and a Benchmade reproduction of the Emerson Commander fighting folder, had an even more unusual weapon—a reproduction of the Vietnam Tomahawk, also a weapon that could be used silently, and at range.

"Quiet steel in Italian, Japanese and Native American flavors," Kowalski quipped in a soft whisper.

Bolan smiled, finding that a simple acknowledgment quieted the blond lawman's asides and wisecracks. He knew the type, rebellious against stern, yet incompetent authority. Only a good commander or a Marine drill instructor could have truly kept him in line. Luckily, for Bolan's vocal cords Kowalski respected the Executioner's leadership.

Bolan took the lead, with Wazdi and Kowalski taking up the rear. None of the three had any illusions that their thrown blades would match a Kalashnikov in close quarters, so it was the Beretta leading the play, hopefully at least getting them something bigger to make the fight more even.

Long, stretched out odds against a highly trained, highly organized force.

Nothing new for the Executioner.

KADAL WAS A MAN who led from the front—any man who did less didn't deserve to be a lieutenant in Ahmur Ibn Laud's Divine Sword. Turiq was behind him, nervous and fidgety, but still staying strong, fighting through his doubts and fears.

Good. He would rather have someone aware of his mortality and what could be a threat than have a blindly charging fool who would stumble into a trap.

They were in the torn hull of the C-130, looking at the mangled corpses of those left behind, American and Divine Swordsman alike scattered in broken, shattered pieces.

No, the trio was not in this part, but the severed head of the C-130 was visible from here, and offered cover from enemy fire. Kadal wasn't certain what kind of weaponry was kept on board, or if the pilots kept anything heavier than pistols in the cockpit and forward flight decks. He reached the end of the hull, Turiq on his back, following tight. The shattered front section of the plane was quiet.

Kadal's dark eyes narrowed, watching the green lump of amputated metal.

He motioned for Turiq to move across their section of the plane. The youth nodded and took off in a low scuffle, keeping watch.

No seeking fire chased him, but the Americans could have been conserving their ammunition for when the battle got to eyeball distance.

Kadal drew his lips tight into a thin, bloodless line.

Tactically, the trio had one real option, to let the Divine Swordsmen bring the battle to them in the cockpit. There, under cover and behind limited access, they would be able to make the most of their close-range handguns and to negate the effects of the Divine Swordsmen's superior firepower. Or perhaps that's what the tall warrior wanted Kadal to think.

Using hand signals, he'd ordered Turiq to watch from the mouth and sent two Divine Swordsmen back to the twisted, ajar ramp of the Hercules. He selected others to follow him toward the cockpit, but he knew he'd have to turn around. On the other side of the C-130's broken tail was their helicopter, its engines off now, conserving fuel for the flight back. The gunners and pilot would be watching, and the sight of Kadal's men guarding the rear would signal that they were to be prepared.

Already, he heard the sound of the engines slowly starting to grind to life.

THE DOOMSDAY NUMBERS tumbled with the beginning whine of turbines, the first slap of rotors on air. Mack Bolan, keeping low to the ground, chest in the sand, saw the Divine Swordsmen stepping out slowly from the back half of the wreckage, moving toward the front. He nodded to Wazdi and Kowalski, and they moved swiftly, crawling on elbows and knees, keeping behind the rambling dunes.

The Executioner's face was a mask of sand as grains stuck to his sweat-covered face. He'd also taken the precaution of pouring sand over his head so it stuck in his hair. Camouflage from head to toe. Wazdi and Kowalski weren't so lucky. Kowalski had naturally sandy hair, and a sand-covered face, but Wazdi's dark features and hair were difficult to conceal. Both men wore dark clothing—totally inappropriate for going unnoticed in the desert. One good look, and it would come to a blazing gun battle. And with the helicopter powering up to take flight, that meant it would be against totally impossible odds.

Wazdi and Kowalski looked to Bolan for a possible change of plan, but the Executioner was continuing. He swung toward the hull of the Hercules, a gaping hole allowing them entry into the dark, protected depths of the aircraft. If they could get the rear security team of the terrorists, then they could grab Kalashnikovs. And maybe they could get to Bolan's gear bag, where he had a separate M-203 grenade launcher.

Bolan would hate to destroy the helicopter and his chance for a quick catch-up, but if it came to the worst, he'd find another way to chase after Laud. For a moment, he remembered Hal Brognola's recounting of a lifetime ago. A policeman had spotted the Executioner taking off after his final target in his Mafia wars. Brognola repeated that "That guy would pole vault after him on his own dick if he had to."

The memory gave him a smile, but Mack Bolan surely was not any superhero, just a man with a plan.

Kill the terrorists.

Get their rifles.

Commandeer the helicopter.

Chase Laud.

Simple.

"Go," Bolan urged, rising as he drew the Beretta 93-R from its holster. He lunged up into the hole, now four feet off the ground, the hull askew in the sand from the hammering it took from the Lockheed. He slid over the bent lip, rolling on his chest.

Body twisting, catlike in agility and grace, Bolan turned and aimed the Beretta toward the front opening. He tapped out two 3-round bursts into the slender young terrorist at the mouth of the yawning half-carcass, quiet rounds chopping into him and heaving him backward with brutal efficiency. The Executioner slid halfway across the floor, waffle pattern tearing at his BDUs and exposed elbow until he splayed himself flat, putting on the brakes approximately two seconds after he lunged through the hole.

A voice cried out behind him in Arabic.

Bolan cursed inwardly for moving so quickly that he lost control of his forward momentum, but speed was of the essence. He rolled over, knowing he was taking too long, writhing and struggling to face the men at his back. Instead of feeling the impact of AK-47 rounds, he saw the shadows of two men leaping through the entrance, arms flinging outward toward the back.

Dave Kowalski dropped to the ground after hurling his tomahawk, a black shadow spinning in a circle of steel death that stopped with a sickening thud. There was a strangled cry and the clatter of metal on metal, flesh thudding against unyielding deck moments later. Orlando Wazdi was still up, and he hurled a second sleek star. The four-pointed wheel of death sliced through the shadows to land closer to center in the chest of the second gunman who was clutching his shoulder, blood pouring from a sliced artery. Metal lodged into breastbone, and the third and final enemy body in the plane hit the floor.

So far so good.

That's when the gunfire started slicing through the air.

KADAL HEARD the strangled cry and knew it was already too late for one of his own men, but sacrifices had to be made in the jihad. He swore he'd get vengeance against these godless heathens and spun, charging back up the sandy trail, AK-47 sweeping ahead of him. The stock was folded and the gun tight to his ribs, finger down on the trigger for a half a clip, firing into the shadows.

A wraith colored like a desert sandstorm scrambled into view, grabbing the slender form of Turiq and tossing him aside like a rag doll, hand filling with the brown and black steel frame of Turiq's Kalashnikov. Kadal triggered his own weapon, firing without aiming and dived to the ground. Sand flew, filling his nose and eyes, but no agony from the thundering response filled the air.

"Down!" he commanded.

His men were already falling. Most from their own incentive, but a few were falling as precision blasts of 7.62 mm rounds chopped into their chests, sending them tumbling.

Nine men so far, slain by these murderous invaders on his soil. And every chance they had, they turned and crushed another of his brothers.

Two more dead, slain in Ahmur Ibn Laud's grand plan to make these vultures cower in terror. More bullets chopped overhead, but a voice barked in English. "Short bursts."

The firing stopped.

Kadal looked back. His men were huddled tight to the sand, waiting for his word.

The Divine Swordsman set down the AK-47, reaching to his web belt and slipping free a grenade. He thumbed loose the pin, rubbing his tongue across his chipped and cracked incisors in painful memory of the time he bit down on another such pin to toss another grenade in training.

Live and learn.

He sacrificed one tooth, just as he'd sacrificed two men. A sacrifice meant to learn a lesson, or to send a lesson. This lesson was how to make your enemies die en masse. His team did likewise, pulling grenades and yanking cotter pins.

The first throw landed short, but other dark eggs of damnation took flight.

It was time for the Americans to learn to give up or die.

"SCREW ME with a chain saw!" Dave Kowalski's voice cut through the Executioner's concentration as he ran and scooped up his smoking, twisted war bag. Bolan turned in time to see Kowalski and Wazdi running and jumping like hell was on their heels.

That's because it was.

One grenade detonated just outside of the gaping maw of the Hercules and a fluttering flight of similar eggs were airborne.

"Go, go, go!" Bolan shouted to them on pure reflex, realizing the command was superfluous. He rushed toward the twisted, half-open ramp.

A shock wave washed over Bolan, sending him skidding hard into a support strut. The half-closed cut on his forehead opened up once again, pouring blood into his left eye.

Bolan dropped the war bag and tore it open. He had no time to worry about the stinging in his eye. He wrenched out the tuned M-16 A-2 and looked it over. The forearm guard was shattered and in pieces, and through it all, he saw that the gas tube parallel to the barrel was broken and cracked. The Executioner set his jaw firmly. The barrel itself looked in pristine condition, but the optics were torn free, and the gas tube had been severed by a chunk of shrapnel from an exploding 77 mm rocket, reducing the rifle to a nine-pound club. Nothing to take out a helicopter crew.

Bolan tossed aside the M-16. So much for high-tech tools. It was time to use his real weapon—his skill and determination.

Bolan looked back and saw Wazdi give him a thumbs-up. Kowalski was sprawled on his gut, shaking his head in frustration. Bolan reached into the bag again and found what he needed—an M-203 grenade launcher. It was originally supposed to be affixed to the M-16, but Bolan hadn't wanted to go

throwing around 40 mm high-explosive bombs inside a city. Instead, he'd left it in the bag with an extra piece of kit.

"Needs a stock man!" Wazdi said.

Bolan pulled out a pistol grip and folding stock. "Call me a
Boy Scout, but I'm always prepared."

Kowalski turned and pulled both halves of the M-203 from
Bolan. "Thanks, I'll take care of things from here."

Bolan nodded, letting the ex-Marine put the M-203 together.
Wazdi was pumping out rounds on single shot, keeping the
enemy off their backs for now, but it would only take a few moments for them to ready another volley of grenades.

And Bolan had an armed helicopter to deal with. He snapped
out the folding stock and shouldered the weapon. He had no
idea the point of aim of the rifle, if it had been zeroed, so he
took a page from Wazdi's book. Single shots. Full-auto might
damage the Huey too much, unless it was armored, in which
case, it would just become a case of wasted ammunition bouncing rounds off the hull.

The M-60D of the port gunner spoke first, sweeping the hull.

"Down!" Bolan ordered. Heavyweight slugs bounced off
the deck behind him, and Wazdi cursed in dismay at suddenly
coming under attack from behind.

Bolan snap aimed the AK-47 and tapped off three single
shots toward the door gunner. The steel-cored 7.62 mm slugs
crossed the space between them, the first two shots sparking off
the door frame. Bolan's third shot was high and smashed into
the face of the gunner, snapping back his head and spraying
blood and bone fragments in every direction. Bolan noted the
windage on that last shot and swung the rifle's muzzle to the
pilot who was starting to pull the helicopter off the sand.

The Executioner tapped out chasing rounds, hot steel cores
sizzling and smashing through glass.

The Huey jerked, and for a moment Bolan wondered if it was
going to topple, those rotors impacting into the sand and shattering like glass. They were close enough that such an impact

would have sent razor-sharp shards hurtling through the opening at hundreds of miles an hour, just as lethal and less discriminating than the M-60 machine gun.

The pilot held on though, and Bolan could see him, trying to turn the Huey. As soon as the aircraft was tail on, the second machine gunner was leaning out the side, hanging on hard and firing off long bursts.

Behind the Executioner, the M-203 thumped and a moment later, the sand shook.

Bolan lined up on the gunner and burned off ten rounds. There wasn't time for precision anymore, not with a 200-round belt of M-60 ammunition tearing at them.

Bolan's fire struck the outline of the gunner, but pinged off his heavy chest armor and helmet, with a few rounds glancing off the sleek bodyframe of the heavy machine gun. A dead on hit behind fifty pounds of metal and another forty pounds of protective gear was worthless. But each hit made it more difficult for the door gunner, his thumbs down on the firing paddle of the twin-handled M-60D. The massive cannon was already rattling hard, making control difficult, and rounds weren't homing in on target.

"Dammit!" Kowalski cursed. Blood was flowing from a fresh graze as he crouched tight.

Bolan's AK locked dry, and so had the door gunner's big weapon, its long belt drained, brass spilled into a twinkling pile unmoved by the desert wind.

Wazdi grabbed the M-203 and fed it a fresh round, a buckshot shell.

Bolan looked back, and the door gunner was wrestling the top of the M-60 open.

"Wazdi!" Bolan called.

Before the FBI man could fire, he stopped.

"Find another round like that," Bolan ordered, trading the empty Kalashnikov for the grenade launcher.

Right now, the big 40 mm cannon was an oversized shotgun.

It wouldn't blow up the helicopter, just send a vast swarm of deadly hornets at the enemy door gunner, getting around his protective gear that had so far made Bolan's fire ineffective.

Wazdi kicked the bag back to Kowalski who began to dig frantically.

The FBI man reloaded and continued trading AK fire with the forces at the front of the wreckage.

The door gunner and the Executioner both paused, staring at each other across the gulf between them. The enemy gunner had the M-60 belt laid into the open breech. The gunner only had to slap the top down and thumb down the spade-shaped trigger to continue laying out slaughtering swarms of 7.62 mm rounds.

Bolan shouldered the grenade launcher. The enemy door gunner snapped the action shut on his M-60.

The Executioner let fly a round that spit out nearly one hundred pellets at more than 1000 feet per second. The sizzling swarm impacted with the door gunner and his M-60, peeling them off the side of the helicopter in a deadly storm of copper-jacketed vengeance. The body and the gun went tumbling into the sand, and the Huey jerked, suddenly off balance. Bolan knew there wasn't time to heft another AK. He unleathered the 93-R.

The Huey was turning, swinging to get some altitude after the sudden shock.

The pilot made the mistake of looking back.

It was a one in a million shot, but Bolan cut the odds by burning off half the 20-round magazine—9 mm slugs slicing across the distance. Two impacted off the pilot's helmet, two smashed through his goggles and another through his nose.

The Huey's controls were released and the big helicopter dropped.

"We have wings," Bolan said. "Now let's make sure they don't get clipped."

6

Kadal shook the sand from his hair, but he couldn't clear the thundering aftershock from his ears, and he glanced over to see more of his men, strewed about. He had only four men left, but through the ringing scream that was blasting across his mind, he heard the distant chatter and thunder of machine guns, real machine guns, like the ones on the helicopter.

The fools had decided to engage the helicopter without finishing their last battle.

It would be a fatal mistake, and Kadal shouted to his remaining men, his head numb, ears cotton-stuffed with postexplosion deafness. Surely after facing the twin, flame-breathing M-60s, there wouldn't be any fight left in the Americans, if they lived at all.

He led the remaining four, moving slowly, not through fear but through injury. His thigh was pouring blood from a massive shrapnel wound. The others were shell-shocked and staggered by the concussive force of the explosions.

How did those men have a grenade launcher? The man so prepared to deal with any war that he'd have a grenade launcher with him on an airplane had to be either a gun-crazy fool, or a consummate professional.

Perhaps it was The Soldier, Kadal thought. The Soldier, a man who appeared and disappeared across the world, fighting for American interests, a seemingly unstoppable one-man army.

Well, The Soldier, no matter what his legend, was still just one man.

Gunfire suddenly broke through the ringing in his ears. The M-60 from the helicopter caught one of his gunners and sent the others diving for cover. Kadal rushed toward the corner of the wrecked back end of the Hercules, slamming his shoulder against the curved hull, pressing tight against it as bullets came thundering and thumping into the sand.

A body stumbled, falling on his arms and face in the sand before him. The man spoke quickly, head wrapped in a bloody keffiyeh, and Kadal recognized the jacket as Sedal's.

"The helicopter! They have the helicopter! Get back!" Sedal gasped.

Kadal reached down, grabbing his man to pull him to safety when he surged forward. An elbow slammed into Kadal's gut, his head bouncing off the hull of the Hercules.

Orlando Wazdi pulled his SIG from where it had been tucked into his pants, and he stiff-armed his handgun. Kadal lunged forward, trying to swat down the weapon as Wazdi was aiming at the three remaining Divine Swordsmen. The men were puzzled when their commander was suddenly being tossed like a rag doll by one of their own. Kadal's arms wrapped around the wire-muscled FBI man and tried to drag him down. Their bodies tumbled into the sand. Behind them, the machine gun had gone silent, only the idling helicopter giving any voice to the strangely silent scene. There were no words, only grunts of effort as Kadal hammered his forearm on the counterfeit terrorist's head.

To one side, a form made the sand bubble and rise, a column of primal force erupting from the shifting grains that poured off like a waterfall. It was like a scene from some Japanese monster movie, a massive shape emerging with grim cold eyes, breathing fire and brimstone as the ground sloughed off the monster who rose to ambush and destroy humanity. This was no movie monster in a rubber suit, however, but a man in desert camouflage fatigues. And the fire and brimstone being breathed didn't come from flaming nostrils and an acid spitting mouth, but two black crafted shapes of Italian steel. One flickered with silent red pencils of lead, the other with burning muzzle-flashes and the crack of high-powered 9 mm ammunition blowing out of a short barrel.

Kadal didn't know the name of this phantom rising from the desert, but he knew the purpose of the grim man as he rose to battle. With renewed savagery, Kadal chopped and punched at the false Sedal, finally knocking his handgun free from his grip and shoving him off. He tossed him back with a strength born of desperation as he watched with helpless impotence. The grim specter of death slammed round after round of 9 mm fury into his three remaining warriors, sending their bodies twisting back, tumbling.

Kadal mentally fought back to battle, abandoning his shock and speculation. He powered another blow off the American's shoulder, knocking him forward. He had no pistol anymore, and was of no consequence, but the other American was armed and had to be taken out as fast as possible.

A spinning star came slicing through the air, catching Kadal in the clavicle, steel jutting and blood squirting from where it violated his body. All the strength ran out of his right arm instantly, the ten pound Kalashnikov dragging his hand down clenched in agony, fingers tightening. Kadal's AK-47 triggered uselessly, wide of its target, who spun at the sound of gunfire.

Kadal saw the cold blue eyes of his executioner as he struggled again to get both hands on his weapon to blow the white man in two.

Then a thin red pencil flickered out at him.

The Divine Swordsman saw no more after that.

"THANKS," WAZDI HEARD the big man say, lowering his Berettas, then stuffing them into their respective holsters on his hip and under his shoulder.

"Not a problem," Wazdi said.

The American lawman walked over and wrenched his star from the chest of the terrorist. He looked down at the wide, lifeless eyes of the leader of this group. The last fighter didn't go down easily, the bruises already forming on Wazdi's face, head and neck attesting to his will to survive. The terrorist leader fought on despite a leg wound, and tried to help the man he thought was his own comrade. Wazdi thumbed the man's eyes closed. Whoever this guy was, he wasn't the easily confused chaff mown down by some movie action hero. He was a man, a fighter for what he believed.

Wazdi stopped that train of thought. The dead man beneath him would have been an admirable warrior but for the fact the Divine Sword of Allah was just one more group of scumbags who, as a rule, waged their war attacking unarmed civilians not engaging in single combat with enemy soldiers.

This man came, guns blazing, expecting injured and broken victims of a plane crash, and was turned back by a small, determined force.

On the one hand, his enemy had shown courage and daring. On the other, he was a murderer who struck at those he thought weak and shattered.

Welcome to the human race.

No one, even cold blooded killers, were one-sided pieces of cardboard.

Wazdi looked back to Bolan, who was watching him.

"Sorry," Wazdi apologized.

The big man shook his head. "No need. Given a chance, he might have be a soldier on the same side. He was just seduced by hatred and the words of Ahmur Ibn Laud, drawn in by a savage who looks for power and prestige, no matter who dies."

"That's why he gets dragged to trial," Wazdi whispered. "To pull him kicking and screaming, and see him face judgment."

"You're still going to arrest him?" Bolan asked.

Wazdi nodded.

Helicopter rotors thumped in the distance. The silence of a thousand unspoken words, debates over the nature of justice that had haunted philosophers for millennia lay like the grains of sand between them. Bolan finally broke the silence.

"Grab some ammunition and a fresh weapon. Laud's not going to be as easy to arrest this time."

Wazdi nodded.

THE EXECUTIONER KNEW the feelings boiling in Orlando Wazdi's heart at this moment. It was one thing to kill someone, a stranger, in the heat of self-defense. Wazdi did what was needed to survive.

But the lifeless lump, the man betrayed by the combined plan of the two cunning hunters, was something that Bolan didn't count on to rise up and slash through Wazdi's determination. The vestiges of dedication and courage, even in someone whose goal was cold-blooded murder, gave proof that this was real life, not a game, not a movie, not a trashy pulp novel. People had layers of noble qualities to mix in with the base hungers and motives of Animal Man.

Bolan had seen too many men forced by circumstances, poverty, ostracism and failure, into a life where they lived only to prey upon their fellow humans, men who hated and loathed their own existence, but still kept going, because to stop moving was to sink and die. The apologies for their actions were many, and the disgust at the turns of their lives was often real, but it still didn't change the fact that they were predators upon the weak.

Bolan long ago came to grips with the fact that looking deeper into the hearts of his enemies would only hurt him. His duty, his War Everlasting, only continued, step-by-step, because he concentrated on those lives he was saving, on those who had to be protected from the unleashed forces of savagery in the world. To do anything else was to throw a burden on his shoulders that could prevent him from helping the innocents of the world.

Loaded down with extra magazines and heavy thoughts, Bolan and Wazdi made it to the helicopter. Dave Kowalski finished pushing the pilot's corpse from where it sat, then froze.

"What's wrong?" Bolan asked, swinging his sack full of magazines into the ex-Marine's hands.

Kowalski chuckled and shook his head. "You'll think I'm crazy."

Bolan scratched his head, feeling more grit and sand coming free under his fingertips. "Try me."

"With your hair all white with sand like that?"

Bolan nodded, knowing what was coming next.

"You are Race Bannon," Kowalski said.

Bolan looked at Kowalski for a couple heartbeats, then ran his fingers through his hair, brushing the grains out. "Careful, or I'll have Dr. Quest send you to bed without dessert tonight, Jonny."

Kowalski laughed and helped load scrounged gear on board the Huey. The laughter was welcome, the flood of a cleansing brook washing away the clotted poison of Bolan's introspection. Even the FBI man seemed to brighten his mood with Kowalski's joke.

With sudden clarity, Bolan realized that it was the marshal's plan all along. While he couldn't bark them into better morale, a friendly joke pulled them back from looking too deep into the abyss.

"Do you fly?" Wazdi asked. He was serious again, urgent to save the lives of his coworkers, but no longer weighted with doubt. It was time to get back to business and save the second-guessing and philosophizing for after the action.

Bolan frowned. "I usually just hitch rides, but I do keep familiar. I ran some extensive course training a lifetime ago on helicopters, and my pilot buddy keeps me on top of my training when I get the chance."

"Right. Just wondering. I don't like going up without a co-pilot," Wazdi said, slipping into the pilot's seat. He dug out a set of headphones the trio had scrounged from the Hercules flight deck and tried plugging it into the Huey's console. It snapped in quickly and cleanly.

Bolan did the same and handed Kowalski a third pair. The soldier's head suddenly stopped pounding, the huge foam-and-rubber cuffs blocking out the thump-thump-thump of rotor slap. The familiar, low crackle and hiss of old and worn wiring and speakers took over in Bolan's ears now.

"Okay, the plugs fit, but can we hear each other?" Wazdi asked, his voice changed to a higher octave, a blade grinding on stone through the wiring.

"You're coming through clear enough," Bolan answered. He didn't expect top-grade equipment, and he examined the console and controls of the helicopter. The intercom system had avoided taking any hits, but there was the sticky blood of the pilot, and a few holes in the top of his side of the control panel.

"McClownburgers, can I take your order?" Kowalski asked. "A little static, there guys."

"When you get your helicopter license, you can have whatever stereo system you want installed on this crate," Wazdi said. "Until then, we just need to hear what's being said, and not scream ourselves hoarse over the noise of the rotor blades."

Kowalski slipped out of comic relief mode for a moment. "Well then, I hear ya. Sounds scratchy, but I hear ya."

Bolan suppressed a chuckle and Wazdi pulled up on the stick. The Huey rose, engines throttling up.

"Did you find a map on the pilot?" Bolan asked Kowalski, leaning back.

Kowalski handed over the hard-laminated map. "Marked off with erasable marker."

"Did they erase anything?" Wazdi asked, keeping his attention on flying the Huey. Bolan knew better than to distract any pilot from flying a helicopter. He heard it said once by his closest and oldest friend, Jack Grimaldi, that any distraction, even a sneeze, turned a helicopter from a flying machine into a blender full of meat, spiked into concrete. A colorful, gruesome mental image, and one of the reasons that Bolan let Grimaldi do most of the flying while he spared his concentration for less hazardous things—like land mines, streams of enemy autofire, and the odd clouds of nerve gas and radioactive chambers.

Bolan took the map and looked at it, seeing the shiny, clear laminate with faint, reddish afterimages, as if he'd been staring at a neon sign for too long, the designs in hard light burned onto his retinas for the rest of the night. "They tried to, but the marker stained. They left the ink on too long."

Wazdi glanced as he turned the Huey. "Where to, Striker?"

Bolan did some checking. "Northwest, heading 312. We've got to cover about 125 miles. It's nothing specific, and we'll be running on fumes when we arrive, but I don't think we'll have a welcome reception when we get there."

"Good. An hour and we'll be back to knocking heads," Wazdi said, looking at the fuel gauge.

The M-60D behind them clacked as its bolt racked. Kowalski looked at them and smirked.

"Except this time," Kowalski said with a grin, "we're bringing some major hurt."

AHMUR IBN LAUD LACED his fingers through Quentin Best's short hair and clawed tight, yanking his head back. In the back of the Bell UH-1 helicopter, his words would be whipped away by slashing wind and hammered under the deck by the thundering pop of the rotor wash. So Laud let his actions speak for him. He tore the hair at the roots, feeling clumps separate from the scalp before smashing the FBI commander in the face with a closed fist, nostrils trailing out thick fingers of red blood, pouring like the flow from a ruptured volcano.

Laud opened his fingers and watched Best's red hair tumble and plummet away in the wind, strand by strand. Best's red-rimmed eyes looked up, watching with a mixture of hate and fear as he struggled against the cable ties that cut into his wrists.

It was a pathetic sight. Once, this was a tall, proud man standing over Laud, gloating and powerful in the knowledge that he had an enemy trapped in the belly of his own aircraft. A complete reversal of fortunes between the two adversaries. Laud struck again, punctuating the humiliation of Best's complete helplessness.

Laud laughed and gave Best another slap, then gripped the FBI man by the neck and yanked him close, to within hearing range. Best struggled, trying to pull away, spattered blood and spittle spraying over Laud's cheek and beard as the Divine Swordsman shouted into Best's ear.

"Looks like Jonny and Hadji weren't wrong about me, idiot," Laud yelled over the hurricane bellow of the helicopter in flight.

Best snarled, face twisting, any noise he made spilling away, words tumbling and ripping out the doorway. Laud read the bloody lips well enough to get the message, though, and smiled. He jerked Best's face into his knee. Blood exploded over the FBI commander's lips and chin, and his eyes crossed for a moment as he shook away the instant of pain. He tried pushing off his knees, but Laud grabbed Best by the ears and twisted him onto his butt, bringing the edge of his hand across the bridge of Best's nose.

The American twisted and writhed in agony, kicking out and spitting through the waterfall of stickiness coating his lips. Laud smirked, feeling his hand. He'd felt bone break with that hit.

Best's eyes were clenched shut now, and he was spitting, spraying droplets, trying to clear his mouth so he could breathe. Laud cupped Best's chin once more and clenched his fist, bringing it down hard, pounding the soft, thin lips of the FBI man between his callused fist and the American's teeth. A second blow and Best pulled his head free, bent into a fetal position.

Laud let him writhe in agony.

The helicopter's copilot handed him a headset.

Laud slipped it into place, and the pilot, Shanir, spoke quickly.

"Sir, I've been trying to reach Kadal and Buraq. Neither is answering."

Laud frowned.

"It might be a communication problem," Shanir offered hopefully.

Laud shook his head. "It's not a communication problem."

The terrorist leader leaned out the door and looked far in the distance. Try as he might, he could not see halfway across the desert to the outcome that he imagined. Somehow, the three Americans left behind had overcome the ten Divine Swordsmen of Allah, and a helicopter armed with two machine guns.

Laud didn't doubt it. He remembered the iron grip, the powerful fingers of the tall, black-haired man who lunged selflessly into unarmed combat against him while trying to save a dying American. Their struggle was brief, but wickedly savage, Laud's fists aching from striking hard muscle that deflected his most determined blows, his throat still feeling bruises from hands that had to have crushed bricks for a living.

He cleared his throat again.

"We have fuel enough to turn back?" Laud asked.

Shanir glanced. "Only if you want to walk across twenty miles of desert."

Laud laced his blood-spattered fingers under his bearded chin, frowning. "All right. Head to the airstrip. We'll regroup there."

Yassif would be keeping the Lockheed there. And if the Lockheed wasn't ready, he had other means of intercepting the Americans.

"MEANWHILE, DOWN on the Farm," Aaron Kurtzman grumbled, stroking away at his keyboard in the Computer Room in Stony Man Farm's Annex. His workstation a clutter of organized chaos, it took him only a moment to find a chewed-up Mickey Mouse pencil and a clipboard.

"Something wrong?" a warm voice asked. Kurtzman knew

who it was without even a glance, but he still looked up to see the stunning blond ex-model who also happened to be the Sensitive Operations Group's mission controller, Barbara Price.

"It's hard to tell yet, but Striker hitched a ride this morning with the Justice Department operation that nabbed Ahmur Ibn Laud," Kurtzman said.

Price leaned over his shoulder. "That's an AWACS radar screen."

Kurtzman nodded. "The captain of the Hercules sent a call out for an AWACS to sweep the desert."

Price pursed her lips, worry wrinkling her otherwise smooth brow. "So where's the Hercules?"

"It was nowhere to be seen when the aircraft carrier launched her Hawkeyes," Kurtzman answered. The computer expert pulled up a couple previous screens. "There were some helicopters in the air, four to be exact. And a fast-moving target."

"No IFF on the fast mover or the helicopters," Barbara said. She didn't sound surprised to Kurtzman.

He shook his head, sighing deeply. "Negative. But then, it's not difficult to shut that off if you know what you're doing."

Price backed away from the cubicle, getting some breathing space and looking at the big screen. "How long ago did the Hercules disappear?"

"We're coming up on thirty-eight minutes," Kurtzman answered. Anticipating Price's next question, he said, "Akira says we'll have satellite imagery of the desert in two minutes."

Price nodded.

"The plane might not have crashed," Kurtzman said. He could see the worry on her face, and knew that she felt more for Bolan than she felt for any of the other Stony Man crew, a relationship that was as arm's length as the Executioner's employment by the government. It was a relationship based on mutual desire and respect, but both knew it wouldn't last forever.

Kurtzman looked up at the screen again.

"Anything?" Price asked. It had been two minutes, and between Kurtzman's working on tracking the missing Hercules and his musings over the romances of the Executioner, time had slipped away like an ebb tide.

Akira Tokaido was working away, earbuds giving off the faint tinny buzz of muffled thrash metal music when he stopped typing, jaw slack with shock.

Kurtzman looked up from his screen at the sound of Tokaido stopping cold. He'd pulled out the earbuds, the aggressive guitar music becoming louder, if not clearer. He heard Price's breath come out in a choked gasp before his eyes settled on the main monitor. Even before he looked, he knew his reassurances were made hollow and empty by the single picture spread across the screen.

Strewed across the desert, broken and smashed to pieces as if by a massive giant, lay the shattered wreckage of the C-130 Hercules, smoke still wafting into desert air. Silence loomed over the Computer Room, as for the first time in Kurtzman's memory, Tokaido abruptly clicked off his music.

7

"I have something to tell you guys that you're not going to like," Orlando Wazdi said.

"I've been watching it, too," Mack Bolan said calmly.

David Kowalski was at the other end of the spectrum as he gripped both of their headrests, repeating a low mantra: "Not gonna crash, not gonna crash, not gonna crash."

"We won't crash. We're just running out of gas," Wazdi said. "And we're still something like twenty-five miles out from that mark on the map."

"Desert I can hump," Ski said. "But two crashes in one day?"

"I'm going to take us as far as the last of the fuel can take us, but it's not going to be an easy hike," Wazdi said. "For one thing, Striker's the only one dressed for the party."

The tall, lean warrior shifted as if uncomfortable in his seat. "I probably clipped a fuel line with my buckshot."

Wazdi shrugged. "No use beating yourself up over it. It was either him or us, and frankly, I'm still picking metal out of my back. Thanks."

"I wasn't beating myself up. Just pointing out the problem and taking responsibility."

"Well, can't we land, fix the fuel line and then go after them?" Ski asked.

The big man shook his head. "No telling where the leak is.

Landing and taking off would take time. We'd be further behind. And there's no guarantee that where we're going will be a permanent base anyway."

"Cheerful, isn't he?" Kowalski asked. "Can't fly a helicopter as good as Hadji, either. My boyhood hero, stripped bare as a fraud and a sham."

Wazdi looked at the ice-blue eyes of the big man for a moment, then the big guy shrugged.

"Was he like this when you told him Santa Claus didn't exist?" Bolan asked.

"What?" Kowalski barked into the headphones.

The fuel gauge crept closer and closer to empty.

THE HELICOPTERS MADE their way in to the airfield, four of them, watched by Kansid Yassif. Hanging from their whirling rotors like overfed bugs, dangling from buzzing, invisible wings, the helicopters looked hideous. He never could understand the appeal of the aircraft, slow and ponderous, such an easy target. To him, flight meant constant forward motion, the ability to soar and to loop and to move up and down, not to stand still and hover. He dismissed the thought and ran closer to the landing pad.

Ahmur Ibn Laud, naturally, was the first man off the helicopter, leaping to the ground, his feet now in boots instead of the slippers he'd been wearing when taken. His fingers were drenched in blood, both his own and the blood of one of the FBI men who was coughing and gagging, his face a wreck of pain and torture.

"You said to meet you when you landed!" Yassif shouted over the declining rotor slap and whine of engines.

"Is the Lockheed ready for another turn out over the desert?" Laud asked.

"I need time to refuel and reload ammunition," Yassif replied. "There is no way I'll be done in anything less than thirty minutes."

"Then a helicopter. You can fly one, can you not?" Laud asked.

"No. I was not trained, and it's an entirely different set of controls. Had I been started on helicopters, I'd know how to handle conventional aircraft, but to fly one without hundreds of hours of training with a copilot..." Yassif said.

He watched Laud's face grow grim.

"I wanted to send up our KA-60 with someone who knew something about ground attack. My helicopter pilots are good, but..." Laud trailed off, as if pondering a new solution.

Yassif had to make his own agonizing decision. He knew that he could work the weapons systems on the Soviet gunship. The pilot glanced up, and Laud's eyes locked with his at the mutual confirmation of Yassif's worst fears.

"The Kamov is a deadly aircraft, with strong armor and even more deadly weaponry. You will be going against a forty-year-old aircraft armed with small arms," Laud said. "And your skills, your knowledge, will prevail for us against these Americans."

"Americans?" Yassif asked. "What?"

"What did you think I was going to ask you to do?" Laud asked.

"To ferry the Kamov to the ship," Yassif answered.

Laud shook his head. "No. The Americans survived your attack with the Lockheed, and they have killed our men and taken a helicopter."

Yassif smiled. "And you just want me to be a gunner to finish what I did not before."

Laud chuckled as the pilot suddenly surged with renewed courage.

"You feel up for battle, but not ferryman duty?" Laud asked.

Yassif mopped his brow and nodded.

"Excellent. Have the crews get the Kamov ready," Laud said, clapping Yassif on his shoulder. "And this time, Yassif, finish them off!"

THE HUEY WAS FLYING on fumes now, and Orlando Wazdi knew he couldn't grab anymore distance. Their wings had failed them, the enemy was too far ahead and despair nearly had him point the nose of the Huey right at the ground, but he held off. The man sitting beside him had faith, that they could catch up and save Quentin Best and his men.

So he tilted the nose up and dropped down slowly, using forward momentum to keep them from plummeting like a rock.

Behind him, he could feel his childhood friend crushing the seat. The intercom was silent save for the background hiss and pop of the aged electronics. Nothing was said, until finally, the skids touched sand with a powerful jolt.

He looked at Kowalski. "How was that landing?"

"Had a nice beat, you could dance to it. I give it a seven," Kowalski answered.

"At least no funny bones were broken in this crash," Wazdi quipped. "Striker, where are we on the map?"

"You did good," the big man answered. "We've only got ten miles to cover."

Bolan looked up, peering into the distance, lips taut.

"Something wrong?" Wazdi asked.

"There was no radio traffic." The big man folded the map and stuffed it into a pocket, gathering up the gear and dividing it among the three of them. "Laud will know something's wrong."

Kowalski checked the M-60 and tried to pull it off its pintle mount.

Bolan stopped Kowalski's tinkerings. "We can't afford that kind of weight. Besides, they'll notice it's missing."

"We're leaving it behind?" Kowalski asked.

"Along with a couple pounds of C-4. Hopefully there's enough fuel in the system to make it a reasonable looking crash and burn."

"Crash and burn. You think they'll send search teams after us?" Wazdi asked.

One good thing about Bolan, he didn't sugarcoat bad news. "Search and destroy teams."

Wazdi snorted in disgust. "Slowing us down some more."

"I'm afraid so. Get moving." He aimed his finger in the direction they should keep going. "I'll stay behind and set up the chopper."

Wazdi gave Kowalski a slap on the back, and the two men started crossing the sand at a ground-eating pace that kept them from overexerting themselves in the hot sun.

The FBI man wasn't quite sure this was what he had in mind when he thought about coming back to "the motherland." He was half-Egyptian, half-Cuban, born in Orlando, Florida, and transplanted to Chicago. Wazdi always felt the eyes of others on him, as if he didn't belong. Too white to be black, too black to be white.

Wazdi studied the languages of his heritage. He was talented in many Arab dialects, as well as with multiple flavors of Spanish. It was a gift—being able to learn quickly. From languages to being a pilot, to learning how to toss little bits of shiny steel with deadly force, he just learned quickly.

He glanced at his childhood friend and thought of how far they'd both come. Kowalski didn't have any gift of natural genius like Wazdi, but what he lacked in learning, he made up in determination. He just didn't stop. He refused to let his fears control him, and though he spoke and gave them voice, he was never paralyzed by them. He just nutted through.

"Keeping up?" Wazdi asked.

"You know it," Kowalski answered. "Sam Gamgee, don't you leave Frodo Baggins alone."

Wazdi panted out a chuckle. "I'm drawing the line at anything that has us running around with hairy, bare feet."

A new voice broke in on the conversation. "Yeah. Besides, you're kind of tall to be a hobbit."

Wazdi looked back and there was Striker, hot on his heels. Wazdi and Kowalski both stopped cold and Striker moved past them, continuing on without slowing. Behind them, they heard the crashing and wrenching of steel being distorted and mangled by plastic explosives. Wazdi looked to Kowalski who shrugged.

"Hmm. Fast on his feet. Tight lipped. Natural leader and born ass-kicker. Maybe he's Strider," Wazdi mused.

"Strider. Striker. Welcome to the new millennium, big guy," Ski said, starting to run again.

"Yeah. Just don't forget us hobbits," Wazdi added.

THE KA-60 BURST over the sand dunes, thundering along on slashing blades, its stub wings sleek and long, bristling with rockets and missiles. Kansid Yassif settled into the gunner's seat, testing his aim with the nose guns, realizing that maybe he could get used to being on board one of these things.

He wondered if he could ask Laud for the opportunity to learn how to fly one of these desert-patterned sky sharks, a fanged monster that seemed even more perfectly tuned for bringing death to his enemies than even the heavily armed Lockheed. Yassif looked at the Sidewinder-style Soviet AAMs on the ends of the wing stubs.

He could even knock an enemy aircraft out of the sky if he so chose.

"Targeting systems are confirmed," Yassif said.

Bahran, the helicopter's pilot, grunted in confirmation. "Excellent."

Yassif scanned the horizon and saw thin fingers of smoke in the distance. "I see something."

"I spotted it, too. We'll be there in a few minutes," Bahran said. "You are not the only one who knows the joys of flying swifter than an eagle."

Yassif heard that as a challenge and smirked. "They also serve, Bahran. I've only ridden in those bloated hogs before."

Bahran chuckled. "Then let me show you something."

The KA-60 poured on the speed, and Yassif checked the speedometer on the aircraft. They had passed 150 knots and were still picking up speed. Beneath them, the dunes blurred.

No, it was not jet speed, but this was how Yassif liked to fly, with the feeling of true speed and power. The surplus gunship swung high and around the smoldering chunk of twisted metal below, the distance between them suddenly eaten up. Yassif swung the cameras on the helicopter over the wreck and scanned it. The power of the helicopter's electronic eyes was awesome, and he was able to see the ruptured helicopter as if he were standing right on top of it. Breathless, he looked at the burning and twisted wreck. The windshield was blackened and scorched, opaque. He couldn't see anything through it.

"Move forward a little bit," Yassif suggested.

Bahran grunted, and the KA-60 edged around in an arc. "Are there any bodies?"

Yassif's lips tightened as he zoomed the camera's focus through a shadowed door. He didn't see anything.

"Base, we have no contact," Yassif said.

The radio buzzed back, Laud's voice filled with gravelly urgency. "You don't, but we do!"

AHMUR IBN LAUD looked at the radar screen. "What range are they?"

"Five hundred miles," the radar operator stated. "Which means they'll be something over a half hour from finding the KA-60 and gunning it out of the sky."

"And they'll find us by our own radar emissions, correct?" Laud asked.

"I'm shifting frequencies, for now. But that's only temporary," the operator said.

"Base…" the radio buzzed. It was Yassif, filled with dread. "We have no contact."

Laud moved to it, keying the microphone. "You don't, but we do."

"Sir?"

"Get back to the base now! Low altitude as well. Stay under their radar," Laud spoke up. "There are two aircraft. We think they might be American jets from an aircraft carrier."

"But…would they suspect us?" Yassif asked.

"We're not taking any chances. Get back to base now!" Laud ordered. He killed the radio.

"Kill the radar!" Laud ordered.

Nohar, one of Laud's lieutenants, stepped forward. "They found no bodies, so that means the Americans are still out there. And look at how close they got."

"I know that. We cannot conduct our search by air, however," Laud stated. He nodded to Nohar. "Get the motorcycles ready."

The Divine Swordsman smiled. "The steeds...yes."

Nohar spun and left the radio tower.

Laud frowned.

So far, the Americans were staying out of their reach, but they were only three men on foot.

Laud was sending out a squadron on motorcycles.

If those men failed, the Americans were still too far behind. The captives would be on his ship in no time, and then, the executions would begin.

Laud grinned.

There was no stopping him now.

MACK BOLAN FIGURED their distance traveled as he knelt in the sand, marking off the map and the amount of time they'd traveled. It was only forty-five minutes since they'd abandoned the helicopter, and he reckoned their pace at around four miles an hour. Three miles. They'd trimmed the distance they had to travel than seven miles. He marked their progress on the map with a marker, then looked to Wazdi and Kowalski, who were both hunched over, trying to recover their breath. Bolan handed them a canteen and Kowalski let his friend drink first.

"We finish off that canteen and bury it," Bolan ordered.

Kowalski accepted the canteen and nodded. "Gotcha, Strider."

"Strider?" Bolan asked.

Wazdi chuckled. "Don't mind him. He's gone from Jonny Quest mode to—"

"Strider. The chosen name of Aragorn, the self-exiled heir to the throne of Gondor," Bolan said.

Wazdi paused.

"Actually, my favorite book is *Don Quixote*, but I've read a lot of Tolkien's work in days gone by." He continued to work on the map, checking his pocket GPS. It was nice to have technology on his side, but he also took measurements by the position of the sun and the time of day. The belt and suspenders approach.

Wazdi was checking his gear. "You think 180 rounds apiece will get us on even terms with whatever we find at the end of this map?" he asked.

"Don't forget your handguns," Bolan added.

"Still. That's long odds."

The Executioner's calculations came out right twice in a row, and he already felt his strength returning. Kowalski hadn't handed him the canteen back yet. "I'm used to long odds. Just follow my lead and we'll have a chance."

"I don't doubt you, Striker."

Bolan looked around for Kowalski, who had wandered to the top of a dune, looking out with binoculars. "Ski, can I get some water before we ditch the—"

"Black riders," Kowalski said.

"What?" Bolan asked.

"Black riders!" Kowalski repeated, ducking low. "I think they spotted me!"

"On horseback?" Bolan interrogated, lunging to his side and dropping to his knees and elbows, looking out across the sands. Wazdi joined him at his other shoulder.

"No," Kowalski said, pointing at the buzzing horde of figures tearing across the sand toward them. "Just your typical Islamic ninja terrorists on motorcycles."

8

"Single shots, rapid fire," the Executioner ordered, readying his own AK as the dark riders roared on their snarling black steel steeds, bouncing the motorcycles toward them.

"I'm sorry, Striker," Kowalski whispered. He made a quick sign of the cross, then shouldered his own weapon. "I didn't meant to attract attention to us."

"This could work in our favor," Mack Bolan told the stocky marshal. "Those motorcycles are better than running across the desert. We can cut down Laud's lead."

Kowalski gave a low chuckle. "You're a regular Pollyanna. When life gives you grens, make grenades."

Bolan shouldered the rifle, getting as much of a cheekweld as he could on the folding-stock rifle. Full-auto with the AK was effective and devastating, but against agile and nimble targets, outnumbered and outmaneuvered, burning off entire clips would put them under the hammer of the racing and darting bikes.

A thump sounded off Bolan's right elbow, and he looked, seeing Wazdi already slinging their grenade launcher and plucking his rifle from the sand. A heartbeat later, Bolan turned and looked for the 40 mm minibomb's impact. A thunderbolt struck the desert, tossing sand and thick black smoke, a high-explosive round detonating a six ounce payload with nerve-shattering effect.

The motorcyclists, if they hadn't seen them before, knew they had found their enemy by now, but they were splitting, racing to keep from presenting a single, easily hit formation. Only one motorcycle had been upended by the initial blast, its rider tumbling. He got up, shaking sand from the folds of his face wrap, his black machine pistol up and spitting out lead.

Bolan swung down on him, the AK barking out two rounds that center-punched the dismounted gunner, tumbling him backward in a lifeless jumble of limbs.

Kowalski was to Bolan's left tapping out single shots. The high-pitched growl of lightweight motorcycle engines split the air as shapes came zooming up and over them.

Bolan spun onto his back, tracking the riders as Kowalski tore one from his seat. The soldier's tracking burst managed to slice into the back of another black-clad biker, sending him crashing and tumbling. The motorcycle fell on its side, the idling engine roostertailing sand as it flailed for a moment and then froze up.

Wazdi triggered rounds from his Kalashnikov, firing faster as a swarm of riders tore around and over him, bodies flashing by so fast that he could barely track them.

Bolan was about to fire a few rounds after the black blurs, but they were out of range before he even gained his windage, their own fire chewing up the sand short of the trio.

"Stay or split?" Wazdi asked, reloading while he had the chance.

Bolan followed suit. "Over the dune, now. Spread out."

He lead the charge as the bikers were finding their range. The Executioner watched as Wazdi executed a forward slide over the top of the sand, legs curling tight, his wiry figure rolling to a halt halfway down as slugs punched the sand on his heels. Bolan took a leap, twisting in midair and tapping off six rounds at the surging horde behind them. His shots hit nothing, but forced the riders to swerve and dodge, their own gunfire spitting far and wide. Still in midtwist, Bolan let himself slam onto his back, skidding four feet in the soft and shifting grains. He braced himself, tucked tight as Kowalski was the last over the dune's top, heaving himself into a barrel roll that ended with him kneeling.

Wave two of the battle was coming, and so far, the score was Divine Swordsmen, nothing, Executioner, three.

Bolan hoped he could keep that lead.

ALI NOHAR BROUGHT the Kawasaki down into the sand, hanging on for dear life. The knobby wheels finally dug in and continued his forward momentum. He looked back at the three men who were scrambling over the small dune, and brought his own bike to a halt. His riders whirled around him in two arcs, getting ready to flank the trio again.

Nohar triggered a short burst, sending a blitz of Parabellum rounds toward the trio as they worked their way up and over the peak, but there was too much distance. One of them was firing back, but the riders were dodging deftly.

This was a disturbing situation. There was hardly any cover for the three Americans, and still they managed to take down three of his speeding bikers without a return shot scoring once. He gave a signal and his riders held up, whirling back to gather around him.

"They're going to be waiting for us," Nohar explained. "Especially if we go over the top."

He looked at the dune. It was a fairly narrow hill, more like a temporary fold in the undulating waves on the golden sea of the desert. The hard wind-packed sand was piled more than twenty-five feet high, but on a slope that could leave someone climbing it with a broken neck should he dare to risk it on foot or wheels. The ridge of the tiny hill was an eighth of a mile across, and considering that the Americans had rifles and his men didn't, Nohar wasn't about to risk his black-clothed riders by charging trained and cool-headed marksmen.

No, the tactics that they had been using only worked well against unsuspecting, untrained men, but against discipline and training, something else was needed.

He keyed his microphone. "We've located the Americans. They're fourteen minutes away from us."

Ahmur Ibn Laud's voice crackled in Nohar's ear. "Excellent. Have you run them down?"

"No. In fact, we've lost three men on first contact," Nohar stated. He waited for rage on the other end. Instead, there was only a chilling silence.

"Sir?" Nohar probed further.

"Just kill them. I'm sick of these Americans hounding me," Laud growled. "Kill them any way you can!"

"Sir!" Nohar snapped back in acceptance.

He looked at the hill, then remembered the layout of the terrain from their approach.

"All right, I'm splitting us into two groups. The first group will dismount, and we'll approach them by foot. The second group will split in two. Half to the left, half to the right. Go to the far edges of the dune," Nohar said. "Don't go up the ridge itself, stay to the ground. You'll be about 125 meters out, and a difficult target to hit. When you pass the dune, don't slow down. Just shoot to harass, and keep your distance."

"But they have rifles," one man spoke up.

"They have rifles, but AKs aren't worth much after thirty meters unless you spend a whole magazine looking for the target. They're firing on single shot, showing they can't spare that kind of firepower," Nohar said. "We'll be able to keep their attention on you, while my group will spring by surprise and bring them down."

Nohar cleared his throat. "But the moment we start in, I want you to turn and press the attack. In close quarters, they could repel us. But without a respite, they will surely be smashed, one way or another."

Nohar fed a fresh magazine into his Steyr, then looked at the top of the dune, the stick of ammo locking in with the finality of a breaking neck.

"May God give us victory."

THE EXECUTIONER LOOKED over the horizon. The motorcyclists were still milling about, on the move, a screen of them. They were five hundred yards out, too much of a stretch for the M-203, and their leader stood with confidence. The Kalashnikov he held might have kicked up sand, or scored a nonvital hit at that range, but except for harassment and wasting ammunition, it was useless.

However, should the cyclists make their charge, they would pass within four hundred feet if they took to the gullys at the ends of the sand ridge. Bolan centered his companions on the ridge, so they wouldn't be an easy snipe if one group decided to swing around one side or the other, but their position was still untenable. They had cover from only one direction, and that could be easily circumvented.

Bolan watched the motorcycles as they suddenly split into two swarming packs, swinging wide.

"They're going to flank us," the Executioner announced. He weighed his choices as the seconds ticked down. "Kowalski, cover our left flank. Wazdi, use the grenade launcher to put out a buckshot blast. Get halfway down the hill to do it."

"But—" Wazdi began.

"Just do it. This way, we won't get swarmed all at once. I'll bat cleanup in either direction," Bolan promised.

Wazdi and Kowalski nodded.

"You watch my friend's back," Kowalski told Bolan, the humor drained off the steel foundation of his voice. "I'll take care of my end."

Bolan gave him a glance. "I'll trust your rifle, Marine. I know you won't miss."

Kowalski nodded, grim for the first time. Bolan knew the determination well. The devotion of a brother, even if he was born to another mother, decades of friendship turned to family. The Executioner had those ties, and he knew the strength of such bonds. The willingness to kill, and to die, for someone else.

Bolan checked over the ridge, and Parabellum rounds cut the air over his head, kicking up sand. He ducked back down, blinking granules out of his eyes, desperately trying to sort out the quick flash image.

Black riders, charging across the sand on steeds of steel and fiberglass, engines howling like demon cats hungering for the flesh of men. The group spread like the wings of a bird, then split into two halves. Bolan shook his head and eyes, fighting to determine the image that had flashed for a brief moment in his memory.

"Waz! Ski! They're splitting into three groups!" Bolan warned.

The Executioner finished wiping the grit from his eyes and brought up his AK-47 in one smooth motion, switching it to full-auto. He looked back and saw the two former blacksuits give him the nod. They spun, bracing for combat.

Wazdi curled tight, bracing his rifle across his knees while he shouldered the grenade launcher. Kowalski was in a classic Marine marksman's prone position—minimum target and maximum stability.

When the dark riders burst around either side of the sandy ridge, hell was unleashed. Wazdi's cone of buckshot spread, slamming three of the motorcyclists off their bikes, crashing them to the ground as lumps of lifeless, pulped flesh. Parabellum rounds wildly sprayed into the sand around him. One shot, and all but two of the charging cyclists on his side were down.

Kowalski was tapping out rounds as soon as the gunners on his side were rolling into view, their wild bursts kicking up sand far short of the prone marksman. His first five rounds took down two. That left five in total, whirling off into the distance, trying to keep outside of his range. It was a good plan that should work well, especially considering there was a third prong to this attack.

But the plan was doomed to fail, because the two blacksuits had the Executioner at their back.

Bolan charged over the ridge. Divine Sword gunmen were racing up and trying to bring their machine pistols to bear, keeping themselves silent to prevent the loss of surprise. They expected the Americans to have their total attention turned on the buzzing riders who charged around to engage them.

Instead, the eight men charging up the incline, machine pistols tucked to their hips, came face-to-face with ice-eyed rage.

The black-clad desert raiders paused. Three unblinking eyes stared at them, the black glare of a rifle muzzle, and the flashing pair of the man wielding the rifle. Their pause lasted only a moment. Bolan tapped the trigger, taking two of the Divine Swordsmen without resistance. His salvo of hellfire chopped into them and sent them crashing loose-limbed into eternity. The others dived for cover, tucking and rolling, coming up firing wildly. The range was only a hundred feet, but firing on the move, their precision was sacrificed.

Bolan did the unexpected. He charged and did a baseball slide, emptying the last of his magazine as the loose surface sand barely slowed his descent. Skidding on his hip and back, the Executioner swept another gunman who was trying to track him, 7.62 mm rounds punching savage holes through his chest, sending him spinning, machine pistol tumbling from lifeless fingers.

By then, the Executioner was among the gunners, rifle empty, no time to reload, and only his pistols to fall back on.

ORLANDO WAZDI HEARD Bolan's warning cry and yanked his AK across his knees, tucking it tight to his stomach before sighting down the M-203. A three-way attack against three out-maneuvered and outnumbered men on a naked dune.

There weren't even sandbags, Wazdi thought with bitter irony. Just sand.

He heard the tinny snarl of the bikes tearing around the corner and braced himself. He'd only fired the M-203 in the heat of combat once before, just moments ago, but had training in the use of the big cannon. Indirect fire hadn't been his strongest point, at least not on his first ever shot. However, with a buckshot round in the breech, the weapon was a simple shotgun that could throw out a volume of buckshot that would make a twenty-foot-wide area uninhabitable for a second.

The motorcycles burst into view, and Wazdi tripped the trigger the instant the black shape broke across his line of sight. The 40 mm charge rammed the launcher against his shoulder, spitting out hundreds of pellets at over 1200 feet per second. He knew in his gut he'd missed the first rider, but the three following were suddenly hit by an invisible wind that swatted them off their motorcycles with explosive force. Ruptured flesh and shattered metal slammed sideways with the massive blast, and Wazdi.was already letting go of the M-203, scooping the Kalashnikov into both hands.

Bullets were tearing up the hill toward him, sand kicking and spitting up in geysers wide and short of him as the riders sent out their initial harassment fire. The FBI man took a shoulder dive, realizing that most of the fire that had been directed toward him was in the air before his grenade launcher slashed the riders down.

Wazdi tucked in tight and.looked back up, watching Kowalski firing with deadly, unnerving calm on the hill. He glanced toward the dark riders who were sweeping themselves wide and away from them.

He didn't blame them. Half their number were dead in what should have been an easy charge.

Wazdi saw Bolan lunge over the top, and listened as gunfire erupted on the other side of the ridge. He wanted to rush to the soldier's aid, but there were still enemies at their back. Instead, he rushed back to Kowalski's side, rifle clenched tight.

Ski was casually putting a fresh magazine into his weapon as the dark riders continued their swirling orbits, keeping at range.

"Striker's dealing with our problems at the back door," Wazdi said. "Think we can clean out the rest of this bunch?"

Kowalski remained quiet, adjusting the sights on the Kalashnikov. He shouldered his rifle, measuring a shot. Wazdi remained quiet.

A single gunshot cracked, sounding ominously loud in Wazdi's ears, and he looked. One of the riders swerved hard, then stopped his bike, tumbling off and scrambling back and away.

Kowalski handed his friend the rifle with a smile. "Here. I zeroed it for you, Waz. You won't miss, even at this distance."

They exchanged rifles, and the pair took aim. "Not going to zero yours?" Wazdi asked.

"I'll do it on the fly. Just take down your guys," Kowalski answered. "Betcha I bag three."

"I'll be glad to bag two if that's the case," Wazdi returned. The friends took aim and began laying down a brutal barrage of fire on the motorcyclists across the desert.

ALI NOHAR DIDN'T KNOW who the tall, long-limbed soldier was who seemed to defy physics as he glided on the shifting slope, but he was deadly with his rifle. Nohar tried tracking the hurtling form with his machine pistol, but all he got for his trouble was an empty weapon. He watched, impotent with rage, as another of his riders was chopped to ribbons.

Then, the wily American was a curled ball, rolling down the hill, something flying away from him. Nohar dodged, then saw it was only the empty rifle, spearing barrel first into the sand as a distraction.

Whoever this was, he was outnumbered now, five to one, and surrounded.

But the man didn't stay surrounded for long. He kept tumbling, rolling out of the midst of them before popping up on his long legs.

Nohar scrambled to reload and fire. He watched as his men shot where the camouflaged soldier had been a heartbeat before, their ammunition spent and wasted without effect. Nohar had finally wrestled his magazine into place when he suddenly saw black pistols appear in the big hands of the soldier charging back among their ranks. From his right hand came loud cracks and bright muzzle-flashes, a small pistol barking and spitting out lead while from his left came hushed and subtle spits of death from a larger pistol with a longer barrel and sound suppressor.

Nohar swung his machine pistol, holding down the trigger and spraying a savage swarm of Parabellum rounds at the swift figure who dropped from his six-foot-plus height to the ground.

Hot, brutal pains stabbed into Nohar's gut as he swung the machine pistol at chest level. He tried to bring the gun down, but his limbs were no longer answering to him, responding only to momentum. Nohar kept spinning, watching the world swirl out of control.

He slammed into the sand and looked up at the tall, grim desert wraith who was rising over him. Nohar sputtered, blood in his mouth. He didn't know where it was coming from.

Then Ali Nohar faded to blackness in an absence of sound or light.

MACK BOLAN LET the hot, smoking Berettas hang at his sides, feeling his shirt starting to stick to his side with fresh moisture. He couldn't be sure if it was sweat or blood, and his adrenaline was kicked too high to tell the difference. He listened. There was no sound of gunfire or motorcycles revving.

Bolan turned, stalking up the side of the hill.

If the black riders had finished his partners, the motorcycles would still be buzzing and snarling, unless the battle had gone down to the last gunshot. If that happened, he was on his own.

Reaching the peak, Bolan looked over and saw Kowalski wrapping Wazdi's thigh with a roll of tape and shredded cloth. Bolan scanned downhill and saw the Divine Swordsmen of Allah strewed like broken and forgotten toys in a schoolyard sandbox.

"You okay?" Bolan asked.

"I took a glancing slug off my leg back there," Wazdi said, pointing to his roost from moments before.

"We have wheels. And more guns," Kowalski chirped happily. "Wheels are good."

"They're on the ground," Bolan noted.

Kowalski winked.

Bolan took a seat and felt pain from the graze he had taken in the wild melee. "We'll patch up my gunshot, then make for their base."

The former blacksuits looked at him, hearing words left unspoken in the Executioner's tone.

They were close now to Laud. Close enough to smell him. The endgame was just over the horizon, moments away by motorcycle.

Then this breakneck pace, this hard pursuit, would come to its inevitable flame-and-blood splashed halt.

Barbara Price paced before the main screen, watching the rescue teams on live video feed. Several SH-60 Seahawks and MH-47 Chinooks assembled around the crash. Some of the helicopters were on search-and-rescue patrol, but there was nothing but mangled steel and dead bodies on the scene.

Price held her breath as the intercepted video was being transmitted.

"It looks like a couple of people were killed on impact," Aaron Kurtzman stated. His deep baritone was reassuring as he rolled his wheelchair beside her. "Four dead in the hold. Their bodies were damaged, but it's apparent that they died on impact."

Price's lips drew into a tight, bloodless line. "Descriptions?"

"None of them were Striker. We have identifying photos onscreen," Kurtzman replied.

Price looked as the four images popped onscreen. On the other side, three more squares with faces appeared.

"Who are they?" she asked.

"The listed flight crew," Kurtzman explained. "They found the pilot and the mangled torso and legs of the copilot. It's presumed that the navigator, Major Al Stewart, was sucked out of a hole in the cockpit."

Price swallowed hard. "Those are file photos. What about the video of the cockpit?"

Kurtzman nodded to Akira Tokaido, who nimbly tapped away. A picture in the lower-right corner showed the footage of the cockpit as rescue crews looked inside.

"Boot prints," Price noted. "Big ones, too."

Kurtzman motioned, and Tokaido froze the image and enlarged it. "Could be Mack's boot print," Kurtzman said.

"He's alive," Price said. "And it looks like most of the lawmen are, too."

"A hostage situation?" Kurtzman asked.

Price shook her head. "It's Ahmur Ibn Laud's chance at making another move against us. He wants to put us in the worst possible light."

She looked at Kurtzman. "Remember when North Korea grabbed that SEAL team?"

"Yeah. Striker and Phoenix barely got them out before their executions were to be carried out," Kurtzman recalled. He smirked. "The Executioner robbed the executioners."

"So far, the best hope we've been displaying overseas has been to send our lawmen out and grab as many terrorists as we can. There hasn't been a lot of news play about it, but these guys are ending up in our jails," Price continued. "But do you think the American public would be willing to risk more American lawmen? No."

"Not only that, but nations that would have normally been willing to help us on their soil don't want to be put in a position where they're sending our people to their doom. The blame games alone could spark trade embargos at the very minimum," Kurtzman stated. "And any shared intelligence between those nations would be snarled up in second-guessing, if not totally dismissed as misinformation."

"And if we don't ask for cooperation from foreign governments and just arrest these guys, wherever we pull snatches, you bet we'll be watched even harder," Price concluded. "All told, Laud can easily screw the government's antiterrorism efforts overseas."

"Well, there's always us," Kurtzman told her.

Price shook her head. "We need the legitimate hunters out there to give our boys cover. Why do you think I've rarely let Lyons off U.S. shores since I took over?"

Kurtzman winced. "Yeah. Ironman does kind of give the State Department a couple of things to think about."

Price grinned. "Though, right now, I wouldn't mind sending them there to help Mack. He's pretty much alone."

"He might not be," Tokaido said. "Three sets of boot prints were found in the cockpit. And I pulled up a roster of the guys who are missing."

"Orlando Wazdi and David Kowalski. Two former black-suits," Price announced. "It's not Phoenix Force..."

"You think those are the two who are with him?" Kurtzman asked.

"Striker's a lightning rod. If he can recruit Carl Lyons or David McCarter, a couple of Feds aren't going to be much effort," Tokaido noted.

"There's that," Price agreed.

"And the two of them would automatically be the others?" Kurtzman inquired. He thought about it a moment. "Then again, we have a stringent selection process. We don't pick cannon fodder, but people with the determination to survive and complete their mission despite the odds."

"Just like Striker himself," Price said. "Just like Striker himself."

QUENTIN BEST FELT himself dragged to his feet and hauled across the floor, fingers knotted in his hair as well as his collar. His shoes scraped, knees bouncing off concrete as he dipped, then was dragged forward again hard.

He didn't know what was being shouted at him, but he knew they wanted him to move, and move fast. Without being able to see—his swollen eyes were tightly clamped shut by the constricting crush of a blindfold—he had no idea where he was going, let alone where to put his feet so they'd keep under him.

Best's shirt rode up and jammed in his throat, choking him, but he managed enough of a kick in his scrambling to get off the ground and suck in a fresh breath. Then he'd lose his balance again and tumble forward, stopped from slamming into the ground by hands hooked under his shoulders, or hard yanking on his shirt collar, which was swiftly feeling like a hangman's noose.

The men stopped, and Best fought to get his feet under him again, but he was yanked and shoved to his knees. His joints jammed harshly against the ground, and over the ringing in his ears and the Arabic babble, he heard helicopters powering up.

God, they were moving him again.

Moving all of his men.

"Good afternoon, Special Agent Best," Ahmur Ibn Laud's voice cut over the still-distant roar of the helicopters.

"What do you want?" Best demanded. His cut and torn lips had swelled, making speech painful.

There was a chuckle. "Your company for a special event this evening. I notice that the American people love the concept of pay-per-view," Laud taunted.

Best wanted to spit in the direction of the voice, but he had no spit left. "So what? We're going to watch some boxing? Wrestling? A movie?"

Laud clapped Best on the shoulder, and he felt himself involuntarily cringing from the contact. Best cursed himself for showing fear of being touched by the terrorist, despite the horrific beating that had smashed his face into a swollen, deformed mask. Laud's cruelty was no joke now, his capacity for evil very real.

Regret churned in Best's stomach as he realized his callous, foolish dismissal of Orlando Wazdi's almost fanatical vigilance in watching over the man who held him at mercy now.

Best made a vow.

To apologize profusely to Wazdi, and his pal Kowalski.

Going off cocksure had been his doom.

"Our pay-per-view tonight won't exactly be a sporting event. Indeed, it would be like shooting fish in a barrel, as you'd say," Laud continued.

"The American people will view as we pay with our lives," Best snarled.

Laud laughed and gave Best's welt-covered cheek a soft slap. "So clever. It's a shame I have to kill you."

"Then why do it?"

Laud sighed. "Because, it's easier this way. Look at how unified your country gets when it has a common enemy, a great evil empire to fight against. The Nazis. The Communists. Al-Qaeda."

Best squirmed, but the men holding him down were too strong.

Laud continued his little rant. "America is the perfect thing for those of us who know what's really going on. The Muslim world probably wouldn't think twice about Americans watching naked *Baywatch* whores and eating greasy hamburgers, and even if they took offense, most of them are the same as your Christians. There are no missionaries left in the world, fighting to convert the 'unwashed' masses, unless you count soccer moms fighting crusades against video games and rap music."

"So you don't think America is evil?" Best asked.

Laud laughed. "You idiot. Your government paints our people as devils. We paint yours as devils. And what does that get? More control."

Best clenched his broken teeth.

"Think about your government. Your Bill of Rights has been trampled over the past decades fighting the war on drugs, fighting the war on terrorism. All in the name of the safety of Americans. Did that stop us?" Laud asked.

"Shut up."

"It did nothing. So you killed off my brothers in the Taliban and al-Qaeda. And they weren't the only ones. Stomp down one group, another one flares up. And you have Americans hating and fearing Muslims, and Muslims hating and fearing Americans, and even when you have all that tension, it doesn't mean a war will spark. Because, if you do actually go into a shooting war, that means you can't maintain your control. You need the threat of an enemy, not someone who you fight, and then suddenly beat down in a year or four."

Laud tilted up Best's chin. "Think of it, Quentin. If it wasn't for me, you wouldn't have a job. Although, if it wasn't for me, you wouldn't be dying tonight on live, streaming video."

Best struggled and lunged at Laud, but something hard hammered into the back of his head, and the blackness was suddenly accompanied by a numbing silence.

ONCE MORE, duct tape was put to use to swathe the trio of bullet creases that the Executioner caught, his skin sliced by three near misses. Torn strips of dead men's clothing went to the bandaging of cuts and scrapes and wounds, and the canteens of dead men were drained of water by the trio of thirsty men.

In the desert dehydration was an enemy just as deadly as flying bullets. Blood lost had to be replaced, by food and water.

The motorcyclists didn't have food, but they brought plenty of water and had 9 mm ammunition to spare for their deadly little Steyr TMPs. Bolan drained the last of a canteen, then twisted and flexed his torso. The bullet wounds hurt, but they were packed with cloth, which would absorb any further bleeding, and sealed off with duct tape.

The motorcycles were sleek Suzukis, the DR-Z400 model according to the markings that hadn't been painted over with black paint applied in sloppy strokes. Scratches where the bikes had crashed and toppled showed that underneath the paint, they were yellow where they weren't chromed. They were a combination of off-road and street-sport motorcycle. The lightweight bikes had power, though, with a 398 cc, 4-valve engine, and range, thanks to ten liter gas tanks.

It took a half hour to drain gas from the assembled bikes to fuel three working vehicles. The Executioner was a well-seasoned car driver, but he'd also spent some time riding motorcycles. This bike was relatively puny compared to the bigger ones that Bolan was familiar with, but those bikes would only get bogged down in the sand with their made-for-asphalt tires and 500- to 750-pound frames. As it was, Bolan, with his fully loaded gear bag, felt a little sluggish in the sand.

David Kowalski was as expert in motorcycles as Orlando Wazdi was with helicopters. From Bolan's complaints, Kowalski spent some time adjusting the suspension, muttering all the while.

Bolan went for a second test circuit with the bike, and it handled better, but his weight in the sand would still slow him. As well, he realized the logic and wisdom of the desert riders for wearing the black head wraps and their goggles to filter the flying sand. He wrapped himself up for his second ride in what Kowalski jokingly referred to as "ninja-biker chic."

Bolan agreed. If he was going to go with the black head wrap, he might as well go all the way and change out of his bloody, torn and worn out BDUs. Bolan wadded up his desert camouflage uniform, after first emptying the pockets, and buried the blood-covered bundle of rags. He reached into his gear bag and removed his blacksuit. Stings of pain jolted from his fresh wounds as he shifted and twisted into the skintight, lightweight fabric. In the desert sun, the black color would attract heat, but this blacksuit was made especially for hot weather. Porous, it allowed the skin to expel heat through sweat and evaporation. More so than traditional fabrics, the blacksuit allowed air to get at him and to wick away the excess heat.

The same principle allowed desert nomads to wear all black and not be broiled to death in their own clothing. It wasn't the color. It wasn't even the layers. It was the ability of the body to eliminate its excess heat.

Bolan sipped water again, before slipping into his battle harness. The water was warm, another vital factor in keeping cool in the desert. Cold water would force the body to warm up to accommodate the sudden relative drop in temperature. The increased body temperature over the long run would do more harm than the good of a quick, refreshing sip of water. Bolan would stay hydrated with warm, tepid water, as tasteless and unsavory as it might be. It was vital to his survival.

"Is your back doing better?" Kowalski asked.

"It'll do. It's not like we can head down to the emergency room and get me some aspirin," Bolan replied.

"The pain might cramp your style, though," Kowalski reminded him.

Bolan shook his head. "Painkillers have never been my thing. They slow your thinking, and worse, if you can't feel pain, then you don't know if you're pushing yourself too hard."

Kowalski sighed. "That's right. Striker, you want we should also pick up on the ninja fashion?"

"That would be a good idea," Bolan replied.

Black tunics and slacks were stripped off two bikers, and the American lawmen discarded the Egyptian street clothes that they'd been wearing all day.

Bolan gathered together a half dozen unfouled Steyrs and handed two to each of his partners, along with ten magazines of ammunition for each. Bolan also distributed fragmentation grenades, again, recovered from the enemy dead. Their enemies had provided an embarrassment of riches for the group.

"Need loose ammunition to fill up your pistols?" Bolan asked.

"My LDA's going to be running low after the next firefight," Kowalski announced with a sigh. "But I can use the refill on my Beretta mags."

Bolan held out his hand. "I'm already dressed to kill. I'll load your magazines."

The soldier got to work loading the pistols for the two temporarily reinstated blacksuits. The time-consuming prep work was a necessary, if boring, evil. They'd been in firefights across hundreds of miles of desert, and this brief pause was a chance for them to replenish not only ammunition, but also strength of body, mind and spirit.

They would need it.

An unknown force was waiting for them only a few miles over the horizon. Lives were at stake, and there was only the three of them primed and ready to stage a rescue.

Bolan had pulled off near miraculous rescues before, but he didn't delude himself that he was a miracle worker. It was equal parts preparation, determination and pure hairy-assed luck.

Ahmur Ibn Laud was forcing the Executioner to fight this war on suicidal terms.

Laud chose the battlefield, and it was a setup that the Executioner didn't even have more than a hint of information about. It was an airfield, and it was big enough to accommodate a large force.

Laud chose the time of the engagement by virtue of having the hostages. There was a deadline, and that meant the Executioner had to move as quickly as possible.

Laud knew that the Americans were coming. He knew the strength and the direction of the Executioner's attack. Laud had bait for what Bolan knew was a trap.

The leader of the Divine Sword of Allah was proving why he was considered such a dangerous enemy by intelligence agencies around the world. The Executioner was outgunned, outmaneuvered, and in terms of strategy, he was left dangling in the wind. This was a case of catch-up, hit hard and watch the pieces fall.

But Mack Bolan had an arsenal of reasons to avoid feeling despair at any hope of victory. He wouldn't stop until he was dead, and he wouldn't fold for any trap. The enemy corpses had provided Bolan and his team with more ammunition, transportation, fuel, even clothing. Laud would be expecting the Executioner to stagger in, weakened, worn out, running on empty.

That was enough for Bolan.

Ahmur Ibn Laud was a monster, but he was a genius at making war. The only thing Laud wasn't counting on was Bolan being an equal to him.

Laud was going to meet the Executioner, and when that time came, they would both learn whether the Divine Sword was a keen enough weapon to stave off an Executioner's wrath.

10

Time was an enemy that was relentless, and someday, the Executioner knew, it would be the ultimate winner. Even if Bolan avoided every fatal bullet, deadly fall and heartstopping blade, there was the persistence of time. Age would eventually kill him.

And then there were times like this. The desert tore past him, the Suzuki pulling him along in the sands that undulated like the waves on the ocean, sand roostertailing like white foam.

Time was ticking away as the sun slowly dropped toward the horizon. Bolan was counting down toward darkness, and he figured three hours. They'd arrive at the enemy hardsite in the barest fraction of that at this rate.

David Kowalski was taking the lead, and Orlando Wazdi was riding parallel with the Executioner.

Deadlines and races.

The race right now was to get to the hostages and stage some effort to free them, but there was another race. A race between two men's views on how to bring Ahmur Ibn Laud to justice. Bolan wondered if Kowalski would be a deciding factor, and then dismissed it.

If they could take Laud alive, Bolan would let the lawmen do their job. He owed them that much. They'd contributed to the effort, they'd fought as hard to survive against impossible odds. The Executioner would be their guardian angel, and he sensed that the two men would sacrifice themselves for him, too.

So Bolan pushed the bike hard, hoping to bring down the cutting edge of their three-man guillotine swiftly. Take out the head, and just to make sure, put a few into the body. Make it count.

That's when, over the snarl of the Suzukis engines, he heard something more powerful.

Hueys.

The next hill cut them off from seeing the base, but he could see them now, big, fat black helicopters rising into the sky with lazy ease. Their bellies were laden with men, and the base's fleet consisted of more than just the four helicopters that had flown away from the shattered C-130. There were a dozen, packed with men, and all taking off. The aircraft rose directly to the north, but the flight formation was swinging around toward the northeast.

Bolan skidded the motorcycle to a halt, watching the helicopters take off, tracking their progress. Ahead, Kowalski and Wazdi turned off too, staring at the helicopters.

They'd come so close, they'd been so steeled for the chance to finish this, and like sand through a screen, everything slipped away. The motorcycles could try to shadow them, but only as far as the coast, which was where they looked to be heading.

They had something on the coast?

Bolan concentrated on what could be done, what could be seen, what could be figured. The battle here was won by Laud without a shot being fired.

The soldier realized that while the massed throb of the fleeing helicopters was fading, one roar was still audible. He glanced to the tiny hill, then shouted over the combined racket.

Kowalski and Wazdi were transfixed by the formation retreating in the distance, too numbed to hear the sound of the Executioner's warning over the rumble and rattle of engines.

Bolan fisted one Steyr and swept the sky with a short burst, the crackle of firepower loud and shocking.

They turned to him, giving him their attention just like he wanted.

But, as they did, their attention was completely pulled from the sleek, sharklike leviathan that rose from behind the hill, nose and wing stubs bristling with weapons.

Too late, Bolan realized, he'd gotten their attention to warn them about the KA-60 gunship that was looming over them.

That's when the first missile slammed into the ground between the three of them, sand vomiting in a gout of blackened thunder.

FLATTENED AND DAZED for the second time that day, Orlando Wazdi just wanted to lay flat on his back, sand sifting through his ninja blacks. He puffed fresh air through the black screen over his mouth as the sun felt as if it was roasting him now that he was still and without the winds whipped by the speeding Suzuki.

The motorcycle in question was several yards away. It was visible between his feet, and still chugging as it lay slumped over. It was starting to choke out, and Wazdi's gaze shifted. He realized one of his eyes was burning, scratched and clawed by grains of sand that had punched through a tiny pebble-sized hole smashed in his goggles.

Whatever hit the ground had sent up a chunk that could have torn out one of his eyes, and Wazdi's blood chilled. Electricity shot through his muscles and he scrambled, fighting his way to his feet and grabbing whatever metal was near him. He needed a weapon, and he came up with the Steyr TMP. He looked around for what fired on them and saw it slashing overhead, trying to follow in tight turns as machine guns chattered and spit.

Kowalski.

He was nowhere to be seen, and the way the helicopter was jerking, it had to be chasing down something fast and agile. A figure in black on the back of a Suzuki, a fireplug of a man, suddenly burst over the top of a dune, hanging in air as the black Suzuki leaped with effortless agility.

The assault helicopter tried to track the U.S. Marshal as he sailed to a landing, again out of sight. Wazdi surged to his feet, running forward as he held down the trigger on the machine pistol, only a half-formed plan blitzing through his brain as he raced.

Parabellum shockers ripped and roared from the polymer powerhouse. Wazdi fired it wildly with only one hand, a tactic that wouldn't allow him to hit the broadside of a barn in most cases. But most helicopters were generally the size of a broadside of a barn, and his magazine wasn't wasted. The rounds flickered and flashed off the cockpit and fuselage of the speeding helicopter.

"Over here you fuckheads!" Wazdi challenged, almost tripping over his motorcycle. He took a short hop, then let go of the Steyr. It dropped against his chest, hanging from a loose sling, and he realized that its twin was cinched more tightly to his back.

Wazdi looked and saw the helicopter sweep around. It had spotted him, but a spray of sparks bounced off the cockpit. He saw that Kowalski was pouring on the speed, swinging off in the helicopter's shadow. The machine guns under the nose kicked up a storm of sand, making the FBI man dive for cover, but the warbird didn't stick around to continue hosing the relatively vulnerable footman.

It wanted the motorcyclist.

Wazdi turned and tried to haul his motorcycle upright when he realized he was getting smoke blowing, choking and hot into his face. Big hands grabbed on to him and yanked him aside before a bright flash and heat washed over him.

Tumbling to the sand, he looked and watched his Suzuki burst apart in a spray of metal and fiberglass, flames leaping and crackling.

A quick glance told him who saved him. The big, grim soldier he knew as Striker.

"One bike down," Bolan growled. He was looking at the helicopter, a combat computer behind those ice-blue eyes spinning at high speed, looking for solutions to the deadly threat.

"Grenade launcher," Wazdi offered. He looked around for it.

"Trashed."

Wazdi remembered that it had been strapped to the side of his own Suzuki. It was now trapped under a gasoline fire that would sear the flesh from his bones should he try to grab for it.

Wazdi pushed to his feet. "Fuck it then!"

The FBI man held down the trigger on his Steyr. Bullets ripped from the stubby barrel, raking the Russian helicopter. To his side, he heard the brief thumping of the heavier Kalashnikov, but the chopper, in its weaving to keep up with Kowalski's frantic flight, wasn't taking anything resembling a center hit. Sparks flickered against the craft's hull, but no smoke issued from any fatal wounds.

Instead, the sleek, sharklike helicopter spun, as if on its heels, and whirled toward them, guns barking and missiles chewing.

"That way!" Bolan yelled.

Wazdi felt himself lifted bodily and tossed a dozen feet by an adrenaline charged shove, and was sent tumbling back into the sand. Blinking grains from his eyes, he spotted Bolan wrestling up his own Suzuki.

In a cloud of spitting sand, bike and rider were taking off at high speed, running away from the deathline of thunder smashing into the sand.

Wazdi tucked and rolled, shock waves smashing into him and buffeting him farther along the dunes.

IT GALLED the Executioner to run from a fight, but he didn't have any weapons that could match the helicopter. Things were further complicated by the fact that he was on a motorcycle.

Simply driving the motorcycle along from point A to point B was all right, if a little breakneck because of the uneven and treacherous looseness of the Egyptian sands. But avoiding being turned into puree by a helicopter was a whole new level of challenge for the Executioner.

The rear wheel slipped out from under him as he took a sharp turn to avoid a shot. Gravity yanked hold of him and hundreds of pounds of motorcycle, threatening to shatter his leg. Instead Bolan's leg landed in the soft sand and the contours of the motorcycle rested around him, keeping him from being crushed between two unforgiving surfaces. A wipeout like this, without the hardshell knee and leg protection of a real motorcycle suit, and on concrete, would have ripped off Bolan's leg.

The Executioner pulled his Beretta 93-R, aiming up at the helicopter. He was a sitting duck now. There was no way to wiggle out from under the bike and take even one step before the thunder of the gunship's arsenal would tear him to flakes of bone and shredded meat.

But damnation wasn't raining on Bolan. The sleek form of the Kamov was in profile and spinning away. The Executioner twisted free from underneath the motorcycle and found his feet, Beretta still stiff-armed at the helicopter. The aircraft had resumed chasing Kowalski, who was continuing his lethal game of aerial cat and motorcycle mouse.

Eventually, the kid's luck was going to run out, and Bolan knew he needed to end the game, decisively, before that happened.

The Kamov's pilot was fast, and he kept flying low, but not so low that the rotors were in danger of clipping the dunes and possibly shattering themselves. Bolan's mind flashed back to a time when his close friends in Able Team threw a roll of barbed wire off a cliff into the rotors of a marauding helicopter, destroying it.

No cliffs high enough. The only way someone could get above those rotors to drop something on them was to do a daredevil-style leap.

Options raced through his brain. Bolan wrestled up his motorcycle again, his shoulders protesting the effort to right the machine, engine twisting, throttle snarling.

He'd seen people use bikes with this kind of power to leap school buses with a sufficient ramp. Around him in the desert, there were plenty of natural ramps of sand. But to coordinate with Kowalski, to get their plan together, while the Kamov was breathing fire down on them? The Executioner had to risk it. He whirled the bike around and took off after the Kamov, gunning the throttle to the redline.

Kowalski was zipping around, doing an amazing front wheel wheelie, spinning the bike on the nose before he rattled off another short burst at the Kamov and sped back toward Bolan.

The Executioner still had to communicate with the man.

Suddenly, Kowalski was skimming beside him, swooping out of nowhere and pacing him as if he were a living, snarling shadow. Bolan looked at him, then put a thumb to his own chest and then to the helicopter. He lunged his hand back to the handlebar as he felt the bike start to swerve.

Hand signals at this speed were out. Bullets began pounding into the ground behind them, and Kowalski tore off hard to the right. Bolan swerved to the left, this time staying upright. He continued the breakneck swoop and found himself looping around to meet Kowalski, who was again slashing a path to meet him.

Kowalski let the Steyr machine pistol hang from its neck strap and pointed to the helicopter, then to Bolan, then made an upward swooping motion with his hand. Bolan nodded.

Kowalski shook his head and pointed to himself.

Bolan shook his head. He pointed to Kowalski, then made a two-signal. If Bolan ended up missing and killing himself, Kowalski would be the option of last resort. He wasn't going to sacrifice the lives of others for his own, nearly suicidal plan.

Kowalski gave him a thumbs-up, popped the Suzuki into a wheelie and took off, bringing up the Steyr and tapping off more shots at the pursuing Kamov as it swung around again, trying to catch the riders. The Kamov took off in hot pursuit again, regarding Bolan as no threat as he wasn't able to shoot and ride the bike across the dunes at the same time.

Fatal mistake.

Bolan brought the Suzuki around hard, his entire body wrenching at the effort of the earthbound acrobatics on the street and dirt bike. If he made it through this, he'd be nursing pulled muscles as he continued his chase against Laud. The Executioner drove those thoughts of dreadful agony and exhaustion from his mind. The soldier lived in the moment.

He was adapting to the motorcycle quickly. It was a fine handling machine, and he regretted the idea of giving it up. But nowhere else did he have a missile large and fast and nimble enough to take out a helicopter. Kowalski was leading the Kamov back now, at an angle, moving away to give Bolan his chance.

Sighting ahead, the soldier spotted a tall dune and gauged his speed, gunning the engine so that he'd be leaving the ground at the same time the helicopter would be passing.

All he had to do was hit a forty-foot-wide dish of a target. The rotors were moving so fast that they'd hit through the motorcycle a dozen times in the heartbeat it would take gravity to pull the Suzuki through. The mass of the bike would probably shatter the rotors easily.

But if the Executioner didn't dismount right, the rotors would pound him into a gooey runoff that would paint part of the desert crimson. Either way, the helicopter would go down if Bolan hit his mark.

And if the Executioner missed, he hoped the Kamov would spare him a mercy burst because laying shattered to pieces in the middle of the desert was not high on Bolan's choice of ways to die.

Acceleration ripped the breath from Bolan's lungs and thoughts of imminent suicide from his mind. The Kamov appeared in his peripheral vision and he spared it a glance. The skyshark was humming twenty feet off the ground, rotors blasting a cloud of sand almost fifty feet high and a hundred feet wide in its wake. This close, Bolan felt his heart echoing the overpressure thump of rotor slap on air. His entire body hummed with adrenaline and energy as he swung in tighter to the blindside of the Russian helicopter.

The Kamov had the potential to outstrip the motorcycles at higher altitude, but the secrecy of the Divine Sword's operation would have made such high flying maneuvers suicide. Moving low and trying to track the nimble motorcycles made it slower than the bikes—and took enough concentration so they wouldn't spot Bolan flashing up in their blindside.

Kowalski's straightaway drive was spitting up a fan of sand in its wake as he pushed his motorcycle to keep one step ahead of the tracking weapons. The Kamov wasn't firing its cannon anymore.

Maybe they were running low on ammo.

Bolan wasn't going to take that chance. He hit the dune and gunned the engine. Gravity tore him down hard in the seat, and he felt the motorcycle starting to pull away from him. The Executioner let the Suzuki fly, the rampaging machinery rocketing from under him as his body tumbled behind it.

KANSID YASSIF HELD OFF on the firing stud. He was waiting for the rider ahead of him to stutter, fall, lose some ground. Already half of the loads for his machine guns were empty.

"Keep on him!" Yassif shouted.

Bahran gave an affirmative grunt over his throat mike, throttling to try to keep pace with the swerving and elusive little motorcycle.

Yassif had to give these three some credit. They survived his Lockheed's assault, a Divine Sword suicide squad, a plane crash and a force of black-clad bikers.

It would almost be a shame to wipe these poor, deluded fools from the face of the earth.

Something moved in Yassif's peripheral vision.

It was the bigger rider, he was bringing his motorcycle alongside them, trying to catch up. Yassif turned back to the gunnery controls. The man didn't have the ability to ride and shoot at the same time. Sooner or later, he'd fall off his motorcycle and snap his own neck or worse, and he'd lay in the sand, flesh baking in the sun for the vultures to tear at.

Bahran gave the helicopter an extra bit of acceleration, and the skilled rider ahead of them was suddenly in his sights. Yassif flipped up the firing safeties on the machine guns, looking to fire.

Something again blurred in Yassif's peripheral vision, time suddenly dragging to a halt as his head whipped around at the sudden movement. He saw two forms—a motorcycle and a man.

The man was tumbling away, arms and legs spread out wide, trying to fall flat, his body like a starfish that was gliding now and falling away in his peripheral vision.

The motorcycle was still going on, and Yassif smiled for a moment.

The big American had just killed himself.

The motorcycle, a plummeting mass of tumbling, unyielding steel and chrome, got closer to the helicopter. They were traveling at angles to each other, and Yassif turned his head back, realizing that the motorcycle would be right above the cockpit within a few seconds.

Yassif tried to shout, calling for Bahran to pull up, but the words were like mush in his mouth. His perceptions were racing along at light speed, but sound was still moving at normal speed.

The Kamov shook violently as the back end of the Suzuki, flying at 150 miles an hour, met its ceramic rotor. Bahran screamed as the helicopter swerved hard.

Yassif wanted to curse, but he was still shouting for Bahran to pull up, to tear them away from the danger. Instead, he could only watch as the fork that held the front wheel tore from the disintegrating motorcycle and rocketed at him, plowing through Plexiglas windscreen as if it were a soap bubble.

There wasn't even time to scream. His brain fired off panicked neurons, thoughts disintegrating into a jumble. The front fork of the Suzuki slammed into Yassif's rib cage and pinned him to his seat, blood exploding from his mouth.

The Kamov was still tumbling forward, and Yassif looked to see that Bahran wasn't all there. A chunk of rotor was sticking out where his head was.

So much for learning how to fly a helicopter, Yassif thought.

His last feeling was absolute failure before tons of steel drove him into the sand, folding and spindling and pulping his dying form.

BOLAN STAYED FLAT and hit the ground on his back, sliding and skipping in the sand like a stone on the water. The impact rammed his spine, but not with shattering force as the blow was deflected.

He came to a halt and stayed still, giving himself a moment to recover. A split second later fuel and rockets cooked off and turned the crashing Kamov into a fireball, a fresh new blossom of devastation in a desert that had seen more than its share of explosions in the past twenty-four hours.

He closed his eyes for a second, then opened them to see Wazdi and Kowalski looking over him.

"You okay?" Wazdi asked.

"Was I out long?" Bolan asked.

"A minute or two. Can you move?" Kowalski queried.

Bolan bent his legs to his chest. His muscles felt like they'd been yanked across a rack until he was a half mile tall, but he could still move and he got to his feet, patting himself down.

One Steyr was lost, its twin tightly cinched on its sling still in place. He felt for his Beretta 93-R in its holster, and it was gone, too.

"Did you see my guns?" Bolan asked.

Kowalski held up a sand-clogged Steyr. "Just this."

Bolan accepted the weapon.

"Feel up to seeing what's in the base?" Wazdi asked.

Bolan stripped the magazine from the fallen Steyr and shook it, adding it to his pouch of spare ammo. "Up to attacking the base?"

Wazdi and Kowalski looked at him, and Bolan stretched out his neck, feeling his muscles recovering and loosening again.

"I've been through a C-130 crash, a controlled helicopter crash, been bombed by a strike fighter, buzzed by a combat helicopter, fought two waves of ground terrorists and a band of ninja bikers for God, and I just used extreme motorcross tactics to knock out an assault helicopter. We've crossed hundreds of miles of desert. It's dark. And you keep calling me Race Bannon," Bolan said.

By the time he reached the end of the list of what had happened that day, Wazdi and Kowalski were grinning, tightening up their grips on their weapons.

Bolan narrowed his eyes, his freshly cleaned and reloaded Steyr locked in his fists. "Yes. I'm up for checking on a base full of Divine Swordsmen ambushers. Are you?"

Kowalski shrugged, looking to his childhood friend. "When he puts it that way, it sounds like so much fun!"

"No more motorcycles. We're hoofing it the rest of the way," Bolan told them. "The engines will only make more noise."

"Good. My ass was killing me," Wazdi said.

Bolan nodded. "Come on, let's get moving."

The Bolan blitz was continuing on.

11

Orlando Wazdi crouched low. On his forearm, at the ready, he had his throwing stars in their buttoned pockets. Both hands gripped the handle and the control grip of the polymer-framed Steyr machine pistol.

The sun was crawling below the horizon as they moved in on the camp. Lights flickered in a large building off to the side of a flattened, hardpacked runway. Torn camouflage netting was strewed about in long tethered messes. Whoever had left wasn't interested in leaving a clean site behind.

As they came over the rise, Bolan motioned for them to keep low, and Wazdi followed the hand command. On the ridge of sand, his black-hooded head exposed, his heart rate increased. He knew nobody down there could hear the hammering of his heartbeat, but it was still unnervingly loud in his own ears.

He thought of the mess before his eyes.

It was as if everyone in the camp had just loaded up and taken off, running like hell.

Wazdi looked over to the soldier who led them. Fatigue was evident in his craggy features. His eyes still scanned the terrain, alert for any signs of ambush in the abandoned airstrip, but all three of them had been using up reserves of strength and endurance in their pursuit of Laud and the hostages. And now, it looked like they were too late.

Wazdi's muscles tensed, wanting to throw him down the embankment to the abandoned airstrip, to be done with it. He longed for this to end here and now. There was simply too much riding on them finding Best and the others for Laud to have gotten away.

Again.

Striker held his hand out to Wazdi, then flashed a two sign. The FBI man handed over two of his throwing stars.

A pointed finger, then a clenched fist, the signal to hold up.

Fair enough, Wazdi thought as he clenched his weapon even tighter. But when the chips started to fall, he was going to be in on the final knockout.

SLIPPING THE PAIR of throwing stars into a belt pouch on his combat harness, the Executioner slithered over the top of the hill and scooted toward the camp, keeping his body low, Steyr leading the way, its unblinking eye probing ahead.

There was no reaction to his sudden movement. No answering fire. Not even any motion from within the main building. Off to the side of it, Bolan could see the nose of a jet poking around the corner. He did some mental calculations and wondered if Wazdi knew anything about flying a jet.

Without Jack Grimaldi, ace Stony Man pilot, on hand to get him around, maybe Orlando Wazdi could pitch in and get him to a friendly aircraft carrier. It wouldn't be much, but at least then Bolan could get in communication with Stony Man Farm and alert them as to the crisis already at hand.

Time was slipping away like the sand sloughing off his blacksuit, and there didn't seem to be any way to catch up. The end of the trail was right here, unless Laud left him handwritten directions saying "follow me here!"

The Executioner moved toward the building at a ground-eating pace, and paused as he was on the approach to the lit windows of the building. It was one-story tall, prefabricated and the next good storm could knock it over. Already it was slouching from shifting sand and winds and most likely the backwash of helicopters and the single little jet on hand.

Still, there was no sign of an ambush force.

That didn't mean much to the Executioner. When he wanted to disappear and hide in ambush, nobody could notice him, either.

Laud's forces were not to be underestimated in skill or determination. Only experience, skill, determination and a dash of near suicidal audacity had kept Bolan and his allies alive this long.

Crouching at the corner of the building, Bolan spied the jet.

It was the Lockheed T33. It had to be the same jet that had blown the C-130 out of the air.

The Executioner had been near enough planes to know that this jet had been cool for a long time. It hadn't been up since its second attack run on the C-130 earlier that day. Even in the dimming light, this close, he could make out its painted-over Pakistani air force markings. It made sense.

The Divine Sword was an offshoot of "the Base," or al-Qaeda as most Americans knew it. And the Base had powerful ties among the rich and powerful from the Saudi royal family to the Pakistani Ministry of Defense. If the government wanted to have proof that the Sword and the Base were still part of the same body, this jet would be a smoking gun that proved that al-Qaeda was still a ticking bomb.

Bolan spotted it underneath the carriage for the nose gear of the jet. It was tucked in tight, but the landing gear strut was defaced with duct tape and a couple black wires.

A booby trap.

Anyone who found this base would tamper and fuss with the Lockheed, turning it into a bomb. How big a bomb?

Bolan didn't know, but he wasn't going to take any chances. He let the Steyr hang on its sling and pulled his Applegate knife, crawling closer. The wires were simple pull fuses. Any movement of the plane would rock it on its shock absorbers. The flexing of the shock absorbers would yank the fuses from the detonators. The detonators would count down like grenades. And the plane would end up spraying itself over a large area.

Bolan didn't have to look at the fuel gauge in the cockpit to know that the Lockheed's tanks were full. Aviation fuel was wonderful in that regard, burning hot and spreading easily. The planeworld would turn into a fireball for a hundred-foot radius, slaughtering anyone within reach.

That didn't include the explosive payloads in the wing mounts. Bolan looked, and sure enough, the artillery rocket pods were reloaded. Explosive cannon shells and artillery rockets would make the Lockheed into a fragmentation grenade of the highest order.

Unless the Executioner could disarm the booby trap.

Fingers brushing the steel cylinder of the shock absorber, he felt the parallel bumps of two parallel wires. Retrieving a pocket flash, he backed from the Lockheed and blinked twice for Wazdi and Kowalski to head over. Fisting the Steyr again, he met them halfway, outside the spill of light from the windows.

"The jet that buzzed us is parked there," Bolan said. "You know how to fly a jet?"

Wazdi shook his head. "I'm good with helicopters, but where would we go with a plane? I am definitely not trained to land on an aircraft carrier."

"All right. Either of you have a mirror?" Bolan asked.

"Bomb," Kowalski groaned. He reached and plucked a flat Plexiglas mirror from his pocket. "Always be prepared."

"I used up a few supplies on my most recent trip. Didn't have time to restock," Bolan answered. "Stay here. If I find something, stay back. If not, we'll do a sweep of the prefab."

"Fabulous," Wazdi mumbled.

Bolan returned to the landing gear and held the mirror toward the nooks and crannies where the wires crawled. No electronic LED lights reflected in the surface of the mirror.

No blatant timers. And in the desert night's still air, he heard no ticking of a wristwatch timer.

The booby trap was a simple one, deadly in its simplicity. Only a truly alert and untrusting eye would be able to spot the out-of-place duct tape. Though his muscles ached with strain and exhaustion, he didn't let up on his vigilance. He did a similar quick check on the other landing gear carriages on the nimble little jet.

Just the nose would set off the bomb. And Bolan wasn't sure how much movement would pull the fuses taut enough to set off their detonators.

All of this was wasting time. Every second the Executioner messed around with the booby-trapped airplane was another mile that Laud could go with the hostages.

He pressed the knife to the two pull-fuse cords and paused. His fingers again felt the ends of the fuses and along their length without applying tension to them.

There was a single wire running along each.

Bolan figured if the circuit was broken, say as in being sliced along with the blunt pull-fuses, a secondary detonator would send the plane—and whoever was toying with the bomb under the nose—into a low orbit to rain down like bloody snowflakes.

Bolan knew he had to take the risk. As long as the Executioner breathed, there was still hope for Best and the other captives.

He took the point of the blade and sliced the cords and the wire free, leaving them to dangle loosely from the landing gear. No longer stretched taut, a movement of the shock-absorber piston would not break the circuit and set off the detonators.

Bolan backed off, then pulled a roll of warning tape and pressed a large X onto the fuselage. Whoever came here after Bolan would know that this was a booby trap and take appropriate precautions.

He rolled from under the plane and pocketed his knife and tape. The machine pistol was back in hand, but it was only an afterthought. If no bullets had riddled him or the others by now, it was unlikely they'd encounter resistance.

But then, Bolan hadn't imagined four tons of bomb to be sitting next to where he wanted to be.

Bolan gave a finger countdown starting at five to make sure the others would keep moving on the numbers.

Getting complacent meant getting dead in this business.

With a boot, Bolan slammed the door inward.

WAZDI TOOK THE LEAD, Steyr up and tracking into the building. It was empty, and inside there was only the distant, gentle chug of a generator at the other end of the building. Other than the steady beat, there was no sound in the place except a soft hiss.

Wazdi led the way, Kowalski having moved in second. Their big leader had risked enough dealing with a booby trap. Now it was their turn to earn more of their keep, Wazdi being on point to make doubly sure that whatever threat lay ahead would be dealt with by a relatively fresh soldier. Kowalski's motorcycle acrobatics and Bolan's near suicidal efforts were more than Wazdi had expended.

By default, that made him the point man, the guy who would take it on the chin.

The hissing sound grew louder and Wazdi could place it now. Still, knowing what was ahead, he stopped his partners and made a slow, step-by-step check, cutting the cake at every corner, sweeping his vision across every potential ambush zone.

The longer end of the building was without walls, only sagging support beams and cubicles. Empty boxes littered the floors as the cubicles were arranged in rows of back-to-back Es. Wazdi went down one way, checking for more traps or hidden gunmen, then came back down the next immediate aisle. No papers or maps, only a few crates and leftover cheap furniture remained for the trio of men to find.

Leftover furniture, and a blank, static hissing television on a stand, hooked up to a generator through a wall to the next room.

"What do you make of it?" Kowalski asked, catching up.

"They took what they really needed and just left us the stuff they could buy at Office Max Cairo," Bolan replied. "And they left a message."

"That's why they left the generator running," Wazdi replied. "They knew we'd never willingly go snooping around in the generator shed if they left the plane booby-trapped."

Wazdi looked over the TV. It was a simple black TV with a built-in VCR. The screen wasn't large, only ten inches.

Bolan stepped forward and pushed the videotape sticking out of the mouth of the VCR into the machine. He pushed Play, and they watched.

The image was blurred, static fizzling through the screen, then the face of Ahmur Ibn Laud glared out of the screen at them.

"You made it," Laud taunted from the other side of a magnetic tape. "I can only assume you made it, because you're playing this tape, Al-Askari."

"Al-Askari?" Kowalski asked.

"The Soldier," Wazdi answered. "A bogeyman vigilante who kills terrorists and disappears like smoke. Some people say he's just like that Executioner guy who went after the Mafia when we were kids. Remember? He was all over the news."

Wazdi looked at Striker, who set his jaw, looking at the screen. For once, the bigman was quiet about the banter between the two of them.

"You have chased me all this way, you at least deserve to know this much about the fate of Quentin Best and the rest of his men. In fact, you might be able to smell a clue about it just now..." Laud continued, his face split by a reptilian smirk.

Bolan remained impassive, except for the storm reflected in his ice-blue eyes.

"He's in the generator room," Bolan said softly.

Wazdi heard the iron in the Executioner's voice, old, weathered iron, harsh and ripping to the touch, but unyielding.

A gunshot cracked on the television, and Wazdi's and Kowalski's gazes were drawn back to the screen.

"I don't think he's alive," Bolan said, "but go check on him."

Kowalski was pale-faced as he looked into the generator room. Wazdi glanced over his shoulder and closed his eyes.

"Consider this a preview of my pay-per-view," Laud prattled on. "I don't want to show you exactly what I'm doing, not now, this is just a taste to get you to tune in."

Manny Bradley was slouched next to the generator. He could tell it was Bradley because of the blond hair, and the overhang of some belly from too many trips to the vending machine. One half of his face was awash in blood, and hard to identify. The other half might have been easier to identify, if they had the time, the tweezers and the superglue to put it all back together on his bullet-shattered skull.

Kowalski pushed Wazdi back behind the door before he could take in a second glance at the horror show before them.

"An even dozen cuts of the blade, before an even dozen bullets to the head. Your Americans will not die as men, Al-Askari. I may have failed in destroying you, but there is no possible way you can catch me in time," Laud bragged. "For once, you Soldier have failed. And for that failure, Americans will die. And all shall know that you, for all your skill, for all your experience, are only human."

Wazdi struggled to get past Kowalski, then stopped, looking at Bolan as he stood, his face an impassive mask, lit by the television, and Laud's face. A wave rushed through the room at that moment, a swirling mixture of rage and calm.

The Executioner continued staring through his emotionless battle mask, his lips drawn tight. Were this any other human being, the television would have been smashed, or shot.

Instead, Mack Bolan simply rewound and ejected the videotape.

"Kowalski, turn off the generator," Bolan ordered. "I'll ignite the booby trap and try to use it as a signal flare for our people."

Wazdi was dumbstruck and turned to Kowalski, who moved with zombielike resolve.

"Striker..." Wazdi began.

"It'll just take a shot of one of my grenades. The explosion will be very visible to the people I know are looking for us," Bolan said.

"I..." Wazdi wanted to say something.

"We have a job to do," Bolan said. "I'm just another soldier. You don't have to worry about anything more. Get outside."

Kowalski had Bradley, wrapped in a blanket, cradled in his thick arms. There were tears were on the blond Chicagoan's cheeks, his voice cracking with the strain of emotional wreckage. "Didn't want him left behind."

"Get moving. I'll set up our improvised flare," Bolan started.

Wazdi reached the door, then stopped cold.

Flaring white lights were cutting across the desert, a storm of whirling rotors filling the once still darkness with thunder.

Helicopters.

Wazdi blinked as he stared right into a spotlight.

"Drop your weapons or die!"

12

United States Marine Corps Force Recon Captain Cable Orion Clemons told his men to hold their fire. There were only three men in the camp and the only form of transportation was a single-seater jet nestled against the only standing structure. That the jet had a big reflective X on it gave him the idea that the three "ninjas" down there were not tangos.

Still, "Drop your weapons or die" was a message that could not be mistaken.

The first guy in the doorway tossed his pair of machine pistols into the sand far away and stepped out into the open, hands up. The guy didn't seem to be eager to divest himself of the holstered handguns but he kept his hands polite.

Another ninja came out holding a body.

"All right! Charlie, Alpha, continue orbital overview. Weapons hot. We're going down," Clemons shouted over the com link.

Clemons's Seahawk, Bravo, landed deftly, and he was first off. He couldn't abide by an officer who led from the rear. Most officers of his rank didn't pack a twenty-pound light machinegun, but then, most officers weren't six foot six with hands the size of baseball gloves.

Clemons looked over the first two black-clothed men. The second man still had the blanketed body of a dead man in his arms. The Middle Eastern features of the first one put Clemons off some, but he was told that one of the trio looked native enough to pass.

"Estas de la Orlando?" Clemons asked, asking if he was from the city in Florida.

"I'm from Chicago," Wazdi stated, making his nationality quite clear.

"We have a countdown ticking," the third man spoke up. He stepped out, and wasn't throwing down his weapons. He was making for the helicopter and not stopping. He looked like a man with a mission, but Clemons stepped in front of him.

"Nobody who is not a Marine boards one of my helicopters with weapons," Clemons said.

The cold-eyed warrior pushed Clemons aside and climbed aboard. "We don't have time for a pissing contest. Shoot me and dump my corpse, or let's get moving. Twelve lives are going to be lost by dawn, and that only gives us ten hours to act."

Clemons leveled his weapon at the tall soldier who handed off his machine pistols anyway, closing his eyes as if he'd take a nap with a half a belt of 5.56 mm in his gut or not. Bolan looked to the other two men and nodded for them to board the Seahawk.

It was going to be a long, silent flight back.

WAZDI DIDN'T KNOW WHERE to look as he sat next to a napping Bolan in the belly of the Seahawk. Kowalski hadn't released the body of Bradley at all, staring straight ahead, his face barely under control, simmering between rage and despair. Bolan himself slept, fitfully, dreamlessly, storing energy for what was ahead.

Clemons watched them like a hawk.

Wazdi couldn't blame anyone. Anyone except himself.

If only he'd dropped the hammer on Laud in the belly of the crashing C-130. If only he'd managed to pick up a heavier weapon to drive off the terrorists. If only he could have squeezed more mileage out of the helicopter, and been able to use its guns on the enemy gunship.

Instead, he was feeling the weight of time and dread crushing him, rolling over him like an avalanche, except in slow motion, one boulder at a time.

Wazdi let his head hang. He could only think of the fact that he was going to be the one held responsible anyway. The Executioner wasn't even supposed to exist, he was just a shadow man, skimming the edges of creation, kicking the same kind of asses he'd always been kicking. If groups like the Divine Sword had a name for him, he was still doing the same business as always.

Kowalski sat across from him, and Wazdi knew he wasn't going to let one drop of the blame touch his childhood friend. It was his failure that allowed this to go on so long. Wazdi would make sure that his friend would be portrayed as being dragged along for the ride. Any dereliction of duty would be swallowed up by him.

"I'm not leaving you out to hang on this," Bolan's voice cut into Wazdi's thoughts.

Wazdi looked over. "You don't even exist, Striker. You're just a dead man."

"I know people who will go to bat for you and sweep this under. You'll come out spotless," Bolan stated, opening his eyes.

"You were asleep a moment ago, man. Now..."

"I was just resting. It's been a long day, and you both need to relax. We won't have time when we get to the ship," Bolan told him.

"But I don't want Dave's career fucked up like mine," Wazdi said.

"Who said your career was in the can?"

"Look at this mess! The world's worst terrorist escapes from two U.S. teams, but he also escapes with hostages, one of whom is already dead," Wazdi blurted out.

"Fine. Stay behind," Bolan replied. "Stress and be worthless, or close your eyes and trust me."

"What do you mean?"

"Laud isn't quite out of our reach yet, Orlando."

"And you still want me on your side?"

"You and Ski have been my aces in the hole for this whole fight. I'm not throwing away my best cards just because we're shuffling a whole new deck."

Wazdi lay back. "Are you sure we'll get another shot at Laud?"

In the darkness of the Seahawk's cabin, the Executioner's voice cut like a razor.

"Nobody gets away from me, until they kill me."

"You've been reported dead a lot of times," Wazdi answered.

Bolan put his finger to his lips. "They never made it stick yet."

THE EXECUTIONER stepped off the Seahawk, the hour-long nap having refreshed him somewhat. His muscles were still knotted, and each step was painful. But he was awake and refreshed.

Men were on deck and they showed up with cups of hot soup in foam cups, and handed them to Bolan and Wazdi, but weren't able to get anything into Kowalski's hands until Agent Bradley was placed on a gurney and covered respectfully with a blanket. Bolan had seen the same bulldog tendency in other soldiers before, an intense identification with the dead, the feeling of loss that came with seeing your buddies lifeless in a field beside you.

Bolan swallowed the last of his soup. With something to digest, he was getting a little more energy now. A little more energy to chip away at another tiny corner of Hell's invasion of the world.

He crushed the foam cup and tossed it into a garbage bin, slipping through a bulkhead where he was greeted by a couple young ensigns who escorted him, Kowalski and Wazdi through a couple passages and then to the captain's quarters. As many times as the Executioner had been aboard an aircraft carrier, he was still amazed by humankind's ability to produce gigantic marvels.

The ship was a thousand-foot long floating city capable of moving around the world. It had a lifespan of fifty projected years and weighed only a shade under one hundred thousand tons. Tall as most skyscrapers at 244 feet, it was a big target, but the dark shapes that the Seahawk sliced over were silent centurions, destroyers and frigates armed to the gills, ready to protect the carrier. Just like the two former blacksuits were ready to take their own hits for him.

Sacrifices.

Bolan was sacrificing himself for twelve men who would sacrifice themselves for the good of their nation and not even blink twice.

He caught the distant agony on Kowalski's face. Sacrifices had been made already. A heroic aircrew who kept everyone on the plane from dying. Brave men who had died trying to prevent the arrested Ahmur Ibn Laud from escape. And Agent Bradley, offered up as a taunt to the Executioner.

Bolan had been here before.

If the footmen of this jihad didn't have this war to fight, they'd find another way to take out their rage on the world. And the men above them, for all their prayers and trappings of holiness were sitting there, loving the full power and weight of their cult of personality. They had more than money and luxury, they had the addictive power to tell men to die in their name.

Even if the Arab nations of the world were at total peace with the West, these slithering serpents would be thrashing through the undergrowth, biting and plunging unholy venom into anyone they met.

All right, Laud, the Executioner thought. You say you are a tool of God? I hear that God is not mocked. Whatever force there is looking over the Universe, he put me on that Hercules for a reason.

The pain dropped away from the Executioner's knotted and strained muscles, and he took the lead into the captain's quarters.

We'll be meeting again soon, Laud, he thought. And we'll find out why we've been put on this hellfire trail together.

CAPTAIN PAUL HETTFIELD looked at the trio who entered his office and immediately had his expectations dashed. He'd heard from US SOCOM that one of these men was a specialist who was returning from some top secret duties in Egypt, and the other two were survivors of the joint team that had been baited and kidnapped by one of the world's most dangerous terrorists. He expected three ragged men, shell-shocked and torn by their harrowing tribulation.

Instead, he saw a pillar of midnight black, muscle, and blue steel determination. The other two showed more fatigue, but they seemed to be plugged into the enormous reserves of the black-haired, ice-eyed leader of the group. Even as Hettfield watched, he could see them turn from putty to the honed steel edge of ready warriors.

"Colonel Brandon Stone, on the deck," the tall man in black said, sharply saluting. "These are Agents Johnson and Johnson."

Hettfield looked at the two men accompanying Stone.

"Any relation?" Hettfield asked.

"Twin brothers," the blonde said, nodding to the swarthy, exotic-looking agent beside him.

Hettfield nodded and blew it off, not needing any more explanation. Not with a presidential communiqué attached to the orders that brought these three into his offices.

"You come with impressive credentials, Stone. The White House says that any operation that we undertake to go after Ahmur Ibn Laud involves you intimately."

Bolan nodded. No joy. No tiredness. No flash of any emotion, except this all encompassing presence that made Hettfield feel the urge to get moving, and fall into rank behind the soldier before him.

"Have your people made any progress in locating Laud while we were gone?"

"We've had Hawkeyes snooping every nook and cranny of the Egyptian coast, as far as we could without making the Egyptian government paranoid about a possible land invasion," Hettfield replied.

"It's a possibility," the big man said. "I'd undertake the mission with minimal assistance from your crew and detachment to maintain plausible deniability."

Hettfield felt his kidneys clench against a blast of icy terror. Stone sounded serious about a one-man invasion of Egypt to continue the hunt for the leader of the Divine Sword of Allah. That terror disappeared as soon as it hit.

Whoever Colonel Brandon Stone really was, he inspired the confidence to charge the gates of hell armed only with toothpicks and mess kit utensils.

"We've located several ships in the Mediterranean that might be a good stop off for helicopters," Hettfield said. "At any time, the Mediterranean has more than enough craft of shady registry that trying to keep track of them would require the concentrated efforts of say, a small floating city a thousand feet long with up to eighty tactical aircraft."

Bolan gave Hettfield a brief smile, then returned grim-faced to look over the charts that the captain was unveiling. Those sharp blue eyes scanned the map like a laser, seeking any and all extraneous markings.

He locked on one within seconds.

"What's this?"

Hettfield looked at the marking, three hundred miles off the coast, moving along at an agonizingly slow five knots. He checked his references. "That would be a pocket-sized oil tanker."

"Pocket-sized?"

"You have the supertankers, which give this tub a run for its money in sheer size," Hettfield said. "This is only 350 feet long, and has at best, two holds. Its superstructure is the size of your average office building, though."

"Name?"

"The Pinnacle," Hettfield stated. He handed over what notes he had on the tanker to Bolan. "It left Alexandria two days ago."

"I need a secure satellite link."

"How secure?" Hettfield asked.

"You have the number you have to dial for me. Dial it, and make sure nobody, not even the operator's listening in."

Hettfield didn't need to be told anything else.

BARBARA PRICE LOOKED at the screen as it burst to life with the hotline call from the aircraft carrier. Voice recognition hardware instantly threw a familiar face up on the screen, the craggy visage of Mack Bolan.

"Striker to Base, Striker to Base, anyone there reading me?" Bolan called across thousands of miles.

"We're here," Price answered.

"Nice to hear from you, Mother Hen. It's been awhile," Bolan said.

"Well, there was nothing on TV tonight. I figured I'd see if you called in," Price lied. "Are you and our two lost goslings all right?"

"We're ready for another couple of rounds," Bolan told her. Price smiled, relief washing over her. When they heard about the initial pickup, in the scramble of information, they'd heard about a deceased FBI agent. She'd wondered if it was one of the two Bolan allies.

She felt regret that she wasn't upset at the death of a lawman. The surge of relief, though, that one of their own was still alive anchored her solidly. Price knew that Hal Brognola and the Justice Department would make sure that the family of the dead agent would get the help it needed to deal with its loss.

"The Pinnacle," Bolan interrupted her thoughts. "It left Alexandria two days ago. Something about this ship blipped up on my radar the minute I saw it."

Price turned to Kurtzman, who nodded to Carmen Delahunt to begin working ship registries. "We're already working on it."

"Check that firm Ironman and the guys hit a while back," Bolan said.

"What firm?" Price asked.

"They were building ships specifically designed for terrorists. We managed to shut down their main shipbuilding operation and put more than a couple of their ships out of operation, but there was no indication how many may have been put out there," Bolan stated. "I'm thinking that the *Pinnacle* was redesigned by the shipbuilders."

"We're working on it," Price answered. "We're also trying to get a good look at the ship right now. It's hard, because it's dark, so we won't be able to get you all the visual intel you need."

"I'll need working blueprints faxed over, if Gadgets managed to get something from them," Bolan said.

Price grunted in affirmation. "Now that we know what we're dealing with, I've got the call out to them."

Kurtzman lifted a hand. "Three-way conferencing, on the line now."

"Non-Sequitur Incorporated. We don't make sense, but waffles aren't slippery," greeted Hermann "Gadgets" Schwarz.

"Good morning, Mr. Wizard," Bolan's voice cut in.

"Striker, long time no hear. What gives?"

"Did you ever get any intel out of those shipbuilders you hit?" Bolan asked.

Gadgets gave a short hum. "You know me, Striker. I'm a pack rat. I have hard drives from around the globe cluttering my garage."

Price feigned shock. "And you never turned them in to us?"

"Just what we thought you could use. Most of what these guys have is Internet porn anyhow," Gadgets stated. "A lot of it the same stuff over and over and over. Not that I memorize this stuff."

"Enough comedy, Gadgets. Does the name *Pinnacle* ring a bell?" Striker asked.

"Mediterranean-bound tanker rebuilt in North Carolina by the same scumbags we introduced to Ironman's bad feelings," Gadgets replied.

"And you never said anything about this?" Price asked.

"Nobody asked, plus I had my own means of watching out

for it," Gadgets said. "You should be getting an alert on the cross-reference about now. Who's referencing the tub?"

"CD," Price gave the initials of Delahunt.

A buzzer went off. Delahunt laughed. "Gadgets programmed us a little subroutine in the Farm mainframe. We begin looking for the *Pinnacle,* we've got its activities tracked by 'conventional' shipping records."

"You can stop bowing now, Gadgets," Bolan spoke up.

"You could see me?"

"Innocuous activities on the *Pinnacle,*" Delahunt said. "The tanker's been at sea most of the time, well offshore."

"No real on-loading or off-loading?" Price asked.

"They go to ports, and there's a lot of activity, but the ledgers look too clean," Delahunt announced. "Transporting ore, or oil, or machine parts, nothing that would attract attention, but there's no losses or breakage reported."

"Absolutely no theft?" Bolan asked. "What about troubles with the crew?"

"Well-behaved," Delahunt said. "Thanks for tying local police records into this, Gadgets."

"Careful, anymore praise and he won't be able to fit his head in a Kevlar pot," Price muttered.

"They're crooked then. Those ledgers are fake if they haven't even had one crate of supplies reported missing," Bolan said. "I've seen too many dummy corporations with perfect records to regard a perfect cargo-shipping record as anything other than bad news."

"It's not a capital offense to be perfect," Price noted.

"No," the Executioner answered, the cold edge of steel in his voice. "But it's a fatal mistake to think you're perfect."

Captain Cable Orion Clemons caught the black blur of the tall man stepping out of the comm center, and paused. Captain Hettfield had told him that the mysterious Colonel Stone would be down here, but he didn't expect Stone to be a whirlwind of activity. The man's big hands held collated files.

"There you are," Bolan stated. "Come looking for me?"

"I heard that you had shown interest in an oil tanker. My Force Recon team has trained Navy SEAL VBSS teams on how to take care of oil tanker takedowns," Clemons stated. "We have a preliminary plan worked out in our ops center, and were hoping to have you come work with us on it."

"Send someone to retrieve Agents Johnson and Johnson," Bolan said. "They're coming with us on this mission."

"Sir, I would like to keep this mostly in the family," Clemons replied. "You're only along because you have some tall orders backing you up."

Cold blue eyes met his own. "They are family. They come with me."

Clemons nodded. "I anticipated your being vehement about this, so we did summon them. They should be in ops when we arrive."

"I don't like pulling rank, Captain. Thank you."

As Clemons predicted, both "Johnson and Johnson" were present, looking not the least bit uncomfortable mixed in with his soldiers. After the few moments of drama back at the airstrip, it was good to see calm among the two parties.

An old teacher of Clemons stressed one thing above all others for successful operations—total unit integrity.

They wouldn't have that. Stone and the Johnsons were total strangers to the Force Recon detachment. They might all be highly skilled, but that didn't matter if there wasn't the trust of one team member to cover the other. There was something to be said for unspoken understandings.

The Marines snapped to attention, out of respect, but they quickly went back to their usual lounging, because Clemons, despite his rank, knew that the members of a team had to be comfortable. When they called him Cable, they meant "Sir."

"All right, we don't have much time to play around. This is Colonel Brandon Stone, that's Orlando Johnson and Dave Johnson," Clemons told his men. "This is my team. We've got our dummy tags on for the briefing, so memorize the names. Once we go black, we tend to forget them."

Bolan nodded in agreement. "Good planning. And I think I have a way around the biggest problem on this insertion."

"What problem is that?" Clemons asked.

"We have two groups unfamiliar with each other. I'm suggesting we split the groups and form two elements with separate battle stations," Bolan suggested.

Clemons smirked. "Halfway decent idea there."

"Johnson and Johnson and I will do a soft probe first. But you'll be close behind, ready to come in hard," Bolan pointed out.

"Soft probe," Clemons mused.

"My team will look for a hole for you to come up in, if there's any antiaircraft weaponry on deck or on the bridge."

"And if there are no holes?"

"We'll make one for you."

Clemons nodded. "We could do it ourselves."

"I don't doubt it, Captain, but we're not quite sure where the hostages are being held. A stray rocket, and we might as well go back home."

"Standard tanker takedown scenario?" Clemons asked.

"Nope." Bolan handed out thermal paper maps to Clemons and his men. "This ship was refurbished at a shipyard in North Carolina."

"The one that blew up," Clemons replied. "They said it was an industrial accident, but unless a civilian shipyard had the amount of gunpowder needed to supply a battleship, I think that's a bullshit story."

"You know a lot about this," Bolan noted, with some respect.

"I'm from the next town over. My dad told me most of what he could find out from the news and what he could find out on his own."

"Healthy curiosity."

"No. Ex-military too. He likes big explosions almost as much as he likes big handguns," Clemons explained. "So the dry dock was modifying ships for tangos?"

"Yeah."

"So what are the modifications on this one?"

"At least the capacity to be used as a helicopter carrier," Bolan pointed out. "It has refueling capabilities. We don't have any information about any weaponry, but the builders thought they could slip the fuel tanks aboard without suspicion as an above the table modification and parts order."

"Nasty," Clemons said. "Any idea what kind of helicopters?"

"They had at least one Kamov KA-60, but we only saw Hueys otherwise."

"All right. We'll drop off the three of you. You'll be able to get to the *Pinnacle* and do your soft probe. But don't forget to call us when it's time to drop the hammer, and stay out of the way when the shooting starts," Clemons ordered.

"No argument here. Now we just need some fresh ammo and gear, and we'll get on our sneaky way."

BOLAN AND COMPANY needed to get ammunition and replacements for their lost and depleted weapons, as well as something more appropriate for the close-quarters killing environment on an oil tanker. Considering that he'd be part of a team earmarked for eliminating possible early warning and threats to the hostages before the Force Recon team staged a full-scale assault, Bolan regretted losing the Beretta 93-R in the frantic battle back at the airstrip. He'd have felt more comfortable with the suppressed machine pistol, but again, the Beretta was only a tool. It was the man himself who was the weapon.

Clemons looked over Bolan's shoulder, literally. The big Marine was wondering what the soldier would choose.

The Executioner found that the Force Recon team's supply of Beretta 92-F's was like new, practically untouched. He selected one, gave it a heft and immediately fit it into his shoulder holster. Perfect fit.

He drew it again and made sure the barrel was unobstructed.

"These haven't even been fired," Bolan said.

"To tell the truth I don't much rely on poodle-popping weapons," Clemons said. He patted the customized Colt 1911 on his hip.

Bolan shrugged. "You have a sound suppressor for this?"

"Why not take a .45?" Clemons offered. "Better stopping power."

"Do you have a sound suppressor for a Beretta?" Bolan repeated, his message clear.

Clemons took a step back.

"AAC suppressor, for either the Berettas or the Colts. The handguns are all threaded," Clemons said.

"Thank you," Bolan said. He glanced at Wazdi and Kowalski, who kept their mouths shut. For the Executioner, the few quiet words he spoke a moment before were the equivalent of the red-faced barrage of abuse that a Marine drill instructor would inflict. He was tired, not physically but mentally and spiritually, stretched across the rack of a hostage deadline and the back-seat soldiering of even a member of Force Recon was something that Bolan was too low on patience and decorum to deal with.

He threaded the suppressor to the barrel and checked it. It was similar to the custom suppressor he'd designed for his Beretta Brigadier ages ago, and updated for the Beretta 93-R. He did a practice presentation, then holstered the gun.

Kowalski was loading up on spare magazines for his Para-Ordnance .45 and Beretta 92-D. Wazdi picked out a SIG-Sauer P-228 as a replacement for the lost P-226.

The trio looked over the racks of long arms, knowing they'd need silence and compactness, but also stopping power and range. Bolan pointed to the 10-inch barreled Colt Commandos alongside the slightly longer M-4 carbines.

Again, Bolan saw the Marine captain's discomfort.

"You have a suggestion?" Bolan asked.

"The M-249 Para model. It works well with the M-4 suppressor, holds two hundred rounds and is light and compact."

"Light for you, but then you're bigger than I am," Bolan answered. "Even the Commandos are pushing the noise limit for the passageways and hatches on a ship. Close quarters full-auto is going to start giving us away the minute I cut loose with any of that, but I don't want to trust ball ammo from an MP-5 SD. Besides…"

Clemons's expression was grim as Bolan paused. A chance to rebuild a bridge.

"Besides, Captain Clemons, what are you going to be using when it comes time for Force Recon to take the decks?" Bolan asked. "I'd rather have that thing giving me cover fire."

Clemons expression lightened. "Shit. I thought you were going for a pissing contest for a moment."

Bolan nodded. "I'm just under some pressure, and didn't need an argument over taste and prejudices."

Clemons nodded. "Well, I've got your back, then, Colonel Stone."

"Couldn't ask for a better man there," the Executioner said, extending a hand of peace.

Clemons looked both ways, then nodded. "All right, you want maximum stealth, and something resembling stopping power? Follow me."

Bolan accompanied the big man to a locker.

"This isn't official kit for us, but we've been evaluating it," Clemons said. He gave the soldier a conspiratorial wink and opened the locker, revealing five rifles.

"DSA Arms SA-58 Offensive Suppression Weapon," Bolan stated, picking up one of the guns. It was a sleek, black workhorse battle rifle, and clearly a new millennium update of the decades-proved Fabrique Nationale FAL rifles. However, the SA-58 OSW had a few improvements that brought it to bear as a close-quarters combat weapon for the twenty-first century. The original twenty-two-inch barrel had been replaced with an eleven-inch tube that extended out to a shade over sixteen inches with a blunt, integral sound suppressor. And it only weighed 7.6 pounds.

"We handloaded the ammunition," Clemons said, "to get the most punch out of the least velocity."

Bolan smiled as he felt the balance of the rifle. "Custom grips. Big tough ECLAN trash-can-style scope. Thirty shot mags."

"You are familiar with the FAL, right?"

"A friend of mine carried one on almost every mission he went on," Bolan said. "I did some cross training with it."

"Think this will do?" Clemons asked.

Bolan looked around and looked for what he needed. He found it, wrapping a set of Kevlar armor around a sandbag. He stepped back, shouldered the rifle and snapped a magazine into the well.

"Fire in the hole," Bolan said.

Clemons took a step back, as did Wazdi and Kowalski.

Bolan tapped three rounds in rapid succession. The effect was no more than a polite cough in the confines of the small armory. He stepped forward and ran his hand over the armor. One bullet had gone clean through the front of the vest, but the other two had been stopped halfway through the fabric, denting the sandbag with enough force to rupture it. The OSW proved itself to be silent and powerful.

"It's not full-auto like my baby," Clemons said. "And it's built in Illinois by Yankees, so it's not perfection, but then again, our Colt .45s are made by those same Yankees."

Bolan spared Clemons a smile of satisfaction. "This will do, Captain. This will do."

14

"Tell me again why we're jumping out of a helicopter in the dark thirty feet above water?" Kowalski asked as he checked his gear one last time. He'd come slightly out of his coma, trying to regain some of his mental energy, and with it, his humor, but the remark sounded weak.

Wazdi shoved the Zodiac raft out the door of the Seahawk, letting it fall on its tether cord down to the sea, where it would anchor them. "It's not jumping out. We're going down a rope. You told me you did this all the time in the Marines."

"I never said that I liked it," Ski snapped back as he, with equal energy, clipped his rappelling harness onto the tether.

"You don't have to like it. You just have to not get killed doing it," Wazdi remarked.

A movement flashed in the doorway, and Wazdi knew it was their leader, sizzling down the tether to the black, glassy water below. Waves lapped, their tips slightly aglow with bioluminescent plankton, just enough to give the illusion of shape to the waters below. Already he heard the Zodiac inflating upon impact.

"Away we go," Wazdi said with enthusiasm he didn't feel. He kicked off and his gloves sizzled against the nylon cord, heat already burning through the thick palm pads. Before he could feel real discomfort, though, he struck the water. Wazdi unsnapped his harness and swam backward a few feet before Kowalski came gliding down the cord and hit the water in front of him.

"All aboard," Bolan ordered, rolling into the fully inflated raft, the compressed air capsules having finished their job of bringing the craft to life.

Wazdi took a grip on one of the inflated cylinders that crimped to form the modified V of the Zodiac, and hung on as he put one leg over the side. Bolan's big hands grabbed his harness and yanked him the rest of the way over.

Kowalski slid into the Zodiac from behind, around the side of the outboard motor. He smirked at Wazdi. "Why did you climb over the big inflated parts?"

Wazdi shook his head and flipped off Ski, eliciting a short chuckle. He looked at Bolan, who pulled a war bag into the craft and unzipped it.

An SA-58 OSW was pressed into Wazdi's hands and the FBI man checked the weapon for function and loaded a round, placing the gun on safe.

"How much of the plan are we going to keep with?" Kowalski asked from the back.

"We're going to make some holes in their defenses," Bolan answered. "We'll do as much as we can on the ship before things get noisy. The minute the ship goes on alert, though…"

"Clemons and his Force Recon will come screaming over the horizon at 180 miles per hour, and come raining shit on Laud's parade," Wazdi said. "And ours, too, if we don't keep our heads low."

"Something like that," Bolan agreed.

"Sounds groovy," Kowalski spoke up. "As long as I'm not jumping out of any other aircraft, I'm going to enjoy the rest of this."

For emphasis, he worked the bolt on his SA-58, chambering a big 7.62 mm round. He slung the stubby weapon around his neck and fired up the quiet, capacitor discharge ignition on the outboard. With barely a growl, the motor sprang to life, white froth trailing behind them before Wazdi felt the acceleration of the near frictionless inflatable boat as it raced across the inky black waters of the Mediterranean, heading for the glowing diamond ahead of them.

The Executioner felt time splattering off of him like the spray spitting over the tip of the Zodiac. The inflatable was light-loaded, and was doing a quick clip at thirty miles an hour, zipping across the waves. It was speed they needed, catch-up speed, desperate minutes and miles eaten up.

But sooner or later, playing catch-up had to give way to violent, brutal action. There were hostages ahead in the cross fire, and Bolan only had a cursory idea of what the layout was, how many enemies there were, and where the hostages were kept.

Again, fighting Laud on his ground, by his rules, at his leisure.

Did the terrorist think that the Americans were coming for him? Did he have the hostages under such tight scrutiny that even the slightest sound would cause Laud to execute them immediately?

Bolan viewed the possibilities in his head.

Ahmur Ibn Laud came from oil money. Big oil money. He dropped almost everything to find a purpose fighting the Soviets in Afghanistan. Trained by the U.S. Army's Green Berets in covert over-the-border operations, he was one of hundreds of young men who battled to the Soviet war machine and sent it limping out of the country.

But Laud, like others of his ilk, wanted more than just liberation for a nation. They took their power, and they did what they wanted with it, damning the concepts of liberty and democracy.

Laud's Divine Sword movement, twice removed from the Taliban, had its bloody origins in that command. And with the worldwide hunt for al-Qaeda, the Divine Sword's defection from the main movement was a ploy to keep the enemies of this hellfire crusade guessing.

The Executioner, however, wasn't guessing. It didn't matter

if there were ten or ten thousand men on the *Pinnacle*. It didn't matter what their politics were, what they really believed, what color their skin was.

They had killed innocent people, they had slain lawmen doing their duty, they had been part of a menace that stretched from Spain to the Philippines and all points between. From rocket attacks in Kenya to homicide bombers in Jakarta, too much blood had been spilled to quibble. The men on the boat in front of him were armed and dedicated. He felt relief that they weren't in a port city. He had only the hostages, Wazdi and Kowalski to worry about.

Everyone else was a free target.

The muffled motor was quiet, but Bolan made a quick motion for Kowalski to kill it as they got within three hundred yards of the ship. He shouldered his SA-58 and swept the deck with the ECLAN night sight. The ship, sporadically lit, had a couple of men on deck, but activity was minimal.

Laud hadn't counted on searchers finding him right away, putting him within easy reach.

The tanker wasn't expecting a visit. Laud probably didn't even think people knew about his boat.

His boat...

Bolan remembered what Kissad said to Yong about having his own boat, telling the Chinaman to go to hell, and doing his best to send him there. With an inward curse, the Executioner realized that it was a small world, and he had been handed a clue as to Laud's operation before he even knew there was anything involving Laud in Egypt.

Bolan handed out paddles, and the men put their backs into rowing toward the tanker. Now that they were closer, Bolan could see that the ship was weighted, low and steady in the water. The railing was only twenty-four feet above sea level, and within easy reach. Climbing would be the slow, excruciating part, especially after paddling three hundred yards through rough water.

Still, twenty minutes, and three sore backs later, they were at the hull, and the bobbing and floating oil tanker groaned and creaked as it flexed on the tidal ebb and surge. The noise of the ship at sea was enough for the trio to feel confident that they could approach without the awareness of the terrorists on the ship. If the *Pinnacle* had been under full steam, there would have been more to mask their presence, but then, there would have been no way for them to catch up, let alone hover next to the craft.

"Crossbow," Bolan whispered.

Kowalski handed it to him. The crossbow had a rubber-tipped grapnel, and was leading a tungsten wire-cored nylon climbing cord. Taking aim, Bolan launched his bolt into the darkness above. This was an area that the Executioner had scanned, and the rail here was ideal—behind the tall bulwark of the cargo bay doors, and out of the spill of lights of the superstructure. Also, there was no sign of any patrolling guards to indicate that the deck was under watch.

Bolan tested his weight against the climbing cord and found that the grapnel was secure. He was set to begin climbing when a hand patted him on the shoulder.

Bolan saw that Wazdi had quickly donned a battered, green Army jacket over his blacksuit and a keffiyeh over his head, like the gunmen they had seen at the far end of the deck. He wouldn't look out of place at all.

"I'll be able to keep an eye out for you," Wazdi said.

"They'll kill you if they see you crawling over the rail," Bolan warned.

"They can try, but I won't fall down until I've given you enough cover fire to get on the deck so you two can do your jobs," Wazdi replied. "I'll be an invisible point man anyway."

The Executioner was divided for a moment. It was risky, and Bolan never felt the need to send someone else probing ahead of him. However, the tactics of the plan were undeniably valid.

"Just remember, if you die, I'll be stuck with Ski," Bolan conceded finally, giving Wazdi a clap on the shoulder.

With a smile, the ex-blacksuit started to scale the hull.

FIRST, THERE WAS the plane crash. Then the battles across the desert. The helicopter crash. The motorcycle ride. The assault.

And paddling across the Mediterranean to catch up with a converted oil tanker.

Now, ten, eleven, twelve feet of climbing up the side of a ship, his muscles stretching and flexing, feeling pulled like taffy. Pain burned across his shoulders, but exhaustion was far from his mind. Adrenaline screamed through his veins.

Wazdi had never felt so calm and focused, yet excited and terrified in his entire life. With fifty pounds of battle gear on his back, the climbing cord cutting through his thick gloves to cut the circulation to his fingers, he was in a whole other universe from the one he woke up in that morning.

It seemed like a lifetime ago that he was just an FBI agent, sent overseas because he knew Arabic dialects with almost innate understanding. Sure, there was the tour of duty at the Farm where Striker worked, guarding the top-secret facility and getting training in more unusual methods of warfare. But he never thought he was all that special, or that he would be part of a relentless, savage hunt for one of the world's most dangerous men.

Funny little world this was.

Eighteen feet, near the top. His boots slipped some as he encountered a slick spot. He gripped tighter and tucked himself down more, using the larger surface of his shins and knees to augment the traction of his boots. He swallowed every grunt, and he could feel his hair matted to his skull with sweat, shoulders now screaming at him in pain, the numbness of excitement being pierced by the ice picks of agony in his muscles.

Why was he doing this? Who was Quentin Best but another blowhard dumb-ass who didn't know any better and deserved everything he got?

There were eleven other men, though. And Best, despite being an ass, was still just trying to do his job, taking dangerous men off the streets and saving lives in the process.

Wazdi gripped the rail with one hand, clamped down with the other and pushed with both feet, heaving himself over the side and landing on the deck clumsily, slipping to one knee and barking it on the hard deck. He scanned both ways, hands empty, and saw no movement.

Nobody had seen him.

He cued his throat mike hooked up to the radio hidden with the rest of his battle harness. "Come on up. Coast's clear."

Wazdi leaned back and pulled a cigarette from the Army jacket. He thought the Egyptian cigarette smelled like shit and tasted twice as nasty, but if someone did happen to turn the corner, he wouldn't seem out of place smoking.

Footsteps clunked against the side of the ship behind Wazdi, and the titanium grapnel strained under the weight of a climber. He took a puff and blew out smoke, holding the cigarette at his side, where he could drop it and rip the suppressed Beretta from his waistband, if necessary. The SA-58 OSW was slung and tucked behind his back, visible enough to be seen as a weapon, but its general make disguised by his body. AK-47s were the order of the day for the Divine Sword.

The clomping of the climber echoed now. Someone was walking around a bulkhead. Wazdi put the cigarette between his lips, letting the smoke accumulate around his face, to better disguise him in the semidarkness away from the main lights of the deck.

"Hamib, is that you?" a voice whispered. The accent was pure Riyadh. This guy was going to die a long way from home. The longer this day was running on, the less sympathy Wazdi felt for these devils.

"No, it's not," Wazdi returned, deciding to make himself sound more Yemeni than Saudi. Terrorists were as regional and cliquish as every other large social group, and this guy might have memorized all the hometown Saudi boys on the boat. "But if you want a cigarette, you're welcome."

The man stepped around the corner, grinning, his hands empty, but yellow-tipped from too much nicotine. "I'm sorry. My name is Ibar."

"Wazdi," he introduced himself, offering the open-topped pack.

"I really shouldn't," Ibar said, taking the cigarette.

Wazdi drew his lighter with his right hand after putting away the pack of cigarettes. He flicked the lighter and the flame flared in Ibar's eyes as his left hand gripped his Beretta and drew it.

Ibar inhaled deeply on the first puff of the cigarette. He leaned back, pulling the cigarette from his lips and letting out a jet of smoke dribble from his nostrils. "You know, the Americans say that this will be the death of me."

"They're right," Wazdi said in English.

Ibar didn't quite get it in time. Wazdi's first shot struck him low, the 9 mm round catching him in the groin. Agony froze the Divine Swordsman's throat long enough for Wazdi to grab a handful of the terrorist's shirt. He levered the Beretta up and under the notch of the gunman's rib cage and fired twice more, muffled coughs signaling the launch of copper-jacketed flesh shredders.

Ibar's eyes grew glassy and his cigarette dropped to the deck. Holding on to the man, Wazdi turned and shoved the corpse over the railing, sending him splashing into the sea below.

Bolan came up over the railing and dropped catlike to the deck, then looked back over.

"First blood already?" Bolan asked.

Wazdi bent and picked up Ibar's fallen cigarette, then tossed it over the railing. "No. Just another statistic for the Surgeon General."

15

Cold sweat trickled down the small of Ahmur Ibn Laud's back as he stood in the middle of the mat, the leather-wrapped handle of the practice sword tight in his right hand. He gripped it so hard, the leather squeaked. His beard matted against his throat.

"Again," Laud commanded.

His four opponents paused, looking him over.

Laud was no longer a young man, but bare-chested, his physique matched that of a man half his age. Thick muscles were interspersed with knife, bullet and shrapnel scars from a lifetime of near death experiences. Dark-skin crisscrossed with the light streaked souvenirs of countless battles. He was an imposing figure, even against the four men he was sparring with.

"Again!" Laud demanded, his impatience cracking through.

The quartet charged, swinging clumsily at him, Laud's blunted practice blade everywhere at once. Thickly corded forearms and biceps absorbed the shock of their strikes against his weapon as he sidestepped, swung, blocked and parried their assaults. This time he took down the slowest of them before he could even think about swinging on the commander of the Divine Sword. With a savage slash, Laud brought the edge of the steel across the man's collarbone, an ugly snap filling the air.

The Divine Swordsman fell, screaming in agony, his weapon

falling from nerveless fingers. One of Laud's other opponents took a desperate lunge to get to the injured man's side, but the terrorist leader whirled, catching him with a wicked smash across his rib cage. The man doubled over, crying out in agony.

It was everything Laud could do not to swing the blade around and bring the blunt edge down on the poor fool's exposed neck. While the blow wouldn't decapitate him, the blunt steel would still shatter the man's neck and kill him. Laud twisted his blade at the last moment and brought down the flat of the steel on the back of his head.

"We are the Divine Sword of Allah! Not the Divine Machine Pistol of Allah, you idiots!" Laud growled to the remaining two men. "Show me the steel in your hearts, not your hands!"

As if shocked out of a stupor, the other two moved in, cautious this time, but not cowardly. They were pressing the attack, looking for Laud's weaknesses. Feints and jabs were presented by the two, and Laud soon found himself working his own blade harder, blunting and deflecting a flurry of strikes. A fresh welt appeared on one shoulder where an opponent's blade struck. A bruise crisscrossed his abdominal muscles where another shot slipped past his defenses.

But Laud wasn't discussing the weather himself. The curved, blunted scimitar swung and looped in a figure eight that made one man drop his sword as a slash jarred his forearm.

The other swordsman moved in tight, negating that defense, and swinging a fist for Laud's already injured gut. The terrorist commander stepped back out of the punch, taking only a fraction of the impact. Instead, he wrapped his arm around his opponent's and swung him over his hip, dropping him hard to the floor.

The last swordsman gasped for breath and found himself looking at the sword point hovering over his throat.

"That was brilliant, Akeem," Laud commended. "You fought with everything you had."

Laud tossed the practice sword into one corner and offered

a hand to Akeem to get him back to his feet. "Thank you for giving me a challenge."

"Few can match you, sir," Akeem said. "But I would be remiss if I did not train to win. The next battle could be against someone I would have to kill."

Laud laughed, then wiped off his chest with a towel. "For that, you have the honor of being my headsman for tonight's activities."

Akeem bowed his head.

"How far away is dawn?" Laud asked, mopping away the sweat.

"We have a few hours," Akeem answered.

Laud ran his fingers though his damp hair, then wiped his hand on his slacks. "Head to the bridge and inform Captain Bhaa to set course, full steam toward broadcast point."

Akeem looked at Laud. "If the Americans see us—"

"They won't see us," Laud replied. "They don't know what they're looking for. And by the time the world gets over the shock of a dozen executions, beamed live into their living rooms, we'll be safe and sound."

"But how can we outrun the planes from an aircraft carrier?"

"The ship will be in Egyptian territorial waters. In fact, we'll be pulling into port," Laud explained.

"But wasn't the purpose of the ship's refurbishing to allow us to strike from offshore?" Akeem asked.

"We have been doing that, yes," Laud admitted. "But I have one last surprise."

Akeem looked doubtful.

"The aviation fuel tanks. It's a simple little job to convert them into Fuel Air Explosives."

Akeem paled.

"Don't worry. By the time we've made the *Pinnacle* an exclamation point to our statement, we'll be long gone from this ship," Laud continued. "But Egypt will not forgive the United States for letting us destroy their docks at Alexandria. And

America's people will not forgive their government for letting their sons die like dogs."

Akeem nodded. It was a bit much.

Laud didn't blame the younger man.

One did not become a living part of history by thinking small.

"Oh darn," Kowalski said.

"Darn?" Bolan tossed Wazdi a quizzical glance.

Wazdi moved to where Kowalski crouched, looking through a vent into the depths of one of the ship's holds. "Please tell me you got vertigo from looking down there."

"Darn, darn, darn," Kowalski repeated softly. "They have helicopters down there, and they're refueling."

Wazdi smelled the fuel and followed Kowalski's finger as it pointed down. He felt Bolan glance over their shoulders, keeping rear security on them.

"That is not good," the Executioner said softly.

"I don't get it. Didn't you say that these guys had new aviation fuel tanks installed on this ship?" Wazdi asked. "Those pumps are feeding from stuff that looks older than you do, Striker."

"That's because they didn't buy the AvGas tanks for refueling purposes," Bolan replied. "Of course Laud isn't going to stick around on a floating target just to get bombed out of existence by the U.S. Navy. Not after planning every single getaway so far."

Wazdi's jaw set. "You mean he's going to turn this into a bomb, except instead of a little inflatable raft up against the hull of a warship…"

"Two fifty thousand gallon aviation fuel tanks," Bolan murmured in a tone that told Wazdi he was doing mental mathematics. "They can pretty much wreck Alexandria's shipping capabilities for the next several years."

"More innocent people killed, too," Kowalski put in.

"This fucker's going to get away with too much," Wazdi growled.

A sigh emanated from the Executioner. "We're not letting him get away with this. Ski, Waz, you have any demolitions training?"

"No," Wazdi answered.

"All right. Find Best and the others. I'll disable the tanks," Bolan told them.

"And if you can't?" Leave it to Kowalski to ask the question that Wazdi didn't want to think about.

"We won't have to worry about exfiltration," the Executioner answered.

THE DOOMSDAY NUMBERS weren't tumbling, they were raining around him in a storm of flaming bits and pieces. The Divine Sword of Allah wasn't just content with gelding America. They were going to make it squirm in the spotlight of major failure.

The very man whom the U.S. had arrested twenty-four hours before would execute the men who arrested him, and set a massive explosion in the port of Alexandria. The force of the explosion would be as close to nuclear as could be. If it happened, only scorched earth would remain. Alexandria was worth more than even the lives of twelve brave American lawmen.

And the lives of the fourteen lawmen, including Wazdi and Kowalski, depended on Bolan succeeding in preventing the massive suicide bomb from going off.

Acceptable losses weren't in the Executioner's vocabulary. If need be, once Wazdi and Kowalski reported that they had the lawmen safe, he'd call in Clemons, exfiltrate the hostages and set off the explosion manually. Once the hostages were safe, and long before the city of Alexandria was threatened.

The Executioner didn't fear death, and he above all didn't fear the need to sacrifice himself for the lives of others.

But the Executioner counted on Laud not picking suicidal maniacs. So far, the men who had come after him were hardened fighters who fought their best, but they fought to win, not to die. Bolan could keep them at bay, give his allies time, and maybe he could stop the ship from detonating and flattening half a city.

Mack Bolan steeled himself for what lay ahead.

Pressed to the hatch that opened to a ladder leading into the hold, the Executioner felt the winds shift. Over the railing, the froth of microscopic life riding the tips of the waves glowed, showing that the water was growing choppier, waves peaking and surging.

The high water was coming.

The Executioner, and hell, were already on deck.

"Welcome to hell and high water," the soldier whispered, throwing open the hatch and grabbing the rails.

NODAM WAAL LISTENED to the tales told by his fellow Divine Swordsmen as they related the events that brought them to the *Pinnacle*. Their tales of Al-Askari peaked his interest, not that Waal even believed for once such a story. He never paid much attention to such fantasies.

One man, alone against thousands? Striking against the pious and holy multitudes after all these years? An utter waste of time, especially when Waal had his own adventures to relate.

The hatch opened above, and Waal's hand instinctively went to the old Colt 1911 .45 auto on his waist.

Winds were whipping through the hole above, the mist of fresh falling rain reaching him.

"Shut the hatch!" Waal spit.

Lightning flashed above, and for a moment Waal saw him.

Tall and slender, yet with an inherent power in his build, he was clad in body-hugging blackness, and in one hand the stranger held a rifle unlike any he'd ever seen before. A red pencil of light emitted from a stubby, fat barrel without sound. To one side, Waal felt a spray of hot and wet stickiness and he turned, seeing one of the storytellers falling backward, his face obliterated by an invisible death punch.

Then lightning flashed again, and the figure was absent from the hatch, sparks igniting along the rails of the ladder. Screams filled the air and a couple of men started to shoot, aiming too high. Waal could finally spot what was happening. The stranger was descending down the ladder on some kind of a rope, one hand on a rail, the other on the rifle, which bucked and spit more pencils of silent red death.

Waal charged the ladder, but nothing landed at the base, and the Divine Swordsman's initial triburst of .45-caliber slugs cut only empty air. No target dropped at the base of the ladder to be ambushed. Instead, the terrorist looked up over his head, as a figure in black somersaulted and landed behind him.

Waal tried to spin, bringing his Colt around to engage this menace who had appeared out of nowhere. He heard shouts of "Al-Askari" from those around him.

Maybe I should have spent time actually listening to these stories, Waal thought as he felt two massive impacts crush his chest.

Darkness made the terrorist tumble backward.

THE EXECUTIONER THOUGHT he'd nearly lost his bid to defuse the tanks when the Divine Swordsman shouted for him to shut the hatch. But on a fresh rappelling cord, he made his charge, kicking off at the last minute to avoid the flying, copper-jacketed death sizzling through the air. Turning away from the corpse of the Colt-toting terrorist, he brought the SA-58 up and around to cut off an AKM-wielding gunman who was just now realizing that death was on the floor with him.

The subsonic rounds were authoritative, smashing through flesh with gory authority, and the AKM-toting goon stopped as if he'd struck an invisible garrote, his rifle flying from his hands. The Swordsman tumbled backward, but Bolan wasn't sticking around to see what was happening. He had to reach the bombs.

Cutting under the hull of one of the Hueys, Bolan barely dodged a spray of bullets that sparked on metal and armor. A single slug bounced and sliced across his bootstraps.

The Executioner paused and swept the legs of the gunmen

behind him, bullets flying as fast as he pulled the trigger, heavy-weight 7.62 mm slugs smashing apart kneecaps, thighs and shins. Screaming as their leg bones were pulverized, the quartet of terrorists flopped to the ground. He spared four more mercy shots that tore through collarbones and rib cages, leaving the wounded mercifully dead.

With a kick, he rolled again. Bolan was on his feet at the end of the roll, checking around him to see if anyone had spotted where he'd gone. One man gave a cry, but a double-tap of subsonic rounds literally picked up the tattletale and smashed him against the bulkhead like a squashed tomato. With long, ground-eating strides, the Executioner weaved around the parked helicopters.

Gunfire chased after him, and he knew the doomsday numbers were against him. Any moment now, there would be a radio call topside. Who knew what would happen then, but at least so far, the attention was on him.

He'd rather have the entire army of the Divine Sword after him here in the hold of the ship than between Wazdi, Kowalski and the hostages. The Executioner hit a baseball slide under the last of the Hueys, spotting the refueling pumps that formed a barricade behind which two of the Divine Swordsmen were hiding.

The Executioner pulled a grenade from his harness and threw it, leaving the pin in place. The fastball bounced off the rusted old tank behind the two gunmen and landed between them.

It was a trick that Bolan had used too many times.

The grenade was picked up, the pin pulled and thrown back.

The Executioner watched the hellbomb arc through the air, landing under the helicopter right next to him.

16

Wazdi was leading the charge through the hallways, his rifle hidden, keeping Kowalski back and at bay. The superstructure was weighed down with the sluggishness of sleepy crewmen and tired terrorists. They passed half-alert, sluggish men who didn't even noticed the fair skin and blue eyes of Kowalski as he was dressed in the same baggy Army jacket and head wrap that Wazdi affected.

It wasn't a perfect disguise. Even the grease that Kowalski smeared on his cheeks didn't do much to match his complexion to the swarthy Arabs on the crew. Every step was one more movement deeper into heart attack territory, and Wazdi didn't even know where the hell Best and the others were.

Wazdi stopped and leaned against the bulkhead and Kowalski pulled in tight, keeping his back to the hall, his blond hair tucked away under the checkered keffiyeh.

"Hadji, this is not good," Kowalski muttered.

Wazdi managed a smile at his friend's lousy accent. "We made it this far."

"There's a bomb on this ship big enough to take out the docks at Alexandria. Striker is either going to disarm the bomb, or he's going to set it off with us on this tub," Kowalski said.

"He'll try to get us out of here first," Wazdi answered.

"Like we'll leave him?"

"So why are you complaining that we're screwed?"

Kowalski shrugged. "I heard somewhere that the more you complain, the longer God makes you live."

"If that's the case, you'll live to see the next millennium," Wazdi remarked.

"That's the plan." Kowalski chuckled. He looked over the bulkhead. "Sword."

Wazdi looked at a black-clad man carrying a sword walking down the hallway.

"Sword?" Wazdi asked.

Kowalski grinned and started off after the black-clad swordsman. "I think we're back in the game."

Wazdi was about to call out to his childhood friend, but instead shut up and followed his pal.

Leave it to someone as audacious as Ahmur Ibn Laud to send a real swordsman of Allah to perform the most blatant execution by the Divine Sword of Allah. Nothing like an actual decapitation to make an entire nation quiver and squirm and yet remain transfixed to the TV screen.

Wazdi caught up with Kowalski who was keeping his tail on the swordsman. The trail stopped at the entrance to a large mess hall. There were gunmen visible in the room and the swordsman paused, giving his blade a whirl as he entered the hall.

Kowalski looked into the room, then nodded.

"This must be the place," he spoke up in his rotten Arabic.

Wazdi felt his heart in his throat, then cinched his rifle tight behind his back. Kowalski similarly hid his long arm. If only they'd been able to get an AK to carry above their coats, but going with their weapons fully hidden under the big old rumpled green jackets would have been equally suspicious.

"So, who wants to die first?" the swordsman asked as Wazdi and Kowalski edged toward the door.

Best was on his knees, glaring daggers. All their compatriots were there, bound, hands behind their backs, beaten and battered. Some showed a little fear, but they remained quiet, keeping their heads up in dignity. They weren't going to deny their fear, but terror wasn't going to master them and force them to cringe.

The swordsman gave his blade a twirl again.

"Who dies first?" the terrorist snarled. The video camera was operating now. It was hooked up to transmitting equipment in one corner.

"How about you, motherfucker?" a voice split the air.

Wazdi turned and looked at Kowalski, tearing off his keffiyeh and charging toward the swordsman. Around the mess hall, the half-dozen Divine Swordsmen looked on in shock.

Wazdi pulled one of his throwing stars and sent it sailing at the blade-toting murderer. He then brought up the SA-58, spitting lead at the momentarily frozen enemy gunners.

KOWALSKI KNEW there was no turning back. With a silenced Marine Beretta in one fist and his sweat-soaked Middle East head scarf in the other, he took a bounding leap onto a tabletop and launched himself across space.

The swordsman brought up his blade, but the red-and-white-checkered cloth snapped around the blade and snagged hard on it. Kowalski hit the deck on bent knees, his Beretta having burned off half its magazine in midfall, pumping rounds into one of the armed sentries who was torn between murdering unarmed federal agents, or taking out the crazy blond newcomer. With eight rounds burning in his torso, the terrorist went to whatever hell was reserved for his kind.

The swordsman yanked back hard, trying to free his blade, but Kowalski swung his Beretta around, trying to bring the weapon on target and end this fight quick.

The swordsman pulled hard on the keffiyeh, pulling Kowalski off balance, and suddenly a boot came arcing around in a circle. The ex-blacksuit ducked most of the kick, but his hand went numb as the waffle tread of the boot smashed the Beretta from numbed fingers. Kowalski cursed as the pistol tumbled away, but yanked himself upright, pulling the swordsman off balance from his acrobatic kick.

A rifleman across the room started shooting at them, but stopped as Kowalski wrenched the swordsman in front of him. Agents dropped to the floor, ducking sparking rounds, but Akeem was not going to end his days as a human shield.

A brutal stomp smashed Kowalski's toes, despite the heavy combat boot he wore, and the blond Chicagoan saw red. He retaliated with a hard left to the goon's ribs.

Akeem elbowed Kowalski in the nose, and he felt it break, hot blood pouring down his upper lip.

In a flash of motion, Kowalski brought out his replica Vietnam tomahawk. The black fiberglass handle rested in his hands as the bearded blade of the ax stood in defiance of the sword.

"Hey, Jonny!" Something came whistling across the mess hall toward Akeem, who brought up his sword, deflecting the blade in midair. Metal sparked on metal, and Kowalski reached out, scooping Wazdi's diverted Cold Steel Tanto knife out of the air.

He let the knife rest against his arm in an ice-pick grip, the foot-long blade and his forearm forming a shield that hovered just under his nose.

"Thanks, Hadji," Kowalski called.

"Ready to dance, man?"

The swordsman sidestepped, keeping his sword tip between them. Kowalski followed, climbing onto a mess table. Out of the corner of his eye, he saw Wazdi keeping the odds even by pumping silenced rounds into the hallway.

"Soon your friend will be dead, and my friends will storm this room, and we'll kill every one of you Americans," Akeem taunted.

"You'll be dead first. So turn it on, Mr. Deadman," Kowalski growled. He lunged.

The tomahawk snapped across, and the scimitar bounced off the curved blade of the hatchet and snapped back to slice through Kowalski's forearm. Instead, steel met the Tanto's blade, only a small slice breaking the skin of the marshal's forearm. Kowalski followed his block with a swinging kick to Akeem's gut, but withdrew his foot just before the scimitar could chop off his leg at the knee.

Kowalski brought the tomahawk around in a speedy arc, and Akeem brought up the scimitar with all his strength, metal singing against metal in a brutal anthem of kill or be killed. Continuing his spin, Kowalski went low, snapping out the tip of the Tanto and nicking Akeem's thigh. The terrorist backstepped, lowering his sword to try to deflect more of the slice, but Kowalski was already coming back.

The Tanto slashed down first, and Akeem bounced blade against blade. That wasn't the end of the third wave of Kowalski's attack though, and he brought down his tomahawk's fiberglass handle, the butt end smashing across Akeem's eyebrow, splitting skin.

A knee rammed the air out of Kowalski's lungs, driving him backward. His foot snagged on a bench and he stumbled, landing on his back. That gave the terrorist his opportunity, bringing up his scimitar and dropping it down.

Kowalski barely got his tomahawk up, deflecting the blow and slashing out with his forearm. The edge of the Tanto knife met cloth and flesh, and Akeem roared in pain as his arm was sliced from elbow to armpit. Kowalski followed up with a boot to the groin that sent Akeem staggering backward across a mess table.

By the time he reached his feet, however, Kowalski was face-to-face with him.

"We have both drawn blood," Akeem grunted.

"There's just a little problem for you, dumb-ass," Kowalski said with a chuckle.

Quentin Best shot Kowalski a big thumbs-up as he and the other agents were finally freed now.

"How...?"

"I dropped my pocketknife off with Best while I was using you as a shield," Kowalski taunted.

Akeem's head snapped left to right. No longer fearful, the exhausted hostages were now taking up the arms of the dead gunmen who had held them captive. Best himself had taken the Beretta that Kowalski dropped.

Akeem gave a savage screech of anger, lunging forward at the tomahawk-armed blacksuit. It was a sloppy attack, and Kowalski could have ended it any of a dozen ways. He decided to pick the one that hurt the most.

Sidestepping the downward chop, Kowalski rammed the tomahawk deep into Akeem's belly and wrenched hard upward. Blood frothed from the terrorist's lips, and his brown eyes looked in horror at his killer.

"This's for Bradley," Kowalski muttered. Then he rammed the eight-inch blade of the Tanto through Akeem's right eye.

The terrorist stiffened, but still hung there, held up by the handles of the weapons rammed into him. With one final, savage twist, Kowalski moved his fireplug-thick body around and centrifugal force ripped the corpse from his blades, smashing him against the bulkhead of the mess hall.

"How was that, Hadji?" Kowalski asked Wazdi as he drew his .45.

"I'd say you just graduated from sidekick school."

BOLAN WASN'T AFRAID to die, but he wasn't going to lay still and be killed by his own grenade, either. There was only one chance for him to survive the next millisecond, and the Executioner took it without hesitation.

He grabbed the bottom of the Huey's door frame and hauled himself up and into the bird, yanking his legs up and tucking them tight to his body. The doomsday numbers hit zero, and the grenade's death roar filled the entire hold. Bolan felt as if his head was going to come apart, the shock wave bouncing him off the floor of the helicopter as it bucked upward.

The steel held, however. No shrapnel tore through to slice him to ribbons.

The Huey began to topple, shaken off its skids and sent sliding to the deck below. Bolan scrambled, grabbing for the lip of the door again, feet digging into the tread pattern in the metal to fight his way out. Metal crunched and the ceramic rotors snapped like twigs as they speared into other Hueys.

"So much for your getting off this tub, Laud," Bolan mused as he somersaulted out of the Huey. Gunfire was again ripping the air around him, but there were confused cries now. In his passable Arabic, he heard someone calling for the terrorists in the hold to head back somewhere.

The others had found the hostages.

The Executioner let the Divine Sword of Allah know that he was not to be ignored, and he drew both Berettas, finding 9 mm salvos of mayhem that swept across the deck. In the firestorm of Beretta thunder and whisper, Bolan's foot kicked the SA-58 OSW, and he stuffed both depleted handguns back into their holsters.

The rifle got a kick flip, tossing it up into the Executioner's waiting hands, and the Divine Swordsmen scrambled for cover, their rifles spraying wildly. The roar of AKs was unnerving in the massive echo chambers, and the soldier was glad his rifle was silenced. He didn't relish the thought of the naked muzzle-blast of his powerful weapon in such close quarters.

Noisy or quiet, though, the SA-58 was a formidable man killer, and three of Bolan's next ten shots were instant kills. He kept putting out rounds, massive slugs splattering against the bulkhead with impacts that sounded like the heartbeats of an ancient giant.

He had his enemies scared, and that was good enough for Bolan. They were shooting sloppy, and they were disorganized, scrambling. The rally to head back to the superstructure and secure the hostages had been put on hold as Divine Swordsmen scrambled to either destroy or escape the man slicing through their ranks.

The two gunmen who were crouched behind the fuel pumps,

the ones who nearly killed him with his own grenade, were in sight now that Bolan had made it as far as the access hatch to the next hold. Their faces looked at him, bug-eyed with terror.

Bolan fired a single round at their feet, the impact of the bullet on steel at this range sounding like the hammerstrike of a god of thunder. "Go away."

The terrorists scrambled away in horror from this monstrous figure who could not even be killed by grenades.

The legend of Al-Askari scored more points for the Executioner.

Fear was always a good weapon, and being a legend had its bonus points.

17

"Striker! Striker, this is Wazdi. Hostages located and secured," Orlando Wazdi called out over the throat mike. "How goes your sitrep?"

Around him, the FBI and U.S. Marshal men were pooling weapons and resources together.

"I'm in the hold with the fuel tanks right now," Bolan answered. "I need you to get those men out of here ASAP. I'm not even sure if we're going to have time to have Force Recon get here to pick you guys up."

"You mean you're going to set those charges off as soon as you can. The minimum safe distance is—"

"Unreachable if I'm swimming for it. Yeah. And just diving underwater will put me underneath a shock wave that's going to squash me like a bug," Bolan replied.

"How about we take over this ship?"

"And risk Force Recon?" Static cut across the tactical radio. "I knew you guys would try and leave us out of having fun."

"Captain Clemons, this ship has enough explosives on it to kill everything for three miles," Bolan spoke up.

"What was that, Stone? Move in immediately and engage the enemy? Thanks for the go-ahead, sir! I know this weather has really got our reception messed up, but I'll do my best for you!" Clemons said up over the other end.

"Some days it just doesn't pay to speak up," Bolan muttered over the open line.

"You can put a boot to his ass later, Striker," Kowalski cut in. "We'll meet Force Recon on deck. Maybe they have something in the air that can stop this tug."

"We're operating on too many maybes," Bolan said. "Get on deck, protect the hostages. Get out and don't stick around for me."

Wazdi gave his throat mike a couple slaps. "I'm sorry. This thing's cutting out on me."

"Dammit!"

"Tell it to me on deck, Striker. We gotta make sure Laud's not getting away."

Wazdi pulled his earplug to avoid any cursing, but was surprised that he didn't hear the beginnings of any.

Then again, the big soldier wasn't a man given to cursing his lot. He just did his job, no matter the odds.

Wazdi loaded a fresh magazine into his SA-58 OSW and poked his head around the corner.

"Best, you look like you took the worst of the beatings, you stick with me," Wazdi ordered.

Best, both eyes rimmed with swollen skin, one nearly puffed shut, gave Wazdi a crooked smile. "I'm sorry I didn't believe Laud was up to something."

"I'm sorry I didn't try to keep my head out of my ass, too. But that's all in the past, okay? We'll laugh about this down the road over beer and pizza."

Best held his Beretta in both hands. He was on rubbery legs, but he wasn't looking for help. Gutsy guy, Wazdi thought.

Wazdi looked at his watch.

Not even a full day, and this morning they'd been at each other's throats.

Worlds can change in a heartbeat.

The group reached a hatchway to the outside, and even in the darkness, with the ship's lights blazing, they could see sheets of rain blowing almost horizontally in a mad wind. Wazdi saw the deck was clear, but didn't quite trust it. He popped his earplug back in.

"Captain! What's your ETA?" Wazdi called.

"From my mark?"

Suddenly five SH-60 SeaHawks burst over the railing of the converted oil tanker. Door gunners in the armored, beetle-shaped aircraft were sweeping the deck, their helmets giving them alien, bug-eyed appearances.

"Oh...give us a few seconds," Clemons drawled over the radio.

WITH HIS M-249 PARA-Saw spitting hot rounds out of its 200-round belt, Clemons added to the mayhem on the deck. The wind and rain were at his back, and he was thoroughly soaked after a 160-mile-per-hour ride at wavetop height.

It was cold, wet and miserable. But there was fire issuing from his weapon. While his Force Recon gunners were hammering the deck with M-60D machine guns, his personal weapon was batting clean-up, firing out short, staccato bursts on full-auto. His rounds would leap out at three times the speed of sound, slicing through terrorist flesh without hesitation.

The heavier 60s would strike a target and smash it to a pulp, smearing flesh and bone across the steel of the deck. In the mayhem of the squall, the terrorists tried to find something to aim and shoot at, but the rotorwash of the five helicopters, hovering in formation, only served to slam more spray and rain into their eyes.

"Where you at, Johnson?" Clemons called.

A light flashed on the deck. Even through the storm, it was a powerful beacon.

"Nice flashlight."

"Thanks. I think it's one of yours," Wazdi answered.

"Probably. Okay. We'll cut you guys some slack. Delta, Charlie, deploy on that hold!" Clemons ordered. "Bravo, we're securing the superstructure."

The quintet of helicopters broke formation, only one staying where it had been. One crossed the breadth of the *Pinnacle* to take up an overlook position opposite its partner. Clemons's SeaHawk and two others spread out, deploying their troops via fast rope.

Clemons was the first out of his bird after he fed a fresh 200-round box to his man-shredder. In a rush, he was dropping down, landing in a practiced featherfall at the end of the rope. Crouching and moving crablike across the deck, he swept for enemy targets.

"You see any tangos, Johnson?" Clemons asked.

"Not from our vantage," Kowalski replied.

Clemons looked at the beacon flash once more. They were three flights up. And those decks were now plunged into darkness.

The Divine Sword was getting ready for battle.

Just the way the Force Recon team leader liked it.

"Stinky, Beamer, kill the rest of the lights. We're going green!" Clemons ordered.

The two Marines lifted their M-4s and fired quick bursts, 5.56 mm slugs leaping out and smashing out any lights still operational in the superstructure. As soon as those distractions were gone, Clemons flipped down his night-vision goggles. The universe turned a fluorescent shade of green, and the night was theirs.

"Tangos! One up!" someone called. Clemons raised his SAW, tracking. Three other Force Recon Marines were going for shots, too, focusing on the unidentified figures in motion on the railing, suddenly sent scrambling by a wave of gunfire.

"Cleared them!"

"We can't see anything!" Wazdi shouted louder than he needed to on his radio.

Clemons held up his men who spread out, two-by-two, taking cover among the pipes and hinges of the deck of the tanker. Two ninjalike forms appeared from where Wazdi had flashed his beacon.

"Dammit, Captain! We're stone blind!" Kowalski added with almost-convincing emphasis.

A quartet of gunmen rushed out of a hatchway, a dozen more started down a stairwell behind them. The two ninjas reacted to the forces bursting out into the open. Clemons opened fire, the Marines dividing up their targets to give the two Americans some help.

"We got the stairwell," Wazdi whispered at a more appropriate volume. "Start getting our men out of here!"

Clemons grinned. "You sure neither of you were Force Recon?"

"That would be telling," Kowalski replied.

THE EXECUTIONER ROLLED two more of his flash-bang grenades out the doorway and slammed the hatch shut. Thundering hammerblows echoed off the wall, and Bolan briefly felt sympathy for the terrorists he left deafened in the converted helicopter hangar.

It was time to continue working, though. He jammed a pipe through the hatch's wheel lock. It'd take a while for anyone to get through, unless they did something truly suicidal like using a cutting torch. And even then...

Something clanged behind Bolan. He whirled and saw a pair of Divine Swordsmen, both armed with pipes, stepping out into the open in front of the converted fuel tanks.

Fifty thousand gallons of aviation fuel apiece. A single bullet through either of them wouldn't cause the explosion Bolan feared, but death would be no less instant and final. A flaming jet of aviation fuel wouldn't even leave his bones. The more conventional explosion, one where vaporized fuel wasn't released into a cloud and then ignited, would only rip out the belly of the ship and force it to sink, all the while pouring gouts of flaming fuel into the water.

The two Divine Swordsmen simply grinned, tapping their pipes on the deck.

"Drop your guns, or you will die," the larger of the pair spoke.

"Well, nothing I do will set off the tanks, if I don't shoot,"

Bolan surmised out loud, setting his chopped and channeled FAL on the ground. He drew his Berettas and laid them beside the rifle. "Shooting one of the tanks. That would be a bad thing."

The bigger one smirked, swinging his pipe up and around, smacking his palm with the unyielding steel. "It's on a timer."

The smaller one looked up at his partner. "He doesn't need to know that."

"Why not? He's going to die in a few moments anyway."

"That's what you think. There's a third option. I drop my weapons, and you die," the Executioner told them.

The Divine Swordsmen glared at him.

Bolan waved them to him. "You first, guys. And hurry up. My ride's waiting on me already."

The big one moved first, lashing with his pipe, but the Executioner saw the move coming far enough away that he could divert his attention to pulling out a garrote that was part of his everyday kit. The pipe crashed down an inch from Bolan's left foot, and he snapped the garrote taut. The wire portion of the sleek weapon was made of tough, space-age flexible nylon. The handles themselves were ergonomic, and also made of nylon, but this was fiberglass reinforced and molded. They tried breaking similar handles, and even with a .50-caliber Desert Eagle round, point-blank, the nylon only bent.

The big guy with the pipe was recovering from his miss, and Bolan brought the wire between them. A hard slash with the pipe and the Divine Swordsman was stunned as his weapon bounced on what seemed like empty air for a moment. Bolan pressed the attack on the off-balance killer with a hard boot stomp to the thug's left knee. Bone cracked and snapped, and the guy retreated.

The Executioner almost managed to avoid getting smacked in the back of his head with the round pipe, but the curved surface struck muscle and curved bone and glanced away. Still it made his eyes cross and his ears filled with the ringing thunder of rushing blood.

That's when the second terrorist decided to step in. He speared Bolan in the ribs as he was still rolling with his larger pal's hit, and the point of the pipe drove the air from the Executioner's lungs. Bolan staggered backward and found the small of his back at a railing.

The large one was limping on one foot, pipe held high, and Bolan kneed up hard, pushing the smaller man's weapon so that he had a grip on it, pushing it skyward. Steel met steel with a spark, and the larger terrorist stepped back, looking in horror at where the flicker of temporary fire hung in the air. Bolan tugged the smaller Swordsman's pipe, using it as leverage to bring his elbow up and into the little terrorist's cheek.

The goon's head bounced and Bolan pivoted, head still ringing from the initial impact, but now he had the pipe. He was bringing the pipe around to introduce some unyielding steel to even the odds in this fight when pain again exploded across the Executioner's body, his shoulders suddenly bearing the brunt of a savage chop. He staggered into the smaller Divine Swordsman who pumped a fist into his adversary's stomach. Again, the wind was knocked out of him, and he knew that this was intentional. Keep an enemy from breathing for just a little while in a fight, you can keep him from breathing for good.

Bolan reached up with both hands with lightning speed, fingers clawing at the sides of the little guy's head before he plunged his thumbs into his eyes. The terrorist screamed, shocked out of his hitting strategy, and the Executioner dropped to his knees, dragging the smaller sparring partner right into the path of a savage figure-eight slash of the pipe. Meaty thuds filled the air above the blood rushing in his ears, and the guy clawed feebly, unfocused.

Bolan drove his fist hard up and into the Divine Swordsman's gut and grabbed him by his belt with his free hand. The terrorist went over Bolan's shoulder like a sack, and the larger pipeman was limping backward, chopping halfheartedly. The Executioner decided to make this fight shorter work, tossing the stunned, injured terrorist on top of the limping giant. Bodies collided and went sprawling on the metal deck as the Executioner drew a set of brass knuckles from another pouch in his kit.

He corrected himself. These weren't brass. Brass had too much metal content to be useful for his line of work. This was another fiberglass-reinforced nylon death tool. With four bold spines around each finger, they were better designed than the knuckle-dusters of old, able to inflict horrific damage.

The big terrorist threw his friend aside, snarling and looking up at the Executioner as he made sure the weapon was snug on his fist. He was getting ready to continue this fight as a wrestling match when the Executioner savagely slammed the knucks right into the center of the terrorist's face. Fiberglass-reinforced nylon shattered bone like eggshells, hot gore spilling all over the soldier's fist.

Bolan flicked his wrist, shaking blood off the knuckle-duster. The terrorist, with a fist-sized hole in his face, was never going to get up again.

The other guy was coughing and struggling to reach Bolan's discarded Beretta. The Executioner owed the guy some mercy so he grabbed a fistful of thick black hair and punched down hard right at the base of the poor guy's neck.

Bone crunched and the guy's spine severed in a body-shaking convulsion.

"Told you there was a third option," Bolan whispered harshly, limping to get his guns.

He turned and headed to check out how the fuel tanks were set up, trying to remember he had a long way to go before the dawn.

CLEMONS KNELT on the deck, keeping watch on the *Pinnacle*. The ship looked softened up enough, but looked and was were two different animals. "Give me some good news, people!"

"We have no hostile movement, all points!"

"Get those Sea Stallions in here, then, dammit!" Clemons

barked. "I want them touched down and loading hostages in thirty seconds!"

Clemons looked at his SeaHawks, which were still keeping overwatch. He knew better than to ask if they saw something. Had there been hostile action noticed, they would speak first with precision fire, then alert him as to the nature of the threat. Still, in the blowing rain on the deck, he wanted more intel.

"Any other good news?" Clemons asked.

"Stone here!"

"What's the news?" Clemons called.

Bolan's voice was grim. "Whoever set this up was good. He set up the tanks with det cord in order to shatter them."

"And of course, that's the major component," Clemons returned. "You get a cloud of explosive fuel and then set spark to the cloud. Everything in the cloud vaporizes once a single ignition goes off."

"The ignitor is a mine with a paper plate and a half-filled balloon duct taped to it," Bolan replied.

"How would that get armed?" Clemons asked.

Bolan didn't sound so grim this time. "The overpressure of the gasoline fumes would set off the pressure on the mine. As the air pressure dropped, the balloon wouldn't be so squeezed against the mine."

"Damn," Clemons said. "Party supplies and an antitank mine."

"They don't have much," Bolan answered. "There. Tape sliced free. So unless someone steps on the mine, the fumes won't have an ignitor."

"We'll scuttle this tub anyway," Clemons said. "Get up here! We're bugging out!"

There was silence on the other end.

"Listen, Colonel, I know you like doing things your way, but rely on someone else for a change. We have two Hornets with Harpoons inbound," Clemons told him. "Whatever is on this ship that can blow up *will* blow up when those things hit."

"I'm not worried about that. Has this ship been cleared, top to bottom?" Bolan interrogated.

"Hostages are loading, sir," came the call from one of the Sikorsky Sea Stallions.

"Great. Tighten up some and keep those weapons hot! I don't want anybody going home with a bullet in his spine!" Clemons shouted. "Colonel, are you coming up?"

Silence.

18

"Go! Go! Go!" Wazdi ordered, pushing Special Agent Quentin Best to lead the ragged band of hostages toward the Sea Stallion. The massive helicopter sat on the deck like an enormous toad, its rotors buzzing overhead.

Kowalski was keeping watch along the decks, unwavering in his vigilance.

Best paused as he was shoving his own men aboard. He looked back at the pair. "Get aboard!"

"No way," Wazdi answered. "We're not setting foot off this tub until you're the minimum safe distance."

"Minimum safe distance?" Best asked. His heart jumped up into his throat. "These guys have a nuke?"

"Not quite so bad," Kowalski answered, backing toward them, still seeking enemy guns. "But not by much."

"Remember the Daisy Cutter?" Wazdi asked.

"Oh fuck. How big?" Best asked.

"At least a hundred thousand gallons of aviation fuel," Wazdi told him. "We're making sure it's disarmed before it crashes into Alexandria, but you and those guys are getting out of here."

Kowalski turned. "Listen. You're going home. Nobody else gets left behind."

Gunfire ripped across the deck. Best flinched and Kowalski's squat form slammed against the side of the helicopter. Best opened fire with his Beretta, aiming at muzzle-flashes but felt a big paw slap him in the chest, driving him into the giant Sea Stallion.

"Get in there!" Kowalski roared. Blood was trickling from his nose, and he leveled the tricked-out rifle in his left hand.

Wazdi shot his friend a look between short bursts. Best was frozen in the doorway, Beretta clenched in his fist.

"Get on board!" Best shouted, his voice shredding into hoarse raggedness.

Kowalski got up and gave Wazdi a thumbs-up, reloading his rifle.

Hands grabbed the back of Best's shirt and pulled him down, Marines slamming shut the Stallion's side hatch.

"There's nothing we can do now!" Bednarek told him.

Best kept his face pressed to the glass, watching the pair moving for cover as muzzle-flashes flickered wildly at them.

"Dammit...dammit make it home you two bastards," Best prayed.

WAZDI AND KOWALSKI rolled over the edge of the hold and landed just as a searing wave of gunfire slashed across the deck at them. Wazdi let his weapon hang from around his neck and pulled his friend down.

"You okay?" Wazdi asked.

"I think I smacked my nose," Kowalski answered, wiping his lip. His mouth was covered with blood.

"Turn around. Can you breathe fine?"

"I got hit in the armor, man. It was just reflex," Kowalski told him.

"If you die, I am going to go ape-shit," Wazdi warned.

"Like you're a paragon of mental health now?" Kowalski asked him.

Wazdi answered with a laugh.

"It never stops, does it?" Mack Bolan asked as he appeared beside them.

"Jesus, Striker," Wazdi whispered. "You ever sneak up on anyone who lived?"

"Not too many."

Bolan looked up over the rail. "It's a mess. Their cover is too good. Lots of steel to stop 5.56 mm ammo."

"And grenades?" Kowalski asked. "We've got the bang for their buck."

"It's risky," Bolan said.

"Those Marines aren't catching a break," Wazdi noted.

Bolan didn't even blink. "Let's go."

KOWALSKI TOOK IT upon himself to lead the charge, his SA-58 held in one fist. His right arm felt numb from where the bullet struck him in the back, and in the slicing rain, he couldn't tell if his back was slicked down with blood, but pain was a small price to pay.

He was a Marine, and Marines were in trouble on the deck.

Duty before comfort, and at worst, Kowalski felt all he had was a broken scapula. A broken shoulder blade wouldn't be life threatening, and the heavy bone had helped save his life. He just didn't want Wazdi seeing that his right arm was all but useless. Being left-handed helped.

He paused at the corner of the hold, looking through a window of the superstructure where muzzle-flashes flared, long tongues of fire clawing out into the night. He ducked back and nodded to Wazdi and Bolan, who crouched.

"I suck at throwing. I'll give cover fire," Kowalski told them.

"On three," Wazdi snarled.

"Three!" Kowalski shouted. He and his partners swung around and hot 7.62 mm lead flamed along the superstructure, bullets pumping into windows. Panicked voices rose.

Kowalski could barely see the dark shapes of the minibombs as they went sailing upward. However, he did spot dead-on the flash and thunder of their deadly effects, blossoming explosions slamming through portholes and viewports.

The gunfire stopped for heartbeats.

"Clemons! Get your people out of here!" Bolan called over the radio.

"In motion! How are you getting out?" the Force Recon commander returned.

"It's a lovely night for a boat trip!" Wazdi snapped. He threw another grenade, and the decks shook again with thunder.

"All right. Alpha and Charlie teams are clear. Get some range and we'll pull you out of the water," Clemons answered.

Kowalski was still scanning the structure when he saw movement. Something huge was dropped overboard, slicing into the water. Bodies went sailing over the railing after it, and he half rose.

"They're bugging out!" he shouted. He charged along the rail, forgetting about the slashing rain and the hail of lead pouring down. Bullets snapped and pinged at his feet, but gunfire continued to hammer from the SeaHawks. It was a battle of wills between door gun crews and the terrorists seeking to keep control of the *Pinnacle*.

And for now, it was an even heat.

Even enough for Kowalski to charge the aft bow, where he spotted a clot of gunmen heaving another inflatable boat over the edge.

"Clemons! Get a ship out here! We've got tangos leaving by the back door!" Kowalski shouted.

Bullets hammered the steel bulkhead he was up against, and he wished right now he had a faster shooting weapon. Instead, he plucked his Para-Ordnance with his off hand, and with the sawed-off combat rifle in one hand and the .45 in the other, he opened fire, spraying the crowd.

Slugs hammered into his chest and slammed him against the railing. The armor held, no fire burning into his lungs, but his head bounced, scalp splitting on unyielding metal. Still he kept squeezing the triggers on both of his weapons, enemy bodies jerking and tumbling in a deadly cross fire.

It was going to be only seconds before these bastards could

get something through or around his body armor, and then, his race would be over. A bullet finally punched through chest plate, and suddenly he couldn't breathe.

It was a hammerblow, followed by the squeezing grasp of a titan, Kowalski didn't have any strength left in his hands, and his weapons clattered onto the deck.

The Force Recon gunship wasn't even on hand to start whittling away at the terrorists escaping from aft of the *Pinnacle*.

The terrorists gave a howl of victory as Kowalski's weapons fell from his numbed hands. He cursed and spit blood. The marshal's left hand slithered toward a weapon, any weapon to continue to deny these animals their victory.

Gleaming silver whizzed over Kowalski's head, taking a slight curve before it split in three, the ribbon of slashing mirror light imbedding into the chests of three Divine Swordsmen. He watched as a pair of blacksuited wraiths leaped over his prone form, pistols barking and bucking, spitting flame both loud and soft into the assembly of retreating killers.

Bolan and Wazdi had finally made it past the slash of sniper fire to make sure evil did not escape unpunished.

As the Executioner and the FBI blacksuit pumped out rounds, Kowalski struggled, picking up his .45 and feeding in a fresh magazine. Blood squirted out of his nose as he bent, and he slumped, coughing, his mouth hot and sticky.

"Striker!" Wazdi shouted. "He's alive!"

"Get him to a SeaHawk, we're moving out now!" Bolan ordered.

There was a grim, dull silence.

Kowalski pressed his gun into Wazdi's hand.

"I think Laud got away," he whispered to his friend.

Wazdi stroked water from his eyes.

"Not for long," Wazdi promised. "But we have to get you some help."

"Just make sure the fucker dies tonight," Kowalski answered.

He closed his eyes, secure in his best friend's grasp.

ANY OTHER TIME, the spectacle of two F-18 Hornets launching missiles into an oil tanker and splitting it apart with an explosion would have been a moment of thrills for Orlando Wazdi. Instead, his best friend was on the floor of a Sikorsky SeaHawk having a sucking chest wound tended to by a Force Recon corpsman. The flare of the orange mushroom cloud lit the sea like a false dawn.

"Your buddy's tougher than a two-dollar steak," Clemons told Wazdi, putting a baseball-mitt-sized hand on his shoulder. "He's going to make it."

Wazdi looked away from the fireball and into his friend's pale face. A Marine was squeezing a translucent bag, pushing fresh air into labored lungs, while another was hooking up an IV bag. Kowalski gave Wazdi's wrist a tight squeeze, then glanced at the medics.

"Anyone else hurt?" Wazdi asked Clemons.

"No. Most of the rest of us had the good sense to keep from standing upright in front of the bullets," Clemons told the half-conscious Marine on the floor.

Kowalski smiled under his mask, then gave Clemons a thumbs-up followed by a middle-finger salute.

"He told me that was Marine for 'You're number one in my book,'" Wazdi said to Clemons.

"No speaking past tense. First off, this Marine has no permission to die yet," the Force Recon captain said. "Second, my corpsmen need the practice on saving lives, not losing patients."

"He's got multiple rib fractures and soft tissue damage. And from the way his eyes are dilated, when he split his scalp, he incurred a concussion," the corpsman spoke up. "Who did he fight, Godzilla?"

"Well, there was a terrorist swordsman, but the real beating came when he tried to stop a dozen terrorists trying to get off the back of the *Pinnacle*," Wazdi said.

The corpsman looked down at the injured Kowalski, who

made a slight shrug. "Next time, you're allowed to call in air support!"

"Did," Kowalski muttered.

Wazdi looked at the other SeaHawks slicing across the water back toward the aircraft carrier at full speed. On one of them was Mack Bolan, and for certain he wasn't going to let the sun rise with Ahmur Ibn Laud still breathing.

The ex-blacksuit wasn't about to let himself get left behind either. Not after all this. As he'd said before, in for a little, in for a lot.

Bolan had policed the corpses on the *Pinnacle* and didn't find their man. At least two Zodiac boats had been tossed overboard, maybe more.

That left Laud and eleven to seventeen of his closest friends to continue on. Once they reached the shore, those men would disappear on the streets of Alexandria, requiring more months, more effort, more blood and slaughter to root him out.

Wazdi squeezed the grip of the .45 that Kowalski had given him. Too many people were dead. Too many good people.

Wazdi looked down at Kowalski, remembering when as little kids, they would pretend to save the world again and again, slaughtering hordes of bad guys.

Save the world. Come home. The good guys weren't hurt, and the bad guys would feed the wolves or whatever mutant monsters off in their secret headquarters.

It was a strong dream, fighting for truth and justice and the American way, strong enough to make both boys grow up to be young men in the military, and then later law enforcement. Somewhere along the way, the childhood friends met again on a small farm in the middle of Virginia, and they were issued skintight blacksuits to patrol and protect the installation at night. During the day, they learned the arts of war and crime fighting from a dedicated core of experts, lead by the mysterious Striker.

"What a trip, eh, Ski?" Wazdi whispered.

"Next time…somewhere safer," Kowalski muttered breathlessly. "Afghanistan maybe."

Wazdi smiled and combed down Kowalski's wet hair.

"Just make sure there is a next time," Wazdi told the man he loved like a brother. "Because if you die, your girlfriend's going to kick my ass."

Kowalski winked. "You'd deserve it, slowpoke."

Wazdi watched his brother slip into unconsciousness.

THE EXECUTIONER hopped off the SeaHawk and looked around for the other helicopter to land. He wanted more than anything to head off while the trail for Laud was still fresh, but there was a man on that helicopter who had all but sacrificed his life to stop a knot of madmen from making it to freedom.

The bird landed and Clemons jumped out, helping off the gurney with David Kowalski, corpsmen holding an IV and a rebreather, rushing him to a medical crew who had set up on deck.

On the carrier, the rain was only a soft drizzle, and Bolan looked at Wazdi, .45 in hand, watching his friend being received and taken care of.

"How is he?" Bolan asked him.

"He'll live," Wazdi answered. "He's not going to live easy for now, but he'll wake up tomorrow, and the day after that."

"I'm sorry about your friend," Bolan said.

"When we were boys, we pretended to be superheroes, and we'd take on entire armies. Occasionally, he'd pretend to get shot up, mainly because he liked that kind of thing, the dramatic sacrifice," Wazdi said.

The Executioner felt the sting of the sentence. "There are no superheroes," he said.

"It doesn't matter, Striker," Wazdi said. "Those guys inspired us to be who we are today. There's a bad guy out there right now, and my friend once again did his dramatic sacrifice, leaving me all on my own."

Bolan caught the dark stare, brown eyes glistening with mixed rain and tears. "Not on your own."

"I'm sorry that it took this long to realize that sometimes, all you can do is kill these vermin before they can hurt anyone else," Wazdi apologized.

"We just need a ride," Bolan said. "The helicopters are going to be too long refueling."

"Well, there's this Bell TH-57 that's all fired up," a familiar voice spoke up.

The Executioner turned and looked at the movie-star handsome features of his old friend Jack Grimaldi. His eyes were baggy, and his jaw was covered in a carpet of stubble, but he was there.

"What's up, Sarge? Need a lift?"

"We've had everything up in the air trying to track those boats, but there's a small problem with tracking Zodiac's on an ocean," Captain Paul Hettfield explained over the radio to the Bell TH-57 SeaRanger.

"Their hulls are made of Kevlar nylon," Mack Bolan answered. He was busy assembling an Uzi in the back of the helicopter. "It absorbs radar emissions, so your Forward-Looking radar wouldn't be able to spot them. Plus, they're small and low to the water, and the men inside and their metal weapons would be even lower profile."

"Can I tell you something you don't know?" Hettfield asked, slightly annoyed.

"Give it to me," Bolan said. "But I'm betting your people spotted some vehicles on shore."

There was cursing at the other end of the radio connection. "How did you know?"

"A pickup party. You were looking at something like eight pickup trucks," the Executioner replied. He locked the bolt in place, lowered the receiver and tightened it up.

"Ten vehicles, total," Hettfield replied. "How did you know?"

"Thirty men were supposed to get off the *Pinnacle* by Zodiac, the rest were going to fly away to safety, so I'd check even further ashore," Bolan explained. "I'm betting the people who were taking off by boat weren't going to be coming to shore in the same spot as the crews evacuating by helicopter. Still, that many trucks, they could split up, and have at least two security teams. With six trucks designated for pickup, pardon the pun, the other four must be security, so we have four crew wagons, at least sixteen gunners on hand, plus four drivers and four guys in the shotgun seat."

"You're not Sherlock Holmes, are you?" Hettfield asked.

That got a laugh from Grimaldi and Wazdi.

"Just someone who pays attention to all tactical openings. Point me toward these trucks on shore," Bolan demanded.

"We can get some air support for you," Hettfield offered.

"It's not going to come in time," the Executioner returned. "I also want to make a confirmed kill."

"Your helicopter is not armed enough for you to take on a force that big!" Hettfield protested.

"My personal pilot brought along some optional extras. We'll make do," Bolan replied. "Where are we going?"

Hettfield rattled off the coordinates.

Wazdi stopped working on an M-16/M-203 and looked over a map with a penlight. "That's along the highway heading into Alexandria. You were right, they'll disperse into the city."

"It's nice to be right for once today!" Bolan exclaimed. "One step behind is not my favorite place to be."

"That's okay, Sarge," Grimaldi spoke up. "I had it in good authority that in the old days, most people didn't like it when you were one step behind them."

Bolan didn't have the urge to smile. "Thanks for bringing me a spare war bag."

"I was passing by the neighborhood at Mach 2.5, and I figured I'd stop off and make sure that you got some fresh gear," Grimaldi stated.

"How long have you been flying tonight?" Wazdi asked the Stony Man pilot.

"If I stopped to count the hours, I might fall asleep at the wheel," Grimaldi answered.

"Now I know how Ski feels when I'm flying," Wazdi muttered.

Bolan gave the ex-blacksuit a nod. "Some friends you can just tell to sit down and shut up."

"I was just guessing that," Wazdi returned. "Too bad we don't have more heavy firepower."

Bolan finished strapping his thigh holster in place, the reassuring weight of the Desert Eagle against his leg. He glanced at Wazdi, weighing the sarcasm in the man's statement. A replacement Beretta 93-R was slung under one armpit, complete with custom sound suppressor. In Bolan's hands was a 9 mm Uzi submachine gun with two taped magazines, and a thigh pouch held more magazines for the Parabellum-spitting flesh-shredder.

Wazdi himself benefited from spare 20-round magazines for his Beretta M-9, and an M-16/M-203 rifle and grenade launcher with a 100-shot Beta C drum in place, and a high-explosive 40 mm grenade in the launcher. On a vest, Wazdi wore various other just HE missiles. Kowalski's Para-Ordnance .45 auto with ten spare magazines from the Marine armory rounded out this arsenal. In addition to the borrowed Beretta and Para-Ordnance, Wazdi also had his SIG-Sauer P-226.

"What are we missing?" Bolan asked.

"Well, a shiny leather trench coat. I'd also like that slow motion bullet-time from *The Matrix*," Wazdi commented.

"What time?" Bolan asked.

"Aww... You were hip to Jonny Quest and the *Lord of the Rings* stuff, Striker," Wazdi said.

"Yeah, but that was before I got...busy," Bolan answered.

Grimaldi looked over his shoulder at the Executioner. "We've got the Farm online."

"Unplug, Waz," Bolan said.

Wazdi looked over, then pulled the plug on his headset.

The soldier hated leaving the young man out in the cold, especially since he'd been involved in the blacksuit program.

Wazdi showed uncommon loyalty, but the security of the Farm would have been compromised. Worse, Wazdi would have been considered a security breach to the Farm. After all the risks the Executioner had taken with the young man's life, he didn't want to leave him open as a possible target of reprisal if a leak occurred.

"We're private. Shoot," Bolan said.

"Striker, we're tracking you inbound to the Egyptian coast," Barbara Price said. "You're not cleared with the Egyptian government to continue your pursuit."

"Who do they think I am?" Bolan asked.

"They think you're a Force Recon team sent to mop-up the last of the Divine Sword. The Egyptians are tap-dancing, looking for someone to pass the buck to about granting authority for you to continue your hunt."

"Sorry. I'm off duty," Bolan answered.

"Striker, G-Force, the Egyptians will blow you out of the sky if you're not careful," she warned. "We have Phoenix en route to help clean them out at the end of today."

"No. Yesterday was Laud's last day," Bolan stated. "I'm not waiting until this evening. I see the shore and he's on that shore. Every minute he's alive, more people die. You've seen the casualties for yesterday and last night. I'm going for the knockout right here."

There was uncomfortable silence on the other end. Stony Man Farm was Mack Bolan's brainchild, and they relied on him for his skills as much as he relied on them for intelligence. But the cold truth was the Executioner was his own man. He was above sanction, and didn't have to obey their orders.

"Be careful," Price whispered.

AHMUR IBN LAUD WAS COLD and soaked to the bone, and he hauled himself out of the Zodiac when it was in four feet of water. It couldn't make him more soaking wet and miserable, so the terrorist leader dived in. He counted on the stainless-steel finish of his "borrowed" Smith & Wesson automatic to keep it from rusting. The AK-47 he snatched from inside the Zodiac would work even if it were completely composed of rust or clogged with three pounds of mud or sand, so he didn't worry about that.

The pickup trucks were battered old Peugeot 504s. Frankly, Laud would have loved to have seen something a little more modern. He wanted to get back to Saudi Arabia and have the comfort of a BMW or an Audi, something that hadn't been covered in layers of sand and rust.

Al-Askari had won for now. He saw the fireglow on the horizon, and moments later heard the rushing thunder of the erupting *Pinnacle*. His hostage execution video was canceled. His destruction of the docks of Alexandria defused.

Laud wondered how many of his men went down with the ship, and knew that however many died, there'd be more to join his circus. He would have an endless parade of manpower as long as there was someone in the world with the feeling that life owed them or someone had screwed them just on the basis of race or religion. He wondered, absently, if he could actively recruit midwestern militias to his cause, and smirked.

Disenfranchised and pissed off, the scum of the world just looked for someone with the charisma, power and willingness to lead them. All he cared about was the power. He might not have made the world shake in terror at the power of the Divine Sword this night, but he did make the U.S. Government quake and spend millions of dollars and man-hours of effort to stop him. Laud's cause was himself, being elevated to a figure of historical impact. All he needed was the right banner to wave, and he had the manpower necessary. Others had taken this route.

Once upon a time, Laud was friends with one such man, and hoped one day to recombine forces openly. But now, he had to get this caravan on the fastest road through Alexandria and down to Cairo. He'd arranged for a flight, and he'd have just enough time to shave his beard and trim his mustache and board the plane incognito.

They'd landed in the elbow of Mandara Bay and had a long drive. He wanted the others to have a chance to spread out, not so much for their safety, but if they did manage to move out, there would be more targets, and it would be easier for them to scatter.

Not that Laud minded. He did the math and knew that as of right now, they had about twenty minutes to disappear into the interior of Alexandria before the Americans could refuel their helicopters and send out their Force Recon Marines or SEALs or whoever those men were.

Laud slogged up the beach and came to one of a dozen men who were busy smoking cigarettes.

"Good evening, Ahmur," Hakkan greeted, flicking his cigarette into the surf. "You're a little early."

"The United States Marine Corps rained on our parade," Laud replied. He shrugged. "We'll have another chance to do some kind of damage."

Hakkan nodded. "Only half of your boats showed up."

"We were under harassment. It was only the storm that kept the helicopters from spotting us and tearing us to pieces with their guns," Laud stated.

"Good. That means the trucks will be less crowded," Hakkan said. He smiled, yellowed teeth glinting in the gray predawn sky. The smile held for a moment, then weakened.

"Did any of your helicopters get away?" Hakkan asked.

Laud turned, his grip on the Kalashnikov's forearm stock tightening.

"Who…"

"Al-Askari!" Laud shouted. "Shoot that piece of shit down now! Scatter! Scatter!"

Hakkan balked, and Laud kicked the pickup man in the shin. He was busy turning his Kalashnikov around and taking aim at the black shape. It was coming in fast, and without operating lights. That would make it harder to hit. He wondered, absently, just how much harder it would be for them to acquire targets on him.

Laud cursed the gods of war.

If Al-Askari was here to finish this mad day, then he would finish it with a chest riddled with bullets!

THE EXECUTIONER perched in the doorway, Uzi clenched in one fist, ready to start spitting its death load as soon as they were within range when the little green bugs in his night-vision goggles slowly began reacting to the manic ravings of one of them. It didn't take broad daylight and a nose-to-nose glance to see who the energetic leader was. His were the first muzzle-flashes flickering in the verdant haze of the goggles he wore. Bolan tucked back and Grimaldi swerved the SeaRanger as more muzzle-flashes lit up the beach, bullets slicing into the air.

"Sarge, I think they spotted us!" Grimaldi called out.

"So much for the element of surprise," Wazdi called out.

"That's okay. I've usually counted on the element lead," Bolan replied. He pulled the trigger on his Uzi and sent a figure eight sweeping onto the beach below him. He knew he wasn't hitting anything except sand and sheet metal, but return fire would at least give them some opportunity to come up with an alternate plan.

In the interim, the Executioner gauged what they were facing. Radar from the aircraft carrier's shore prowlers and spy birds detected several vehicles. They were a mix, six truly dedicated pickup trucks, with gunmen seated in their backs, firing from their elevated position before Uzi fire and rotorwash made them flinch and cower from the blasting combination. The other four vehicles were station wagons, truly crew wagons now. Bolan figured they could have packed eight people into each of the vehicles present. Things could have been worse, then, they could have been fighting up to eighty armed killers.

Too bad, Bolan thought, we killed half your friends getting

away by boat, and all the ones getting out by helicopter. It's just you, and your closest friends, Laud.

The SeaRanger swooped around and Bolan looked at the beach. It was relatively secluded, a half mile from a row of hotels. He looked and saw that the guards at the entrances of the hotels, tiny specks in the distance, were slowly moving into action.

"Wazdi, take a listen in on the local military channels. See if the Egyptians are getting any major reaction to all this shooting going on," Bolan suggested.

"Gotcha, Striker," Wazdi answered. He fired off a few bursts from the M-16 and dropped a grenade into the sands below. A gout of thunder erupted from the shore, and terrorists ran screaming, their concentration on shooting down the SeaRanger broken. He leaned back into the helicopter and wrapped his arm with the rifle's strap, then began keying in the radio.

The Executioner looked below, noticing that the grenade had hit between two trucks, tearing the door off the driver's side of one. Smoke poured into the sky from between them, and the second truck looked lopsided, its rear passenger wheel snapped off at the axle. A good shot, but then, Wazdi had been proving a damn good shot with the grenade launcher all day long.

"Well, up until that grenade hitting the beach, they were thinking of sending someone over here to look in on the situation. Now, they're saying that they wanna have someone else check it out," Wazdi explained.

Bolan fanned another truck, forcing the men behind it to duck, their rifles silencing for the moment. "That means they're going to want to send some fast movers here. I'm not sure how fast they're going to scramble them."

"I can give you about five minutes, Sarge," Grimaldi answered. "Then I'm going for a quick spin out of here."

"Jack, I spotted a dune," Bolan called out. "It's got a good view of the road, but it's high enough that it'll give you some cover when you drop us off."

Grimaldi looked over one shoulder and nodded. "One hot LZ touchdown coming up."

"All right. Get us there, and get out. We'll meet you where we hooked up after we took care of those smugglers working for the Chinese," Bolan told him. He turned at the sound of Wazdi's M-16 chattering a long burst, the Arab American taking advantage of the extra-sized drum to bring some headaches down on the enemy.

Grimaldi gave the SeaRanger a twist and swung the chopper sideways over the dune, giving both Bolan and Wazdi the opportunity to pour lead out the open side door of the helicopter, hammering slugs down and into the clot of terrorists and their trucks.

Grimaldi's steady hand brought the SeaRanger hovering down to a yard above the weed-entangled sand. The Executioner was out first, landing in a half crouch, then moving forward, Wazdi hot on his heels.

"Take care, Sarge!" Grimaldi called.

"Don't forget, you're our ride home," Bolan answered back.

The SeaRanger took flight, tearing into the sky and spiraling away. Bolan looked at Wazdi, who was feeding a 40 mm hellbomb into the M-203's charge tube.

"Ready to finish this day off with a bang?" he asked.

"I'm ready to finish the whole damn year off. Laud's dead, then I take a nap," Wazdi growled. He snapped the launcher shut.

Bolan fisted the Uzi in both hands and charged up the sand dune, burning off a blast of Parabellum rounds. "There's plenty of time to sleep...when your enemy's dead."

WAZDI TOOK the Executioner's M-16/M-203 and swung it to bear even with a Peugeot 504 and let fly with yet another 40 mm charge. This particular round he wasn't sure of, as it was grabbed out of a shoulder sash bandolier while on the run, but he didn't expect the warrior to go into battle with pop caps and noisemakers. The recoil was akin to a shotgun, but it was something he was used to by now.

The sound of the launch was completely different from the others, though. This was a hollow, buzzing sound, a swarm of dozens of brutal hornets streaking out of the 40 mm tube and spreading out into a cone of devastation. The truck he hit shrugged to one side, peppered with hundreds of hits. Men behind the truck screamed in bloody agony as pellets went over, under and through the sheet metal of the pickup truck. The buckshot round finished its recoil when the punctured fuel tank of the Peugeot went up, an oily fireball licking skyward and finishing off the wounded who were too slow to escape.

"Oh, I gotta get me one of these," Wazdi said appreciatively, moving his trigger finger back to the M-16 and hammering out a short burst at another truck.

"I'll see what I can do," Bolan replied, throwing his grenade overhand. It sailed into the darkness, and Wazdi wasn't sure if the big guy could hit the target. However, thunder split the night moments later, men screaming in agony as hell rained upon them.

Wazdi popped up, scanning for running figures and spotting them, tracking the M-16. The barrel flared hot, flame exploding from the nose of the rifle. Bodies tumbled as he raked the weapon. Muzzle-flashes lit the night as gunmen tried to return fire, but the terrorists were of the type encountered around the globe. To them, the mere fact that they were men who had taken on the mission of soldiering for God made them expert marksmen. They didn't have much training other than how to load a magazine and work the safety and the trigger. Their gunfire was wasted on empty air by the time Wazdi was on his belly, face down in the shoreside weeds.

Slugs sliced the night above Wazdi's head, and he looked over, seeing the Executioner in full run, letting his Uzi drop on its sling. The big figure was swinging around to the road, drawing both handguns as cones of light came burning around the dune.

Suddenly, the ex-blacksuit made the realization. The Divine Sword terrorists were getting their acts together and trying to escape.

The terrorists had wheels, while the Executioner and Wazdi were on foot. A Peugeot sliced down the road past the black-clad soldier as his paired handguns exploded and shattered the darkness on the road.

The Executioner let Wazdi do his thing from on high. His weapon had more punch, and more range, to turn the beachhead into a slaying ground for Ahmur Ibn Laud's forces. His precision fire against their ragtag potshots would make the disparate odds even. And if Wazdi's tactics weren't enough, he still had a half dozen more 40 mm HE grenades to smash to a pulp whatever was left standing.

Bolan's current mission was to get around the side of the dune and block off the road in case any of the wheelmen decided to get a clue and put pedal to metal. So far, they'd only accounted for the disabling or destruction of four vehicles sitting on the sand.

That meant there were six sets of wheels, and six powerful, reliable engines capable of snatching up the leader of the Divine Sword of Allah, and whisking him away to points unknown.

That wasn't going to happen, not this night.

A vehicle came lurching up the road, and Bolan triggered a short burst from his Uzi when it locked open and empty. Just a short sputter, and then the weapon failed. No time for anything but a New York reload, Bolan knew. Weapons and steel had failed him enough, but all weapons failed. It was the soldier who couldn't fail.

The New York reload was developed by New York cops back

in the forties and fifties, when they had only 6-shot revolvers against guys with rifles and shotguns and even the occasional tommy gun. Six shots wasn't much, and they were mandated to only carry 6-shot weapons. But they were never mandated to how many of those six-shooters they could carry.

The Executioner had been a fan of the concept all his career—two guns meant that he almost always had firepower to spare. Uzi empty, his hands plunged toward both holsters, left hand tucking up to rip the Beretta from its shoulder leather while his right hand pulled the Desert Eagle from its quick-draw rig.

The Peugeot, a wagon, was within spitting distance when both weapons were in hand, and Bolan tripped the triggers on both weapons, a triburst of 9 mm rounds from the suppressed Beretta being drowned out by the belching fireball of the Desert Eagle's .44 Magnum slug launch. The wagon jerked and swerved from the Executioner, but continued charging down the road. He pivoted and sent off another salvo, aiming above and between the glaring, glowing red eyes of the taillights of the wagon, but knew instinctively from the way the vehicle lurched drunkenly that he didn't need to put out the extra rounds.

Everyone who wasn't dead in the Peugeot was spilling out the passenger doors, their weapons belching and spitting, flares spitting off into the night, trying to track the phantom who had opened up on them. Bolan hit the dirt before the Divine Swordsmen actually fired up enough of their brainpower to begin aiming, let alone remembering where the muzzle-flashes that had stopped their vehicle had originated from. Rolling twice, each time the Uzi jamming hard into the Executioner's ribs, Bolan was out of the line of fire. The respite was only temporary, but the soldier was counting muzzle-flashes and marking positions.

His Desert Eagle bucked and hammered out as he cut loose with a savage 4-round display of mayhem. Recoil made his arm sing, blood pumping in response to the shock waves from the Isreali-designed hand cannon. Two men flopped lifelessly, bullets smashing through heavy ribs and spongy lung tissue in a nonstop gore blast. Another screamed as his leg was blown apart, a softball-sized chunk of muscle and bone vaporized by the hollowpoint's impact. The fourth intended target, the last of the gunners from the Peugeot, gasped in terror as Bolan's missile struck sheet steel instead of flesh, caroming away into the night.

Bolan turned the Beretta on the terrorist he'd shot in the leg and fired off a swift, silenced burst that quieted the cries of pain, then swept the 93-R to under the Peugeot. He spotted a pair of feet backlit by the taillights of the vehicle, and cut loose with another 3-round burst, suppressed rounds leaping and tearing through leather to chop and chomp into flesh and bone.

The terrorist wailed and fell forward, his rifle clattering from his hands, feet and ankles reduced to mangled pods of shattered flesh. With a surge of motion, the Executioner was on his feet, pumping the last round from his 93-R into the wounded man's head, the mercy shot ending this conflict.

He heard motion behind him and realized that engines were revving all over the place. Strong hands grabbed the Executioner and pulled him back from the road as splashes of light and the rip roar of automatic weapons swept the dirt where he'd been moments before. Autothunder filled the air and packed sand was gouted skyward as bullets chewed it free and spit it up.

Wazdi held on to Bolan, making sure he wasn't thrown unceremoniously to the ground, only pulled out of the way of near-certain death, then cut loose with his SIG-Sauer and Beretta, both 9 mm pistols kicking out hot brass as he swept the passing Peugeots with them. The Executioner dumped his empty Uzi magazine and slammed a fresh load of Parabellum rounds into place. Topped off, the Uzi lashed a tongue of liquid fire at the last of the vehicles in line.

"How many got away?" Bolan asked.

"Two," Wazdi answered. "One with Laud, the other with a truckload of West Alexandria good ol' boys with rifles."

"Come on. We're borrowing the crew wagon," the Executioner said, running toward the first of the escapee vehicles. He was about to slip behind the wheel when Wazdi cut him off, yanking out the dead driver before he could.

"What?"

"Listen, you shoot better than I do. Chances are, you jump onto the backs of trucks better too. I'll drive, you get the shotgun, the Uzi, even the fucking M-60 if we had one."

Bolan nodded. The soldier accepted the M-16/M-203 stuffed into his waiting hands, and raced around to the other side. "Right now, it's too early for anyone to be putzing around the roads by the hotels, but if they head deeper into the city..."

"I'm not letting these assholes get away," Wazdi said. He ground the clutch and worked the stick on the Peugeot. Gears slipped for a millisecond before power roared into the wheels.

The vehicle shot off, tearing after the retreating taillights in the distance.

AHMUR IBN LAUD THREW one arm onto the roof of the pickup's cab to secure himself as he stood in the bed of the Peugeot. The Divine Swordsman looked back at the station wagon roaring to life in the distance. Once more, his enemy began his hot pursuit. In a flash like a flame, Al-Askari swept down upon them and now the beach was covered in corpses and wrecked vehicles.

This wasn't a human being, this was a one-man storm, an elemental force of nature wrapped in the illusion of flesh. Every step of this path, the Soldier had been on his tail, breathing closer and closer. They'd almost been within touching distance on the *Pinnacle*, so close that Laud threw himself over the railing thirty feet to plunge into the dark Mediterranean waters to escape with his life.

At his knees, one of his fellow Divine Swordsmen clutched his bloodied stomach, crying out, praying to God for mercy and release from his injuries.

"Shut up!" Laud spit. He pulled the Smith & Wesson he'd taken from Rafferty, just the morning before this, and fired into the dying man's head. "There's your release! If you're too wounded to fight, you're too wounded to live!"

The other Divine Swordsmen in the bed of the pickup, and the next truck over, looked at the executed corpse.

"Al-Askari dies today!" Laud hammered on the roof of the pickup. "Draw him in close! You! Pull away and sneak up on him from behind!"

"He could gun you down!" Hakkan shouted from the other truck.

Laud sneered and holstered his Smith & Wesson, pulling the Kalashnikov from the dead Swordsman's clawed hands. He kicked the corpse off the back of the truck and fired a burst toward the wagon that was gaining speed on them.

"Do your worst, Al-Askari! Fill my chest with lead if you can!" Laud shouted. He held up the AK again and pulled the trigger, searing the night with a blade of white fire, the muzzle-flash of the rifle sweeping its arc mercilessly.

In the distance, he saw sparks light on the frame and front of the pursuing Peugeot.

Laud's teeth clenched tight, a grin stretching across his face.

"Come on, Soldier. Let a bloodred sun rise upon one or the other of our wrecked bodies!"

LIGHT STREAMED over the horizon as the Earth spun. The pair of pickups were racing away from them to the east, and Bolan held on, M-16 clamped in his fist as he watched a body being kicked out the back.

Wazdi swerved hard, avoiding wrecking the undercarriage and the shock absorbers by hitting the once-living speed bump. The Peugeot carved grit and dust, choking clouds pouring off the fenders and streaming into the Executioner's face, making him turn away and spit. He blinked the grit from his eyes, keeping crouched.

"Damn!" Wazdi cursed, bullets suddenly sparking all over the front of the speeding wagon.

"Do your worst, Al-Askari!" came the roar from the pickup down the way. More rounds sliced into the air, this time the jumble and jostle of the road and Wazdi's swift steering denied them their intended target. Bolan watched as Ahmur Ibn Laud held his rifle, drenched and grinning, lips peeled back in a feral snarl mixing joy and hatred.

Bolan didn't have to hear his enemy's words to know that this man relished the chance to finally end this brutal battle. A full day of cat and mouse had left them with a respect for each other.

But then, the Executioner always respected his enemies. Any one of them could kill him, just as he had the power to kill them.

Bolan stroked the trigger on the M-16, milking the 30-round magazine. He aimed low, trying to fight the bounce of the two racing vehicles and the potholes they couldn't avoid. He chewed up dirt and road, and the pickup lurched as one tire suddenly went flat. Gunmen in the pickup ahead of him screamed, but Laud kept firing his AK.

The windshield turned into a shattered mass of broken safety glass, pebbled cracks making it impossible to see through. Bolan leaned back in when Wazdi yanked on his Uzi, twisting it on its strap. "Mind if I borrow this?"

"Go ahead," the Executioner allowed, leaning close enough so that Wazdi could maneuver the agile little machine pistol.

Wazdi held down the trigger, blowing through the half-destroyed windshield, letting open air through. Bolan snaked out of the Uzi's strap and Wazdi swung hard, using the hammer-shaped submachine gun as a mallet, pounding out the last bits of broken windshield. When they could see the road before them, all they saw was one of the pickups, Laud kneeling in the bed, fighting to feed his weapon a fresh magazine.

"Trade back," Bolan said, taking back his Uzi. "You got all the M-16's magazines."

"Damn, sorry," Wazdi growled, hitting the gas and cutting the distance between the wagon and the pickup to ten yards.

"Not your fault," Bolan returned. "But I'll take out some aggression anyway."

Bolan, his Uzi recharged, swept the pickup again, bullets leaping the distance between the speeding trucks at over a thousand feet per second in relative velocity. A gunman screeched and tumbled off the enemy truck, his chest riddled with eight burning slugs. Wazdi swerved again, then took a look.

"Dammit!"

"What happened?" Bolan asked. He pulled his Uzi back from the dashboard, recoiling as Laud threw his rifle in frustration, the weapon landing on the hood and skidding almost between them. The wooden stock bounced on the hood and slammed hard into Bolan's forearm, shocking it numb momentarily, throwing off his aim with the Uzi.

The Uzi fire went high again.

Whatever remained of the rear window in the Peugeot now exploded as rifle fire came hammering in at them, Kalashnikov rounds punching at sheet steel looking for vulnerable mechanisms and the fuel tank.

"We lost the second truck. It must have moved while we were blinded," Wazdi said.

"We've been concentrating on him, so Laud sent his boys around to harass us from behind," Bolan surmised.

The dashboard split and cracked as a single round punched through and Wazdi yelled unintelligibly, holding his arm as he continued to steer. "Dammit!"

Bolan looked back. "How bad are you hit?"

"A scratch," Wazdi growled. "But I'm sick of this shit. Take the wheel!"

Bolan lunged for the wheel, grabbing hold of it and steering as Wazdi grabbed the M-16/M-203 and wrestled with it, ramming a fresh charge into the barrel. The FBI man twisted in his seat, pointing the assault rifle grenade-launcher combo out the rear window as Bolan continued to wrestle the speeding wagon. The Executioner saw that Wazdi had his foot jammed practically into the floor as he held down the accelerator, his entire body pushed tight between the wheel and the driver's seat.

"Just a couple seconds more!" Wazdi begged.

"By all means, take your time," Bolan returned.

Wazdi snarled. "Throw terrorists at me, I throw grenades at your fucking terrorists, Laud."

The 40 mm grenade launcher chugged, a hollow whomp filling the inside of the Peugeot wagon. Bolan turned his head, looking back. He spotted the wobbling shape of the 40 mm round spinning out the back window and tumbling toward the grille of the pickup truck hot on their tail.

The impact between one small little bombshell and the two-ton pickup was violent, noisy and messy. Shredded steel, flaming fuel and pulped flesh flew in all directions as the pickup crumbled in on itself. The six ounces of high explosive transformed into an invisible fist thanks to the impact primer in the nose of the hellbomb. Devastation swirled in a spiral of churning oily smoke behind them.

Wazdi and Bolan returned their attention to the madman ahead of them, and ducked below the dashboard, his silver pistol hammering and thundering, .40 caliber bullets pounding at the remnants of the hood and dashboard.

"I'm glad this is someone else's car," Bolan spoke up, unleathering his Desert Eagle and ripping out a withering burst of return fire.

AHMUR IBN LAUD watched Hakkan's truck detonate, disappearing in a flash of violent thunder. Frustration, anger and dread writhed in his gut like a nest of serpents, slithering and slinking, entwined and knotting more and more. He pulled Rafferty's Smith & Wesson again, checked the load and began shooting, trying to put rounds into the driver and Al-Askari.

He recognized the driver. It was Hadji, from the plane.

The two of them followed him across how many miles of

desert, and now, they had swung around almost in a perfect circle.

He recognized the stretch of shore. They were nearing his yacht.

If he could reach his abandoned yacht, or maybe steal another boat, he could continue his escape. There was no way that their engine could keep going with all the sheer damage punched into it. Laud realized he was pulling the trigger on an empty autopistol, the silver slide locked back, and he popped the magazine, feeding in a fresh stick of .40-caliber slugs. The weapon clamped back into battery, ready to fire again when the truck shook. The tailgate he was crouched behind exploded as a series of half-inch holes suddenly pierced through it. A massive muzzle flare exploded from the shattered remains of the wagon's windshield.

"Oh God! Oh God! My legs! My legs!" the last Divine Swordsman in the bed of the truck howled.

Laud looked over, sparing a moment and he saw bare white bone and dripping strings of meat where the shins of the terrorist used to be. He was soaked through with blood, and despite having had his legs smashed apart, he was still trying to pull a pistol from his belt.

He aimed the weapon, and Laud saw that the weapon was dented and twisted by the savage, bone breaking impact of a 240-grain hollowpoint round. The Divine Sword commander started to call out, then snaked into a ball, curling up.

The handgun exploded, the crushed slide and barrel trapping the gases of the 9 mm bullet and turning it into a bomb.

The terrorist howled, his fingers blown off. Laud looked back and saw that the poor man's face was a maze of slashes and cuts, flesh shorn through by the shrapnel of the exploding pistol. Blood flowed from eye sockets that stared imploringly toward Heaven.

"Go to Allah," Laud whispered. He aimed the Smith & Wesson and finished the job that Al-Askari had started. The terrorist jerked as his forehead exploded into a fountain of fresh brains and bone splinters.

Mutilated. That's how his people were ending up. Mutilated and chopped apart. Blown to component atoms by missiles slamming into ships. Slammed into putty by grenades.

The Divine Sword lived by the sword, but it was dying by the gun, by the bomb.

And Al-Askari was laughing all the way.

Laud felt the handle of the scimitar on his belt, the "badge" of the Divine Sword of Allah that he had grabbed up in the spur of the moment and stuffed into place. It was an unconscious maneuver, but he knew that it was fate.

The Divine Sword was being carved to pieces, and the only true way to determine if the Sword would once again be raised above the heads of the West, was if he proved that they truly were the swords of Allah. This war would only end on the sharpened edge of steel, and Ahmur Ibn Laud grinned.

"Come closer," he growled, drawing the sword. Laud rose, the pistol and the sword gleaming steel extensions of his hands, firing a flurry of slugs into the cab of the pickup truck.

The truck lurched, and in that moment, Al-Askari and Hadji came too close.

Sword range.

The Divine Swordsman leaped, swinging his curved steel high above his head.

21

Bolan couldn't believe his eyes as he watched the madman he'd chased for a thousand miles suddenly shoot his own get-away driver, then leap from the back of his getaway vehicle, sword shining above his head. He was reloading the Desert Eagle, and normally he could perform the reload as unconsciously as he breathed.

But Mack Bolan didn't even breathe or blink as he watched 175 pounds of psychotic terrorist sail through the sky, gleaming steel in each hand, soaring easily eight feet off the ground. Time snapped, distorting as Bolan tried to force the magazine even faster into his Desert Eagle, pushing to beat the deadline, before Laud came crashing down.

Laud brought his feet forward in the leap, swinging his knees up to his chest and plunged the point of his sword toward them. Wazdi was pushing hard on the steering wheel, fighting physics, feet below the oft-punctured dashboard jamming onto brakes. Bolan felt the Desert Eagle magazine slam into place and the savagery of the reload drove his aim out of whack, the gun twisting in his grip. He felt himself losing control. He would have regained it had Laud's booted foot not come slamming into his hand, ramming the frame of the big Israeli pistol into his chest. Breath exploded from his lungs, and Bolan felt a rib snap, the jolt of pain traveling faster, despite the slow-motion effect of stress on his senses. Pain still moved at three hundred yards per second, and still arrowed into his brain.

With the breaking of his rib, and then the snapping of his right trigger finger, Bolan burst back from slow motion, driven deeper into his seat as Laud slid into the excavated windshield. Wazdi exploded with a scream as the point of the scimitar sliced across his trapezius muscle, only barely deflected by the Kevlar body armor that he wore. Blood flew from where Laud's steel slipped around armor and plunged glancingly into skin and muscle.

Laud struggled to bring the sword around and carve the Executioner into sandwich meat when the Peugeot stopped violently, slamming into the rear of the pickup truck. Both vehicles locked together in tangled metal, tons of machinery skidding and finally slamming to a stop against the side of a building. Inside the Peugeot's front, Bolan and Wazdi were thrown forward, slamming into the dashboard and steering wheel. Laud slithered down the hood as inertia took over.

In a half daze, the Executioner looked at his surroundings. They'd cut past several hotels. That was good, given that Egyptian hotels had groups of armed soldiers out front, providing security for the tourists, and to keep the tourists themselves from causing trouble. As it was, overhead Egyptian air force fighters were flying a search pattern because of the firefight and helicopter sighting at the beach.

Bolan hoped that Grimaldi got away, but knew that the ace Stony Man pilot would be able to handle himself. Around him, he heard the sounds of children's voices and his gaze focused, figuring out that the pair of Peugeots had slammed into a small apartment building. Small faces with large brown eyes looked at him in a mixture of awe and fear, and he hit the door release. It popped open, and somewhere in his scrambled brains, the Executioner realized that this fight had suddenly dropped off in the center of a civilian area.

Worse than that, there were children up and about, getting

in early-morning chores or playing while the air was still cool from the nighttime breezes. Bolan's inner soldier demanded he pull himself to his feet and end the threat of Laud before any innocent children were harmed. If he took a hostage, or killed a child, none of this chase would have been worthwhile.

Bolan looked over at Wazdi who was clutching his chest, blood pouring from a busted lip, or perhaps worse considering the crash. The steering wheel might just have done enough damage to kill them, but he remembered once more, the body armor they both wore.

Laud was sliding off the hood, climbing over the tangled metal of the rear fender of the pickup and the front grille of the wagon, but the Executioner wasn't going to leave until he was sure his partner was all right.

"Waz—"

"Get that asshole. I'll live!" the former blacksuit hissed. No pink froth issued from his mouth, just the steady waterfall of blood from a torn lip or tongue.

Bolan kicked out the Peugeot's door and stepped out, legs giving out from under him. Pain stabbed deep into him, and he couldn't rule out a punctured lung. The Desert Eagle tumbled from his nerveless right hand, and already his trigger finger was swelling to twice its normal size.

Laud grinned at the soldier. He was still holding his sword.

"We've taken this fight down to the knife, haven't we, Al-Askari?" Laud taunted. He gave the sword a whirl, but it was evident that the Divine Swordsman himself was equally shaken up. His voice turned to a demented singsong as blood and spittle dripped down into his beard. "But mine's bigger than yours."

Bolan reached for his Uzi, but the blade swung hard, steel striking steel in a shower of sparks. The submachine gun tumbled away. He started for his Beretta, but Laud shook his head.

"Blade to blade..." Laud said.

Bolan reached for his knife. It was a third the length of the scimitar, and he wished he had some extra backup.

A knife dropped and skidded onto the ground by Bolan's foot.

The Executioner looked down and saw the familiar handle of a Tanto knife in its sheath. He looked over to Wazdi who was leaning against the Peugeot, panting, blood still dripping from his busted mouth.

"Gotta help..." Wazdi panted. The FBI man's features twisted in a mask of sadness. "Goddammit... No!"

Bolan's and Laud's faces turned to masks of confusion when they looked around. Shell-shocked children were around them, looking on in numbed horror. Wazdi slipped back down behind the bumper, then came back up with a tiny, bloodied figure in his arms.

"Gut that baby-killer!" Wazdi demanded.

The Executioner turned to the Divine Swordsman, stooping to scoop up the Tanto with his off hand. "A child."

"One more dead," Laud answered. "What's it matter to you?"

"Everything."

Laud swung his sword in a figure eight, the tip swirling around. Dropping his knives into ice-pick grips, the Executioner brought up his forearms, each protected by a foot of steel, punching away the savagely slashing ribbon of death in the hands of the Divine Swordsman. Bolan lashed out with a foot, but Laud was too disciplined to leave his shins and knees exposed to a kick. The scimitar's tip lashed down and tugged at the American's calf.

Bolan backpedaled and snapped out with his knife. Steel rang as blades collided, Laud barely blocking the stroke. The soldier kept his pivot, flipping the Tanto into a fencer's grip and slashing forward, feeling the chisel tip tug against clothing and skin. The terrorist snarled, recoiling and swinging his sword down in a loop. It was everything the Executioner could do to bring his arm back in tight to his body to keep the scimitar from cleaving off his arm. As the sword swung upward on its follow-through, Bolan continued the pressure, dropping his weight to one foot long enough to bring his right knee hard into the terrorist's belly.

Fetid breath and bloody spittle sprayed in the Executioner's face, but that wasn't going to be the last of this fight. Bolan stole a page from David McCarter's brawl book and snapped his forehead forward hard, skull meeting the nose of his enemy. Blood and snot squirted into his eyes, but Laud went stumbling, trying to keep his balance, sword tip pointing between them as he stood on rubbery legs.

The Executioner pressed his advantage, lunging in, both knives held in tight against his forearms. Laud swung again, and the edge hit Bolan right at the hairline, a glancing cut that sliced his scalp and staggered him. His ice-blue eyes rolled for a moment, the concussion of the stroke slowing the warrior. The Divine Swordsman laughed, sputtering through the fountain that used to be his nose, and raised the scimitar again to chop down.

The Headsman's pose left Laud open, though, and the Executioner dived head and shoulders into the terrorist's belly. Laud's legs kicked against his chest as the two bodies slammed against the bent wreckage of the shattered Peugeot, flesh and bone hitting the unyielding mass of mangled metal.

In the tackle, Bolan had lost his knives, but he made up for it with a full-powered kidney punch that crashed hard into Laud's side. Bolan felt the flat of the sword drop onto his back before bouncing away, and he hammered again into the terrorist's back, making Laud jerk as if he were being snapped on a whip. A knee came pistoning up into Bolan's breastbone, the impact aggravating his broken rib and driving the breath from him. An elbow jammed down hard onto the big American's spine, and a fist that caromed off his head followed that.

Bolan shoved the Divine Swordsman back across the hood of the crumpled pickup, then grabbed one leg to keep his adversary off balance. His off hand struggled to grab for Laud's free leg, but that swung around, bashing across the Executioner's cheek, making his head roll with the impact. Laud swung his leg again, but Bolan was able to trap it, both arms wrapping around the terrorist's ankles.

Laud struggled to turn over so he could get a better grip on the hood of the Peugeot pickup, but Bolan yanked back hard, stepping away from the vehicle. Laud's hands skidded on the hood, dragging behind, and his chin bounced off the folded fender of the pickup. The Divine Swordsman clawed to get up higher and Bolan pulled back again, yanking the man into the air, then dropping him.

Laud came down, forehead bouncing off the fender, and his body dropped, bent at an odd angle against the crashed truck. He clawed to get up when Bolan lunged forward, stomping his boot into the small of Laud's back, the hollow thump of the impact filling the air.

Bolan took the moment in the fight to run his forearm across his eyes, wiping away the torrent of blood. He could barely see out of one eye directly under the nick that Laud had scored, and he was certain he might have incurred more than a little blunt head trauma from the impact. He couldn't quite tell. Exhaustion had him as ragged on his feet as he would have been if he was suffering from a concussion. That he could stand at all was a sign that he wasn't suffering a sidelining injury, but he was still slowed.

Laud rolled over and kicked out, catching Bolan on his right ankle, driving his foot from under him. Hitting the ground, the big soldier was stunned. The Divine Sword's leader pounced, hands extended like claws, grabbing at the Executioner's throat, but the soldier was too experienced to fall for that, tucking his chin deep into his chest. With his shoulders sucked up to his ears, the stranglehold was nothing more than a groping grasp of blacksuit and Kevlar vest, and Bolan swung a short punch into the ribs of the terrorist.

Red spray exploded all over Bolan's face again, spewing from Laud's shattered mouth and nose. This maniac had shot himself out of the sky to cripple America's efforts in chasing and arresting terrorists abroad. He still possessed a bottomless reserve of strength, releasing Bolan and quickly pounding the Executioner in the face, head and upper chest. The soldier fought to heave Laud from his chest, but the terrorist was maintaining his balance too well, shifting his weight to brace against the soldier's struggles.

Laud suddenly lurched, diving to the dirt as a metal star imbedded itself in the wheel of the pickup they were lodged against. Bolan pushed to a half-crouched position, kicking out sideways and catching the Divine Sword's commander in the gut with the full tread of his boot, lifting and tossing him a couple feet. Panting, the soldier crawled his way to the hood of the pickup in order to stand again. He didn't trust his legs to help him stand, but Laud was on all fours, draining more of himself into the sand. Bloodshot eyes glared at him from behind the bearded maniac's crimson face.

"You too weak?"

Bolan didn't answer with words. He took two strides and brought up his boot, kicking Laud hard in the face, snapping his head back. The Divine Swordsman nearly flipped, twisting in the air before landing on his back. The Executioner continued his assault, each kick forcing Laud to roll and retreat lest he suffer crushed bones.

Laud reached up, trying to block another kick, but forearm bones shattered, and the hand hung from yet a new hinge in his arm. It was the Divine Swordsman's scream at his arm being destroyed, folded and mutilated by this last kick that snapped Bolan out of his sudden rage flash.

He looked at a blood drenched, crumpled form, curled against a wall, jaw slack, teeth missing from where they'd been kicked free. Idly, Bolan noticed that there was a tooth imbedded in the toe of his left combat boot. Bolan sucked air into his lungs, trying to regain his oxygen as the blood rushed and swirled in his head. Wildfires of pain from broken bones, cuts and bruises raged across his entire being as he looked down on the defeated terrorist before him.

"Go ahead. Arrest me. Or kill me," Laud said, words spilling out with the blood over his broken lips.

He was gasping, trying to breathe enough to curse the enemy that had destroyed him, but to the murdering psychopath's credit, he managed to get his message out.

"Either way, I've proved expensive to you. Eliminate me, and others take my place, and now I have proved the cost to your people in blood."

The Executioner looked down on the man, looking at him against the wall. Yeah, it was an expensive battle. Pulled muscles, lacerations, a broken finger and a broken rib, Bolan was sure now that he was suffering a concussion on top of all of this. All this, atop the two trucks crashing, and only a single day, a lone frantic, bloody day of brutal warfare and hard pursuit. He weighed the worth of the lives lost in this savage game of one-upsmanship started by the man before him. Dragging him before the court of public opinion, putting him on trial and smashing him even more, it could conceivably be a victory.

Those lawmen, and the crew of the Hercules, were brave souls who were sacrificed to bring this piece of scum to a brand of justice that Bolan believed in with all his soul, even if he didn't deliver it. He heard shuffling feet behind him and looked out the corner of his eye.

Wazdi stumbled alongside Bolan, pistol out. It was Kowalski's .45. "I tried to stabilize the kid."

Bolan saw the man's ashen face.

"He didn't make it," Bolan surmised, his words sounding slurred and drunken.

"Ah, Hadji," Laud sputtered. "Welcome to the party. Going to decide who gets me?"

Bolan felt the turmoil clearing from behind his dark eyes, his jaw set. Sadness had draped over his face like a burial shroud. Wazdi looked at Bolan, then shook his head, conceding defeat on one hand before the sharp edges of hatred ripped through his shroud of sadness.

"When one of us falls," Laud continued, "we shall take twenty of you."

"You ran over a child, you sick bastard," Wazdi growled, lifting the Para-Ordnance pistol. No need to cock the weapon, no need to flick off a safety. The LDA fired with a stiff pull of the trigger. Laud probably didn't know that, probably expected a dramatic cocking of the hammer. "You killed a child!"

Laud shrugged one shoulder, wincing as he tried to move the other. "Acceptable losses."

"You have the right to remain silent, asshole," Wazdi said, his voice creaking with a mixture of rage and sorrow. The Para-Ordnance thundered, the big .45 auto flashing brightly, spitting out one deadly round. Laud shook as it smashed through his forehead, a spray of dark wetness glistening on the wall behind his head. "If you give up the right to remain silent, too fucking bad. You're dead."

Wazdi lowered his pistol, looking at the executed terrorist, the burial shroud of sorrow once again darkening and deadening his face. "Makes you wonder if this was all worth it."

Bolan knew full well the feeling. The lives of innocents run down by Animal Man. The lives of brave men murdered in the pursuit of containing the beast. Victory against them was only rudimentary, temporary. And the deaths didn't bring satisfaction, only a slight lessening of the odds against you in the next round of battle.

No cheers.

No parades.

Just a dead body left sprawled and leaking in an alley.

No medals.

No commendations.

Just aches and pains and exhaustion finally crashing in on both men.

The Executioner spoke softly to Wazdi. "Think of the lives that won't be damaged by Laud and his men. Think of the lives you saved, the families you've kept whole because you and Ski didn't quit."

"That what keeps you going?" Wazdi asked.

"Yeah," Bolan said. "The lives saved, and the fact that there are others out there fighting the good fight. If I were truly alone, I don't think I could walk another step. Stick with Ski. He'll need you, and you need him."

Wazdi looked at Kowalski's pistol, then stuffed it back in his waistband. "It'll take awhile, but we'll be back out there again, Striker."

Bolan nodded.

"And if you need help…"

"It's appreciated."

The men turned and started walking into the morning, back to the rendezvous with Jack Grimaldi.

New ghosts of the friendly dead surrounded Bolan, good men and women, innocent children, to remind him that no victory was without loss. The Executioner wished in his heart of hearts that he didn't ever need to have physical and spiritual reminders ever again about the agony of "acceptable losses."

But, at least for a short time, a fellow soldier walked beside him, easing his burden.

Epilogue

Barbara Price touched the freshly unwrapped chest of Mack Bolan, her slender fingers tracing the darkened bruise where his rib was healing. The bed was warm, feeling more like a real comfort rather than a shelf where she stuffed herself during the times when the world faced a threat. Bolan watched her long, delicate fingers brushing his chest and managed a slight smile.

"Everything pass inspection, sir?" he asked her.

She leaned in close and kissed him, her lips soft and warm on his, then she pulled back some, nose to nose with him. "You passed inspection there, soldier."

Her thumb ran across the freshly closed line along his scalp. The Executioner was recently freed from stitches and tape, and while he was a little stiff from his full-body pounding, she appreciated more the fact that he was plenty stiff and in need of a full-body massage. It had been too long since they'd been together, and even if all he did was lay still for her body to wrap and slink around, it was enough for her.

Ever the dutiful soldier, though, Mack Bolan returned kiss for kiss, caress for caress, embrace for embrace.

"So you said you had more news for me," Bolan spoke up. "Work?"

"We've got Phoenix Force and Able Team taking care of business," Price said. "If the world is coming to an end and only you can stop it, we'll direct you to the nearest phone booth, Superman."

Bolan tugged her tighter, grinning and nibbling on her neck, breathing deeply her scent. "So what's the news, Supergirl?"

She grinned and stroked back Bolan's hair, then rolled onto her side, propping up on her elbow. The big man's hand rested on the curve of her hip as he kept his blue eyes locked with hers. His trigger finger was still wrapped loosely in a flesh-toned gauze bandage, but flexible. It beat the metal splint that had been wrapped around it the past couple days.

"Well, Kowalski and Wazdi are both doing better, health wise. Kowalski just got into physical rehab," Price said. "Pretty good for someone who was in an ICU in Germany a week ago."

"Pretty good for someone who was just shot in the chest a week ago," Bolan qualified.

Price nodded. "Wazdi's been by his side, and even arranged for Kowalski's girlfriend to get to the hospital today."

"Did Hal manage to smooth things over with their agencies?" Bolan asked. "They both went AWOL for all intents and purposes."

"Hal wasn't the only one pulling for Waz and Ski. Quentin Best put them in for high marks and recommended them for commendations."

"I guess Wazdi and Best kissed and made up." Bolan chuckled. He winced. "Reminder, no chuckling for a while."

"I'll put it on a sticky note," Price answered. "Hal talked with Wazdi and made an offer to hire him full time as a blacksuit."

"Kowalski, too?" Bolan asked.

"It'd be like breaking up the Lone Ranger and Tonto."

Bolan dropped his head back to the pillow. "Enough with the pop culture identity switches!"

Price laughed, burying her face in Bolan's shoulder. She looked up at him, and he smiled at her. "I heard that someone asked Hal to make that offer."

"Those kids are good. And they're young. None of us is bulletproof, or immortal, so it might be time to start building up the standing blacksuits into something we can cull replacements from," Bolan stated. "Plus, I need Kowalski to teach me some of his moto-cross tricks."

"When do you need to ride moto-cross?" Price asked.

"I needed to in Egypt," Bolan answered.

He sat up. "I needed to do a lot of things in Egypt. And I need to do a lot of things period. Rest and relaxation is one thing, but I'm feeling my roots starting to set in."

"You can't save the world by yourself."

Bolan looked back over his shoulder. "I know that. Going after Laud proved that, if not the dozens of missions before that with Able Team or Phoenix Force."

She nodded, stroking his shoulder. It was knotted as tight as steel cable.

Bolan stood, stretching his shoulders, then bent, grabbing his clothes from the bedside.

"You're going out?" Price asked.

The Executioner tugged on his pants and pulled the shirt over his head. A pair of athletic socks and a pair of Magnum SWAT boots finished his clothing, except for the shoulder harness for his Beretta 93-R. That he slid on last, making sure the pistol was loaded and both spare magazines were set in place.

"I'm going back to work," Bolan said. "I'll stop by the Computer Room to see what's showing up on the threat board."

Price watched as he shrugged into a leather jacket, slipping it over his shoulder holster. He looked tired, but it was the exhaustion of the soul.

"You think that Waz and Ski will take the job?" Price asked.

Bolan paused, shrugging tighter into the jacket, then turned to her, his mouth drawn into a grin.

"Even if they don't, they'll still be out there, doing their thing. Whether it's inside or outside the law, it's always good to know you have friends somewhere."

She tugged him back to sit on the bed, and gave him a deep

kiss, arms wrapping around his neck. "And you still have friends here, with us."

Bolan stroked back her hair, still enjoying the taste of her on his lips. "I never doubted that for a minute."

··· James Axler
Outlanders®

MASK OF THE SPHINX

Harnessing the secrets of selective mutation, the psionic abilities of its nobility and benevolent rule of a fair queen, the city-kingdom of Aten remains insular, but safe. Now, Aten faces a desperate fight for survival—a battle that will lure Kane and his companions into the conflict, where a deadly alliance with the Imperator to hunt out the dark forces of treason could put the Cerberus warriors one step closer to their goal of saving humanity...or damn them, and their dreams, to the desert dust.

Available August 2004 at your favorite retail outlet.

Separation

*Available June 2004
at your favorite retail outlet.*

The group makes its way to a remote island in hopes of finding brief sanctuary. Instead, they are captured by an isolated tribe of descendants of African slaves from pre–Civil War days. When they declare Mildred Wyeth "free" from her white masters, it is a twist of fate that ultimately leads the battle-hardened medic to question where her true loyalties lie. Will she side with Ryan, J. B. Dix and those with whom she has forged a bond of trust and friendship…or with the people of her own blood?

DEATH LANDS.

Death Hunt

*Available September 2004
at your favorite retail outlet.*

Ryan's razor-sharp edge has been dulled by the loss of his son Dean—but grief is an emotion he cannot indulge if the band is to escape the chains of sadistic Baron Ethan. Now with the group's armorer, JB Dix, imprisoned and near death, Ryan and the others are forced to join Ethan's hunt—as the hunted. But the perverse and powerful baron has changed the rules. Skilled in mind control, he ensures the warriors will not be tracked by high-paying thrill seekers. Instead, they will hunt each other—to the death.